MIKHAIL BULGAKOV

Diaboliad and Other Stories

MIKHAIL BULGAKOV

Diaboliad
and Other Stories

EDITED BY

Ellendea Proffer & Carl R. Proffer

TRANSLATED BY CARL R. PROFFER

INDIANA UNIVERSITY PRESS

BLOOMINGTON / LONDON

Published in Canada by Fitzhenry & Whiteside Limited, Don Mills, Ontario

Library of Congress catalog card number: 76-172127

ISBN: 0-253-11605-8

Manufactured in the United States of America

Contents

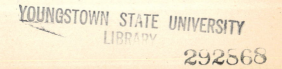

Introduction

THE IRISH *filid*, OR POET, frequently used his magic talent for satirical purposes, and ancient Irish laws suggest that the authorities came to regard these poetic satirists as a serious social problem. Thus Aithrine the Importunate was eventually walled into his fortress with his sons and daughters and burned. He was not the first nor the last satirist to suffer at the hands of societies and governments fearing the metaphorical swords of the written word. If rats can be rhymed to death, and humans can be skewered on their own folly, so artists like Bulgakov who perform these ritual murders with great skill have never been loved by proponents of systems or men holding power.

A parabolic path led Bulgakov to writing. It began in Kiev, where he was born, the son of a professor of theology in 1891, and swerved to a literary career in Moscow, where, blinded by neurosclerosis and filled with pain-killing narcotics, he died in 1940. Despite boyhood dreams of the theater, he went to medical school at Kiev University and spent his first adult years in ignorant rural areas amputating limbs and healing infections (venereology was his specialty), rather than composing dialogue. When World War I and Revolution raged around Kiev, Bulgakov lived through the city's fourteen changes of power in the refuge of his family's apartment—later transformed into the home of the Turbins in his brilliant first novel *White Guard* (1925) and in his famous play

Days of the Turbins (1926). He abruptly abandoned medicine in 1919, and after a hungry stay in the Caucasus, where he wrote stories for newspapers and plays for local theaters, Bulgakov moved to Moscow in the bitterly cold winter of 1921.

It was the beginning of the New Economic Policy,[1] and Bulgakov's real literary career began with stories about what Zoshchenko called the "grimaces of NEP." In memoirs one can read about cafés which turned into bordellos at night, bordellos where thieves, prostitutes, and writers mingled. Pornographic books and postcards were sold in front of churches, gambling casinos were widespread, and the crime rate was very high; in the area known as the "catacombs," now the site of the Gorky Street Post Office, there was an unfinished building in which several murders a week supposedly took place. In the "Bar" restaurant, the cabaret entertainers were available, as were cocaine and heroin. The "Bar" ended its flourishing business when a tax-collector found out the restaurant's profits were much greater than reported. Ehrenburg wrote that Moscow at this time was like a mixture of the nineteenth-century gold fever in California and an exaggerated Dostoevskian moral climate.

Given all this and the massive campaign by the new order to reeducate or coerce the populace into building a socialist society, the period offered plenty of the rotten fruit which satirists feed upon. The decade before the Revolution had been remarkable for its paucity of satirical literature, but dozens of satirical publications appeared during the twenties. By the mid-twenties satirical novels such as Alexei Tolstoy's *Ibikus* and Valentin Kataev's *The Embezzlers* began to appear, but at first inexperience and a critical shortage of paper dictated the dominance of newspapers and short forms; thousands of feuilletons were hastily written for such papers and magazines as *Red Pepper, The Red Journal, Red Panorama, Red Gazette,* and *The Megaphone* by Bulgakov and his colleagues. Using pseudonyms such as Emma B. and M. Ol-Rayt, Bulgakov wrote for all of these, but he published regularly for only two: (1) the émigré newspaper *On the Eve* (*Nakanune*), the literary supplement of which was edited by Alexei Tolstoy for fourteen months between 1922 and 1923—a paper published in Berlin, but sold in the U.S.S.R. because of its conciliatory politics, (2) *The Whistle* (*Gudok*), a paper of the transport workers, whose stable of writers included, besides Bulgakov, several men who were to be famous— Zoshchenko, Ilf and Petrov, and Olesha (who wrote poetry under the pen name Zubilo).

Diaboliad and the other stories in this collection represent the first stage in Bulgakov's career as a prose writer. Besides the dozens of stories Bulgakov wrote in the years 1921–25, he also completed what is probably the best Civil War novel (*White Guard*). The feuilletons were written strictly for money, the novel was a labor of love. The *Diaboliad* collection and the first parts of *White Guard* were both published in 1925, and, with the exception of two slim booklets of reprinted feuilletons (1926), this marked Bulgakov's last appearance in print until after the death of Stalin. Bulgakov's satire was neither gentle nor primitive, and thus could have no success with Party-oriented keepers of the faith. *Diaboliad* provoked a furor of criticism;[2] the journal in which *White Guard* was serialized (*Russia*) was shut down by the Cheka; and Bulgakov's plays *Days of the Turbins* and *Zoya's Apartment* (1926) were subjected to a bewildering sequence of bannings, rewritings by the theaters, and "unbannings." To this day *Diaboliad* is not in the open card catalogue of the Lenin Library in Moscow, and the copies of the almanac *Nedra* have had the stories "The Fatal Eggs" and "Diaboliad" torn out and Bulgakov's name expunged from their tables of contents—this no doubt a relic of the Stalin era.

Despite official criticism and forced revision of the text, *Days of the Turbins* was a great success, indeed a milestone in the history of the Moscow Art Theater. For the rest of his life, and even until the unexpected publication of his novel *The Master and Margarita* in 1967, Bulgakov was known as a playwright. *The Crimson Island,* based loosely on the story of that title in this volume, premiered in 1928 at the Vakhtangov Theater; but it was quickly banned. Bulgakov wrote seven other plays: *Flight* (1926–28) deals with the Civil War and émigrés; *The Cabal of Hypocrites* (1929–36) is about the life of Molière (Bulgakov also wrote a biography of Molière); *Adam and Eve* (1931), *Bliss* (1934), and *Ivan Vasilievich* (1935) are science-fiction satires; *Last Days* (1934–35) treats the duel and death of Pushkin; and *Batum* (1938) deals with the life of the young Stalin. While all of these plays reached various stages of acceptance and even rehearsal, only one, *The Cabal of Hypocrites,* was played in Bulgakov's lifetime. It was rehearsed by a senile Stanislavsky, and in spite of his high-handed but pathetic attempts to make it acceptable ideologically, the play was immediately attacked in *Pravda* and banned after a few performances. None of Bulgakov's plays was published until long after his death; *The Crimson Island, Zoya's Apartment, Adam and Eve,* and *Batum* still have not been published in the Soviet Union.[3]

By 1930 the critical attacks had become so ferocious and the bans on his works so strict that in fear he burned many of his manuscripts. Then, however, he wrote a bold letter to Stalin, recapitulating the campaign against him and while obviously not wanting to become an exile, asking for permission to leave the country if he would not be permitted useful literary work in the future. Apparently struck by Bulgakov's candor and happy as usual to surprise everyone, Stalin arranged a minor post for Bulgakov at the Moscow Art Theater; and in 1932 the government, presumably Stalin again, gave the theater permission to revive *Days of the Turbins.* Bulgakov could not be said to have lived a secure life, but after this he and his third wife Elena Sergeevna (they were married in 1932) survived on a small salary as literary consultant for the theater (1930–36), royalties from *Days of the Turbins,* and stage adaptations of Gogol's *Dead Souls* (1932), *Don Quixote* (1938), and from four libretti written for the Bolshoi Theater (1936–39).

Bulgakov is an important Russian dramatist, but it is as a writer of prose fiction that he made his most important contribution to Russian literature—*White Guard, Theatrical Novel* (1936–37, a parody of Stanislavsky and the Moscow Art Theater which may or may not be finished), and *The Master and Margarita* (1928–40). All through the dark years of the thirties Bulgakov used his "own" time to write and rewrite his satirical masterpiece about the Master, his beloved, and the Master's novel about Pontius Pilate. *The Master and Margarita* is one of the finest of all Russian novels, and if for no other reason Bulgakov's early fiction deserves attention. Many of the themes, characters, and devices used in *The Master and Margarita* developed from the early satirical tales.

"Diaboliad" belongs to the tradition of Russian stories about "little men" and civil servants started by Gogol in "The Nose" and "The Overcoat" and continued less successfully by Dostoevsky in *The Double*. Character types are similar, including civil servant heroes suffering from sexual isolation and menacing superiors. The systemizing world of bureaucracy reduces people to categories, prizing sameness over individuality—and thus it produces frightening doubles. The boundaries which separate people begin to disintegrate, as does the sanity of the hero; when this happens the distinction between the "real" world and a fantastic world is not far behind. Madness and fantasy are age-old satirical devices. Gogol's Poprishchin ("Notes of a Madman") imagines noses living on the moon; Bulgakov's Korotkov sees Underwarr turning first into a phosphorescent black cat (forerunner of Behemoth in *The Master and Margarita*) and then into a white cock smelling of sulphur. Dostoevsky's Golyadkin Sr. loses his identity to an arrogant serial self and Korotkov loses his identity to a similar upstart—through documents, for as Soviet satirists have noted, without identification papers a man is not a man. In Gogol, without a nose a man is not a man.

Stylistic grotesqueries accompany thematic ones. Comic similes and realized metaphors appear on every page (Underwarr has a voice "like a copper pan"; after the first reference in the simile it is always "clanged the pan" or "rang the pan"). Ordinary verbs of saying are rare; the dialogue is marked by all kinds of "squeaks," "sings," and "mutters" rather than "he saids." Inanimate objects such as typewriters or teapots sing and talk to characters. People are turned into synecdoches (usually colors or clothing), and many minor characters remain nameless except for some dominant feature ("the blond one," "the *kuntush*").

Neither in the use of fantasy nor in stylistic grotesqueries is Bulgakov unique for the mid-twenties. The short story was the dominant genre, and there was a great deal of experimentation in the realm of verbal stylization and fantasy—much of it more radical, and ephemeral, than Bulgakov's style. This was particularly true of the group known as the Serapion Brothers—named after a character in E. T. A. Hoffmann. Their leader, Lev Luntz, wrote a story entitled "Outgoing No. 37" in which a little clerk so fears for a lost document that he turns into that document (as Gogol's hero in *Vladimir Third-Class* turns into that medal). The Kafkaesque atmosphere and fantasy of that story is much like that in "Diaboliad." Among the better-known writers one had such experiments as the primitivism of Zamyatin, the ornamentalism of Vsevolod Ivanov, and the brilliant narrative inventions of Zoshchenko. In all of these stories, as in Bulgakov's, characterization suffered at the expense of style—true, sometimes as an intentional reduction of the characters to the status of robots. One of the ways Bulgakov does this—and it is obviously borrowed from Gogol's "The Nose" and Dostoevsky's *The Double*—is the exaggeratedly detailed registering of Korotkov's physical gestures and changes of location.

Korotkov's mortal plunge provides a natural ending, but it is not "the bone of the bone and the blood of the blood of the beginning," as Robert Louis Stevenson has said endings of short stories must be. It is typical of Bulgakov (for example, "The Fatal Eggs," "A Chinese Tale," "No. 13") that what seemed harmless fun and fairly mild topical satire should unexpectedly end in death— which is no laughing matter. Of course, the mixture of satire and death is not unusual; (indeed it has ancient roots[4]), and this is found in works by the best Russian satirists of the twenties—in Zamyatin's *We,* for example, or Zoshchenko's *Tales of Nazar Ilich Sinebryu-*

khov. But as is frequently the case (recall Gogol's "The Overcoat" again) the reader is faced with the problem of sympathy. If Korotkov has been made flat and ridiculous in the beginning, can we feel his death as a real tragedy? The problem of irony which undercuts irony is one which Bulgakov faces in other stories too, including "The Fatal Eggs."

"The Fatal Eggs" is the most famous and ambitious story of the collection. The Serapion Brothers had helped renew interest in stories with interesting plots (generally classical Russian literature has little plot interest), and works describing adventures enjoyed great popularity. Nor were science-fiction elements entirely new to Russian literature in the twenties. Zamyatin's anti-utopian *We* is the best-known example; Alexei Tolstoy's pro-Soviet tales "Aelita" and "Garin's Death-Ray" soon followed, and Bulgakov returned to this kind of literature in the short novel *Heart of a Dog* (1925) as well as in his later plays. In "The Fatal Eggs," using the plot of H. G. Wells' *The Food of the Gods,* Bulgakov created a horrifying picture of the catastrophe that results when the state interferes in scientific endeavors. The story is brilliant in its details, but as allegory it is somewhat unclear.[5] Although it is the leather-jacketed Feyt and the journalist Bronsky who are responsible for getting the government interested in using the ray for chicken breeding, it is some unknown person who switches the reptile and chicken eggs. This means that the *direct* cause of the reptile invasion is an accidental switching of boxes—which seems rather pointless. Bulgakov's critique of the Revolutionary handling of scientific inventions and the attempt to circumvent natural evolution is presented far more lucidly and logically in *Heart of a Dog*—written only a few months after "The Fatal Eggs."

Feyt himself is at first portrayed as an extremely unpleasant man with a Mauser at his hip—but then we suddenly discover that he had been a flute player before the Revolution and that he has a nice wife and is really just a kind, simple man. We are told all of this in chapter eight, which is devoted to an idyllic (and humorous) description of the night on the Sovkhoz: Feyt is fluting, his nice wife is listening—and the next day she is crushed by a giant reptile in a scene described in horrifying naturalistic, clinical detail. This is a shock from which the reader never really recovers; although the deaths that follow are many and frightening, they are expected—except perhaps for Persikov's death at the hands of the Moscow mob.

The reptiles and ostriches, like Napoleon, are finally destroyed not by the Russians, but by an incredible frost. The frost comes at the end of August in true *deus ex machina* fashion.[6] While interesting on first reading, the plot itself is not all-important, which one can conclude from the fact that Bulgakov's basic plot differs from Wells' only in that Persikov is killed—Wells' persecuted scientist escapes the mob and lives out his days in safe obscurity.

Bulgakov's originality consists in the way he adapts the story to the Russian environment—the Deaconess Drozdova's story, for example, is all his own invention. Also in evidence is Bulgakov's great talent for arousing readers' interest by creating an air of mystery and suspense. However, all of these abilities are as nothing when compared with Bulgakov's ability to make the fantastic seem real—as in the description of the giant reptiles ravaging the land. Scientific precision and a proclivity for naturalistic detail might explain the extraordinarily powerful effect of these descriptions of horrible events—but only partially. Perhaps it is explained by the visual nature of Bulgakov's imagination, the fact that whatever he described he had "seen," if only in a nightmare. Elena Sergeevna Bulgakova has related how when dictating Bulgakov would stand staring out a window, interrupting himself only to correct a detail which he could see but was describing imprecisely. In *Theatrical Novel* there is an obviously autobiographical description of a dramatist "merely" transcribing the pictures which of themselves appear before his eyes.

The visual side of Bulgakov's imagination is perhaps most effective in the six scenes of "A Chinese Tale." This story is somehow enchanting in its description of a Chinese coolie in the Red Army. Bulgakov's repeated evocation of the coolie's childhood under the hot sun is an effective and touching contrast to the cold of Moscow and the Kremlin wall. The repetition of certain key details, details which are packed with memory and meaning for the character—the kaoliang, the keen-edged shadow, the buckets of ice-cold water—is typical of the mature Bulgakov's prose. The cocaine dream with its careful incorporation of details from the coolie's immediate past and mystical foreshadowing of the future (the Chinaman being rewarded for a decapitation) is another successful feature of the story. (The irreverent references to Lenin make the story unpublishable now.) Bulgakov later used the cocaine, the Finnish knife, and Hellish vision of a Chinese dwelling in Moscow in his play *Zoya's Apartment*.

As noted by critics at the time *Diaboliad* was published, "A Chinese Tale" appears to be a polemic with Vsevolod Ivanov's celebrated story "Armored-Train 14–69"—which was made into a play and put on at the Moscow Art Theater shortly after Bulgakov's own *Days of the Turbins,* with much less trouble politically. Ivanov also has a Chinese hero, but a *real* hero who joins the Bolsheviks and intelligently and consciously serves the cause. In the end he deliberately sacrifices his life for his comrades, throwing himself under the wheels of a train which has to be stopped. Contrast Bulgakov's coolie, who owes his original acceptance by the Red Army merely to his utterance of three words, the Russian national oath ("Fuck your mother"), and who serves and kills strictly for bread, with not a whisper of ideology.

"The Adventures of Chichikov" is one of Bulgakov's "Gogolisms." The title is the title which Gogol's censors insisted he use above *Dead Souls*. Basically the story uses characters and lines from *Dead Souls* (both Part I and Part II), but other works by Gogol, including *The Inspector General* and "The Nose," are also incorporated parodistically. Much of the narration is composed of bits and pieces of sentences from Gogol—such as the last sentence of the story, which from "again life went parading before me" is from the end of a Homeric simile in *Dead Souls*. Bulgakov's ironic "dream" ending mimics both Gogol's original version of "The Nose" and the denial of reality in the preface to "The Tale of How Ivan Ivanovich Quarrelled with Ivan Nikiforovich"—the narrator claims it is all fantasy, but the reader knows that it is all too real. For this reason, Bulgakov was attacked by politically minded critics who, like the critics mentioned in *Dead Souls* ("they will come scurrying from their crannies"), saw the story as unpatriotic slander. There are several examples of Gogol's works being updated during the twenties, including Barkanov's long story "How Ivan Ivanovich Made Up with Ivan Nikiforovich" and Meyerhold's surrealistic production of *The Inspector General.* Later Bulgakov was to be the author of the stage version of *Dead Souls* which has been a standard at the Moscow Art Theater for nearly forty years, and he wrote film scripts for both *Dead Souls* and *The Inspector General.* Even before "The Adventures of Chichikov," which is really an overgrown feuilleton, Bulgakov used Gogolian epigraphs, characters, themes, and parodies in several of his feuilletons for *The Whistle* (see especially the hilarious "Inspector General with a Kicking Out").

"No. 13. The Elpit-Rabkommun Building" (from *Rabochaja kommuna*—Workers' Commune) is also a feuilletonistic piece. Its themes (the housing shortage, problems of communal living, "ignorant" or "uneducated" people—*temnye ljudi*) recur in Bulgakov's early humorous works and then in his plays (*Zoya's Apartment, Bliss*), as well as in *The Master and Margarita.* Indeed, the number of the fatal apartment—50—is used again in *The Master and Margarita* (Berlioz's and Woland's apartment), and No. 13 was the Bulgakovs' address in Kiev. In this story the narrator's sympathies seem to lie primarily with the old order, and the ignorant people, the unwashed multitudes represented by Annushka, are to blame for tragedies of this sort. The repeated images and metaphors (the naked stone girl, the fire as beast), the secret servicemen, hints of demonism (the devil is disguised as a snowstorm), allusion to Meyerbeer's *The Huguenots,* and the sudden intrusion of electrifying death are all typical of Bulgakov's fiction.

Introduction

Three of the feuilletons published in a tiny book called *A Treatise on Housing* (the title story, "Four Portraits," and "Moonshine Lake") are characteristic of the best of Bulgakov's early newspaper humor—which is not to say much. They are not really fiction, and are of interest now mainly for the topical humor—after all, Bulgakov was rather bold to poke fun at pictures of Lenin and Marx. They are also useful for a study of Bulgakov's narrators. Typically these early works had quotations from Worker Correspondent Reporters as epigraphs. Bulgakov would then bring the epigraph to life—a frequent device was a mix-up caused, say, by the combination of a snack bar and a library, or what would occur when the political indoctrination class, choir practice, and the movie "The Daughter of Montezuma" would all take place simultaneously. His success with feuilletons is due in large part to Bulgakov's natural abilities as a storyteller—since feuilletons are unified by the narrator rather than by plot. The narrator-storyteller was one that was natural to Bulgakov, and he employed him in most of his prose. This narrator is especially visible when a work is long and tends toward the comic. For example, the narrator is fairly unobtrusive in "Diaboliad," but he makes his presence felt in "The Fatal Eggs."

The need for refuge in the midst of real and metaphorical storms is a theme which runs through most of Bulgakov's fiction. "Psalm," however, is very unusual for him. He had written feuilletons in which dialogue dominates, and some of the impressionistic devices are used in other stories (especially "The Raid"), but "Psalm" is wistful, personal, and delicate in a way unusual for the early Bulgakov. Here we have no satire, no science fiction, none of the grotesqueries which dominate virtually all of his other early stories —only a quietly lyrical set of scenes between a lonely man and a lonely woman. It is a touching story, affecting partly because Bulgakov has his characters transform homely details, such as the buttons, into apt symbols of complicated and pathetic situations in a way which we recognize as very human.

Abram in "The Raid" also has a very human triumph, a minor

victory of quiet inner dignity over the indignity of physical ridiculousness, the arrogance of Yak, and the torment of Revolution. In manner "The Raid" is close to the battle scenes in *White Guard,* and to a certain extent, some scenes in "A Chinese Tale." This happens when the narrator's mind merges with that of the main character and we see things, estranged, through the eyes of a wounded man—Abram recalls the warmth and unfinished watercolor as the Chinaman had the kaoliang. Stories about the Civil War were probably numerically dominant in the early twenties, and the naturalistic description of physical cruelty can also be found in the tales of Vsevolod Ivanov, Mikhail Slonimsky, and Nikolai Nikitin. The metaphorical, impressionistic description of the storm and attack also owes something to the ornamentalism typical of the twenties, although the light effects are typically Bulgakovian.

"The Crimson Island" was published in the Berlin newspaper *On the Eve* in 1924. "Islands" and "journeys" are ancient devices for presenting utopias or anti-utopias, and obviously Jules Verne, from whom Bulgakov borrows characters and situations,[7] is the most important forerunner in this genre. Both the island and the journey were used frequently by Soviet writers—from Mayakovsky's *Mystery-Bouffe* (1918) to Ehrenburg's *Trust D. E.* (1923) and Valentin Kataev's *Ehrendorf Island* (1924). Bulgakov's story appears to be a parody of the kind of propagandistic stories written after the Revolution, allegories in which history is simplified and characters are either heroes or villains. It is full of hyperbole, gross caricature, incongruous juxtapositions, and funny non sequiturs. It is an amusing piece, but hardly significant; one would not give it much attention if Bulgakov had never written a play called *The Crimson Island*. The play was written in 1927 and premiered at the Kamerny Theater in December 1928. While the play was very popular with the public, the critics violently denounced it as "talentless, toothless, humble" and a "pasquinade on the Revolution." The play is quite different from the story—in fact the basic story is made into a play within the play, and the main theme becomes censorship. So *The*

Crimson Island served as the final piece of evidence in the trial by press of Bulgakov, and soon he was run out of Russian literature.

A complete picture of Bulgakov's early prose would also have to include such diverse genres as "Notes on the Cuffs," the stories which make up *The Notes of a Young Doctor,* and *Heart of a Dog.* The first of these is a curious work—a fragmentary autobiographical account given the appearance of a fictional feuilleton describing Bulgakov's literary life in the Caucasus (with many famous writers such as Mandelstam and Pilnyak appearing briefly) and then in Moscow's labyrinthine corridors. The six stories which form *The Notes of a Young Doctor,* told in the first person, are again closer to *White Guard,* with little grotesque satire, more in the realistic vein. There are strong echoes of Tolstoy's story "The Snowstorm," Pushkin's story with the same title, and such Chekhov stories as "The Enemies." Here one again finds a hero, common to many of Bulgakov's works at different periods, who suffers agonizing self-doubt, but survives inhuman trials because of his aristocratic sense of human dignity and humane compassion. The young doctor is an aristocrat in ability, as are the scientific heroes of "The Fatal Eggs," *Adam and Eve,* and *Heart of a Dog.* All three of these works describe the confident misuse of knowledge which, while promising human good, leads only to injustice and inhumanity.

Bulgakov once referred to himself as a "mystical writer"—but he is only mystical in that he believes there is more to the world than common sense can know. There is no absorption in the other-worldly in his works—even in *The Master and Margarita* he describes Yeshua and his character, not God and His divinity. Bulgakov's world is moved by the desire for justice here and now, and his most powerful satire comes from the frustration of that desire.

ELLENDEA PROFFER
CARL R. PROFFER

February 7, 1971
Ann Arbor

NOTES TO THE INTRODUCTION

1. The New Economic Policy, known as NEP, was begun in March 1921 as a result of agricultural disasters and a labor paralysis. It was considered a betrayal by many Communists because it allowed a partial restoration of free trade, gave peasants the right to sell surplus goods independently, and allowed private enterprises to be set up, leased from the government. The Nepmen realized from the beginning that this period of freedom was only temporary, and many of them hurried to make their money and emigrate—often with the collusion of Communist officials.

2. Bulgakov was called a "bourgeois" writer, and his name was sometimes joined with Zamyatin's for purposes of attack. For example, in I. Novich, "The Tree of Contemporary Literature," *On Literary Guard*, No. 3 (1926) there is a picture of the "tree of literature." On the next to the lowest limb sit caricatures of the "bourgeois writers" Bulgakov, Zamyatin, and Ehrenburg. (Anna Akhmatova, the famous poetess, is on the ground with the "living corpses.")

3. The first complete publication of the Russian text of *The Crimson Island* and the final version of *Zoya's Apartment* was in 1971.

4. It is thought that satire was born in improvisations to Phallic Songs sung in fertility rites, to the carrying of huge poles in the shape of phalluses; and the satirist was often the scapegoat (or *pharmakos*) who was executed after ritual beating on the genitals.

5. At least one critic turns Persikov into Lenin [S. Orlovsky, in M. Bradshaw (ed.), *The Soviet Theater* (New York, 1954), p. 55]. There were violent attacks on the story as some reviewers thought it was counterrevolutionary, but others noted that the story's points seemed to be contradictory. See reviews by V. Pravduxin, *Novyj mir*, No. 5 (1925), pp. 287–89 and D. Gorbov, *Novyj mir*, No. 12 (1925), pp. 147–48.

6. The last chapter is entitled "A Frosty *Deus ex machina*" (*Moroznyj bog na mashine*). Mirra Ginsburg's good translation has only "A Frosty God"—since it is based on the émigré edition.

7. Hatteras is from *The Adventures of Captain Hatteras*, Michel Ardan from *From the Earth to the Moon*, Lord Glenarvan and Paganel from *A Voyage around the World* (native names from this trilogy are also copied or closely imitated). The erupting volcano, duel scene, chapter titles and subdivisions are also take-offs on Verne.

Diaboliad

Diaboliad

The Story of How Twins Destroyed a Clerk[1]

[I]

THE EVENT ON THE 20TH

AT THE TIME when everyone was jumping from one job to another, Comrade Korotkov[2] worked steadily at MACENTSUP-MATMAT[3] (Main Central Supply of Match-making Materials) as a regular appointment clerk—and he had served there for eleven whole months.

Thus sheltered by MATMAT, gentle, quiet, blond Korotkov completely exterminated from his mind the thought that the so-called vicissitudes of fate do exist in the world, and in its place he inculcated certainty that he—Korotkov—would work at the Supply until the end of his life on earth. But, alas, it did not turn out that way at all . . .

1. "Diaboliad" was first published in the almanac *Nedra* [The Depths], No. 4 (Moscow, 1924), pp. 221–60. The *Nedra* publishing house also did the entire *Diaboliad* collection the following year.

2. The name Korotkov derives from *korotkij,* meaning "short," and is thus in the tradition of depreciating names for the civil-service heroes of phantasmagoric Petersburg tales (e.g. Akaky Akakievich in Gogol's "The Overcoat" or Golyadkin in Dostoevsky's *The Double*).

3. The new Soviet acronyms were notorious for their comic ugliness, and all satirists seem to have made fun of them.

On the 20th of September 1921, MATMAT's cashier donned his disgusting, huge-eared cap, put the lined pay sheet in his briefcase and left. This was at eleven o'clock in the morning.

At four-thirty in the afternoon the cashier returned, wet all over. When he arrived he shook the water off his cap, put his cap on the table, put his briefcase on his cap, and said, "Don't crowd so close."

Then for some reason he rummaged around in the table, went out of the room, and returned after fifteen minutes with a large dead chicken which had had its neck wrung. The chicken he put on his briefcase, and on the chicken—his right hand, and he said, "There'll be no money."

"Tomorrow?" cried the women in a chorus.

"No," the cashier shook his head, "there won't be any tomorrow either, or the day after tomorrow. Don't crowd in, comrades, or you'll tip my table over."

"What is this?" everyone shouted, including the naive Korotkov.

"Citizens!" sang the cashier in a whining voice, shoving Korotkov away with his elbow, "Please!"

"But what's happened?" everyone shouted, and this comic Korotkov loudest of all.

"All right, but please," hoarsely muttered the cashier, and taking the pay sheet out of his briefcase, he showed it to Korotkov.

Written in red ink across the place where the cashier jabbed his dirty fingernail was: "Pay this. Senat signing for Comrade Sub-botnikov." Written below this in violet was: "There isn't any money. Smirnov signing for[4] Comrade Ivanov."

"What?" Korotkov shouted alone—and, puffing, the others all attacked the cashier.

"Oh, my Lord!" he moaned desperately, "What have I got to do with it? My God!"

Hurriedly shoving the pay sheet into his briefcase, he donned his cap, stuck the briefcase under his arm, flourished the chicken,

4. "Signing for" because people in posts of responsibility were never there.

shouted, "Let me through, please!," and knocking a breach in the human wall, disappeared out the door.

The pale registrar wearing high, sharp heels ran after him with a screech; her left heel broke off at the door with a crunch. She toppled, picked up her foot, and took off the shoe.

And barefoot on one foot she was left in the room—as were all of the others, including Korotkov.

[I I]

THE PRODUCTS PRODUCED

THREE DAYS AFTER THE EVENT just described the door to the separate room where Korotkov worked opened part way, and a tearful female head said maliciously, "Comrade Korotkov, go pick up your salary."

"What?" Korotkov exclaimed joyfully, and whistling the overture from *Carmen* he ran to the room with the sign "Cashier's Booth" on it. He stopped at the cashier's table and opened his mouth wide. Two thick columns made up of yellow packages soared up to the ceiling itself.[5] So as not to answer any questions, the sweaty, upset cashier had tacked to the wall the pay sheet, on which there was now a third inscription in green ink:

"Pay them in the products produced.
Preobrazhensky, signing for Comrade Bogoyavlensky.[6]
I agree—Kshesinsky."

Korotkov walked out of the cashier's office smiling broadly and stupidly. In his hands were four large yellow packs, five small green

5. Bulgakov himself was once paid for a story in mathes, and they are still sometimes used as small change.
6. The names Preobrazhensky and Bogoyavlensky derive from "transfiguration" and "annunciation."

ones—and in his pockets were thirteen blue boxes of matches. In his own room, listening to the hum of amazed voices in the office, he packed the matches into the two huge sheets of the day's newspaper, and without saying anything to anyone he left work for home. At the entrance to MATMAT he almost got run over by an automobile someone was driving, but who specifically Korotkov did not make out.

Arriving home, he unpacked the matches on the table and looked at them admiringly as he backed away. The stupid smile had not left his face. Then Korotkov mussed up his blond hair and said to himself, "Well, sir, there's no reason to spend a lot of time moaning. I'll try to sell them."

He knocked on the door of his neighbor, Alexandra Fyodorovna, an employee at GUBVINSKLAD.[7]

"Come in," said a hollow voice inside.

Korotkov went in and was amazed. Alexandra Fyodorovna had come home from work early, and she was squatting on the floor in her overcoat and hat. In front of her stood a row of bottles filled with dark red liquid and corked with newspaper. Alexandra Fyodorovna's face was tear-stained.

"Forty-six," she said and turned around to Korotkov.

"Is that ink? . . . Hello, Alexandra Fyodorovna," the astounded Korotkov uttered.

"Church wine," his neighbor answered, sobbing.

"What—you too?" Korotkov gasped.

"You got church wine too?" Alexandra Fyodorovna said, astonished.

"We got matches," replied Korotkov in a fading voice, and he twisted a button on his jacket.

"But they don't even light!" exclaimed Alexandra Fyodorovna, getting up and shaking out her skirt.

"What do you mean, they don't light?" Korotkov said in terror, and he rushed to his own room. There, without losing a minute, he

7. Province Wine Stores.

grabbed a box, unsealed it with a crackle, and struck a match. With a hiss it burst into greenish flame, bent over, and went out. Choking on the acrid sulphur odor Korotkov coughed feverishly and lit a second. It shot out and two sparks spat out of it. The first landed against the windowpane, and the second in Comrade Korotkov's left eye.

"Aie!" screamed Korotkov, dropping the box.

For a few moments he picked his feet up and down like an overheated horse and pressed his eyes with the palm of his hand. Then he looked into his little shaving mirror in horror, certain that he had lost an eye. But the eye was in place. True, it was red and oozing tears.

"Oh, my God!" Korotkov said in confusion. He immediately got an American individually packaged bandage out of his chest-of-drawers, tore it open, wrapped it around the left side of his head, and came to look like someone wounded in battle.

Korotkov did not turn off the light all night; he lay in bed striking matches. Thus he used up three boxes, during which he managed to light sixty-three matches.

"She's lying, the fool," Korotkov growled, "they're excellent matches.

By morning the room was filled with a suffocating sulphur odor. At dawn Korotkov fell asleep and had a silly, terrifying dream: it was as if a huge, live billiard ball on legs appeared before him on a green meadow. It was so revolting that Korotkov screamed and woke up. In the murky darkness it seemed to him for about five more seconds that the ball was there, beside the bed, and that it smelled strongly of sulphur. But then all of this vanished; after turning over Korotkov went to sleep and did not wake up again.

[I I I]

THE BALD MAN APPEARS

THE NEXT MORNING Korotkov pushed back the bandage and satisfied himself that his eye had almost healed. Nevertheless the excessively cautious Korotkov decided not to take it off for a while.

Turning up at work extremely late, the sly Korotkov went straight to his room so as not to arouse idle chatter among the lower-level employees; and on his desk he found a paper in which the director of the personnel division asked the director of the Supply whether the typists would be issued uniforms. Having read the paper with his right eye, Korotkov took it and set off down the corridor to the office of the director of Supply—Comrade Chekushin.

And there at the very door to his office Korotkov bumped into a stranger striking in his appearance.

This stranger was so short that he reached only to the waist of the tall Korotkov. This shortness was compensated for by the extreme broadness of the stranger's shoulders. His square torso rested on crooked legs, and the left was lame. But most remarkable of all was his head. It was formed exactly like a gigantic model egg set on the neck horizontally with the sharp end forward. It was also as bald as an egg, and so shiny that electric light bulbs burned constantly on the stranger's crown. The stranger's tiny face was shaved blue, and his green eyes, as small as pinheads, sat in deep hollows. The stranger's body was clothed in an unbuttoned service jacket made out of a gray blanket, under which one could see a Ukrainian embroidered shirt; his legs were in pants of the same material and he was wearing the low-cut boots of a Hussar of Alexander the First's time.

"What a character!" thought Korotkov, and he headed for Chekushin's door, trying to pass by the bald man. But quite unexpectedly he blocked Korotkov's path.

"What do you want?" the bald man asked Korotkov in a voice that made the nervous clerk shudder. The voice was absolutely like the voice of a copper pan and was distinguished by a special timbre which caused everyone who heard it to feel, at every word, as if someone were dragging a rough wire across their backbone. Besides that, it seemed to Korotkov that the stranger's words smelled of matches. In spite of all this, the short-sighted Korotkov did what he should under no circumstances have done—he took offense.

"Hm . . . this is rather strange. I'm going along with a paper . . . And may I inquire who you are to . . ."

"Do you see what's written on that door?"

Korotkov looked at the door and saw the long-familiar sign: "Don't enter without a report."

"And I'm going in with a report," Korotkov said stupidly, point-ing to his paper.

Unexpectedly the bald square got angry. His eyes glittered with yellowish scintillas.

"You, comrade," he said, deafening Korotkov with his metallic tones, "are so undeveloped that you don't understand the meaning of the simplest office signs. I am positively amazed that you've held a job this long. In general there is a lot around here that is interesting —for example, these black eyes at every step. Well, never mind, we'll get all that into order. ("Aie!" Korotkov gasped to himself.) Give me that!"

And with these last words the stranger tore the paper out of Korotkov's hands, read it in an instant, pulled a chewed-up ball point out of his pants pocket, held the paper against the wall, and wrote a few words across it.

"Get moving!" he bellowed, and jabbed the paper at Korotkov in such a way that he almost poked out his remaining eye. The door to the office howled and swallowed up the stranger; Korotkov was left petrified—and Chekushin wasn't in the office.

Confused Korotkov came to himself a minute later when he ran up very hard against Lidochka de Runi, Comrade Chekushin's personal secretary.

"Oh!" gasped Comrade Korotkov. Lidochka's eye was wrapped up in the same sort of individual material with the difference that the ends of the bandage were tied in a coquettish bow.

"What happened to you?"

"Matches!" Lidochka replied irritably, "the damned things!"

"Who was that?" desolated Korotkov asked in a whisper.

"You mean you don't know?" Lidochka whispered. "He's the new one."

"What?" squeaked Korotkov, "And Chekushin?"

"He was fired yesterday," Lidochka said furiously, adding as she jabbed her little finger in the direction of the office, "And what a ninny. What a screwball he is. I've never seen anyone so repulsive in my entire life. He yells! Fire him! . . . Bald underwear!" she added unexpectedly, making Korotkov bug his eyes out at her.

"What's his na . . ."

Korotkov did not finish asking. Behind the office door a terrifying voice thundered, "Messenger!" The clerk and the secretary instantly flew off in different directions. Hurtling into his room, Korotkov sat down at the desk and made the following speech to himself: "Ay-ay-ay . . . Well, Korotkov, you've botched it. This thing will have to be corrected . . . 'Undeveloped' . . . Hm . . . The boor . . . All right! You'll see just how undeveloped this Korotkov is."

And with his one eye the clerk read what the bald man had written. Slanting words crossed the paper: "In proper time all typists and the women in general will be issued soldier's underwear."

"What a great idea!" Korotkov exclaimed ecstatically, and he shuddered voluptuously, imagining Lidochka wearing soldier's underwear. He immediately took out a clean sheet of paper and in three minutes composed the following:

Telephoned telegram.

To the director of the personnel division period.

In answer to your memorandum No. 0-15015 (6) of the 19th comma CENTMATMAT informs you comma that in proper time all typists and the women in general will be issued soldier's underwear period Director dash signature Clerk dash Varfolomey Korotkov period.

He rang and to the messenger Panteleimon who came he said, "To the Director for his signature."

Panteleimon chewed his lips, took the paper, and went out.

For four hours after this Korotkov listened carefully without going out of his room, calculating that if the new director should decide to inspect the building he would definitely find him sunk in work. But no sounds reached him from the terrifying office. Only once a vague iron voice reached him, seemingly threatening to fire someone, but whom specifically Korotkov could not make out, even though he pressed his ear to the key-hole. At three-thirty in the afternoon Panteleimon's voice rang out behind the office wall: "He's left by automobile."

Everyone in the office immediately started making noise and leaving. Last of all to leave for home, in solitude, was Comrade Korotkov.

[I V]

PARAGRAPH ONE—KOROTKOV IS OUT

THE NEXT MORNING Korotkov happily satisfied himself that his eye was no longer in need of treatment, therefore he got rid of the bandage with relief, and immediately changed and became more handsome. Drinking his tea on the run, Korotkov extinguished the primus and dashed off to work trying not to be late—and he was fifty minutes late because instead of taking route six the trolley took circular route seven, rolled off into distant streets lined by small houses, and there broke down. Korotkov managed two miles on foot and gasping for breath ran into the office just as the kitchen clock of the Alpine Rose was striking eleven. In the office he was awaited by a spectacle which was utterly unlikely for eleven o'clock in the morning. Lidochka de Runi, Milochka Litovtseva, Anna Evgrafovna, the senior bookkeeper Starlin, the instructor Gitis, Nomeratsky, Ivanov, Mushka, the registrar, the cashier—in a word everyone in the office was absent from their places at the kitchen tables of the former restaurant Alpine Rose—and they were standing jammed into a tight group by the wall on which there was a quarter piece of paper nailed. An abrupt silence set in as Korotkov entered, and everyone lowered their eyes.

"Hello, comrades, what is this?" the surprised Korotkov inquired.

The crowd parted silently, and Korotkov walked to the quarter. The first lines stared at him confidently and clearly, the last through a tearful, stunning mist.

Order No. 1

1. For his impermissibly lackadaisical attitude toward his duties, which has resulted in a scandalous mix-up in important organizational documents, and also for appearing at work looking hideous, his face apparently smashed in a brawl, Comrade Korotkov is herewith fired this 26th day of the month, to be paid trolley fare through the 25th inclusively.

The first paragraph was simultaneously the last—and beneath this paragraph in large, prominent letters was the signature:

UNDERWARR,[8] DIRECTOR.

For twenty seconds ideal silence reigned in the dusty, crystal main hall of the Alpine Rose. During this time greenish Korotkov was silent the best, most profoundly, and deadest of all. At the twenty-first second the silence cracked.

"What? What?" Korotkov's voice tinkled twice exactly like an

---

8. In Russian the character's name is Kal'soner, which Korotkov confuses with *kal'sony*—"underpants."

Alpine glass being broken by a heel, "his surname is Under-warr? . . ."

At the terrifying word the office people spurted in different direc-tions, and in an instant they were seated at their desks like crows on a telephone wire. The rotten-mould green of Korotkov's face changed to a spotted purple.

"Ay-ay-ay," rumbled Starlin in the distance, looking up from his ledger, "how did you make such a boner as that? Eh?"

"I th-thought, I thought . . ." crackled the last splinters of Korotkov's voice, "I read 'Underwear' instead of 'Underwarr!' He writes his name with a small letter!"

"He doesn't have to worry, I'm not going to put any men's shorts on!" tinkled Lidochka like crystal.

"Shh!" Starlin hissed like a snake, "what's the matter with you?" He dove down, hid in his ledger, and covered his face with a page.

"But he's got no right to say that about my face!" cried Korotkov quietly, starting to get white as ermine instead of purple, "I burned my eyes with our goddamn matches, just like Comrade de Runi!"

"Quiet!" squeaked Gitis, who had turned pale, "what's the matter with you? He tested them yesterday and decided they were excellent."

Dr-r-r-r-r-rrr the electric bell over the door rang unexpectedly . . . and in that same instant Panteleimon's heavy body fell from its stool and rolled through the corridor.

"No! I will explain! I will explain!" sang Korotkov in a high and thin voice—then he dashed to the left, dashed to the right, ran some ten paces in place, distortedly reflected in the dusty Alpine mirrors; he emerged into the corridor and ran toward the light of the dim bulb hanging over the sign: "Private offices." Gasping for breath, he stopped in front of the terrible door and found himself in Panteleimon's arms.

"Comrade Panteleimon," said Korotkov anxiously, "please let me by. I must see the director this minute . . ."

"Impossible, impossible, I have orders not to admit anyone," croaked Panteleimon, stifling Korotkov's determination with a horrible odor of onion, "impossible. Go on, go on, Mr. Korotkov, or I'll get into trouble because of you . . ."

"But I have to, Panteleimon," begged Korotkov, his voice fading, "don't you see, dear Panteleimon, there's been this order . . . Let me by, dear Panteleimon."

"Oh, my Lord . . ." muttered Panteleimon, turning around toward the door in horror, "it's impossible, I tell you. Impossible, comrade!"

A telephone rang suddenly in the office behind the door, and a heavy voice crashed against copper: "I'm on the way! Right now!"

Panteleimon and Korotkov moved aside; the door was flung open, and Underwarr careened along the corridor wearing his service cap and with his briefcase under his arm. Panteleimon ran after him coweringly, and behind Panteleimon—after hesitating for a moment —darted Korotkov. At the turn in the corridor Korotkov, pale and flustered, skipped under Panteleimon's arms, overtook Underwarr, and ran along backwards in front of him.

"Comrade Underwarr," he muttered in a broken voice, "allow me to talk to you for one minute . . . It's about the order . . ."

"Comrade!" the preoccupied Underwarr's voice clanged furiously as he hurtled along, brushing Korotkov aside on the run, "Can't you see that I'm busy? I'm on my way! I'm on my way! . . ."

"It's about the ord . . ."

"Can't you see that I'm busy? . . . Comrade! Go see the clerk."

Underwarr ran out into the vestibule where the huge, abandoned organ of the Alpine Rose was located on the landing.

"*I'm* the clerk!" shrieked Korotkov in horror, breaking into a sweat, "Hear me out, Comrade Underwarr!"

"Comrade!" Underwarr howled like a siren, paying no attention; and turning around to Panteleimon as he was moving, he shouted, "Take measures to see that I am not delayed!"

"Comrade!" croaked Panteleimon in fright, "why are you delaying him?"

And not knowing what measure should be taken, he took this one: he grabbed Korotkov around the torso and pressed him lightly to himself, like a beloved woman. The measure turned out to be effective; Underwarr slipped out, sliding off the stairs as if on rollers, and hopping through the front door.

"R-roomm! B-rroom!" a motorcycle rattled outside the glass; it backfired five times, and enveloping the windows in smoke, disappeared. Only then did Panteleimon release Korotkov, wipe the sweat from his face, and wail, "Trou-ble!"

"Panteleimon . . ." Korotkov asked in a trembling voice, "where is he going? Tell me quickly, he'll get someone else . . . don't you understand . . ."

"To CENTEQUIP, I think."

Korotkov flew down the stairs like a whirlwind, tore into the cloakroom, grabbed his overcoat and cap, and ran out into the street.

[V]

A DEMONIC TRICK

KOROTKOV WAS LUCKY. A trolley had come even with the Alpine Rose at just that moment. Leaping successfully, Korotkov swept forward knocking against the brake wheel and then against bags on backs. His heart was burning with hope. Somehow the motorcycle had been held up, and now it was rattling along in front of the trolley; and Korotkov would sometimes lose sight of it, sometimes again locate the square back in a cloud of blue smoke. For about five minutes Korotkov was knocked around and crushed on the platform; finally the motorcycle stopped at the gray building of CENTEQUIP. The square body was enveloped by passers-by and disappeared. Korotkov tore off the trolley while it was still running, spun around, fell down, bruised his knee, picked up his cap, and just getting missed by a car, hurried into the vestibule.

Covering the floor with wet spots, dozens of people were walking toward Korotkov and overtaking him. The square back flashed on the second flight of stairs, and gasping for breath he hurried after it. Underwarr was going up with weird, unnatural celerity, and Korotkov's heart sank at the thought that he would lose him. That is what happened. On the fifth landing, when the clerk was totally exhausted, the back dissolved in a mass of physiognomies, hats, and briefcases. Like lightning Korotkov flew onto the landing and for a second he hesitated in front of a door on which there were two signs. One was gold on green with old orthography: "Dortoir Pepigneroc." The other was black on white in new orthography: "Nachkantsupravdelsnab." [9] Guessing, Korotkov swept through these doors, and there he saw huge glass cages with many blond women running around between them. Korotkov opened the first glass partition and saw some man wearing a blue suit sitting behind it. He was leaning on the desk and merrily laughing into the telephone. On the desk in the second compartment were the complete collected works of Sheller-Mikhailov,[10] and beside this set an unknown middle-aged woman wearing a scarf was weighing on scales a bad-smelling, dried fish. In the third incessant thunder and little bells reigned—six light-haired, small-toothed women were sitting there behind six typewriters typing and laughing. Behind the last partition a large space containing six puffy columns opened up. There was an unbearable clatter of typewriters in the air, and he could see a mass of heads—female and male—but Underwarr's was not among them. Bewildered and whirling around, Korotkov stopped the first woman he came to—she was running by with a little mirror in her hands.

"Have you seen Underwarr?"

9. Head of the Office of the Management of Supply.
10. A. K. Sheller-Mikhailov was a talentless author of problem novels in the 1860's.

Korotkov's heart jumped for joy when the woman replied, making huge eyes, "Yes, but he's leaving right now. Catch up to him."

Korotkov ran through the becolumned hall to where a small white hand with brilliant red nails was pointing. Having dashed across the hall, he found himself on a narrow and rather dark landing, and he saw the open maw of an illuminated elevator. Korotkov's heart leaped . . . he had caught up . . . the maw received the square blanket back and the shiny black briefcase.

"Comrade Underwarr," shouted Korotkov, and his extremities went cold. A large quantity of green lights started jumping around on the landing. The gate covered the glass door, the elevator started, and the square back, turning around, was transformed into a Bunyanesque chest. Korotkov recognized everything, everything: the gray service jacket, the cap, the briefcase, and the raisin-like eyes. It was Underwarr, but Underwarr with a long Assyrian crimped beard flowing down onto his chest. This thought immediately occurred to Korotkov: "He grew the beard when he was riding the motorcycle and coming up the stairs—what is this?" And then another: "It's a fake beard—what is this?"

And meanwhile Underwarr was beginning to descend into the becaged abyss. First his legs vanished, then his stomach, beard, and last his little eyes and a mouth shouting tender, tenor words, "It's too late, comrade, come Friday."

"His voice is disguised too," pounded in Korotkov's skull. For about three seconds his head burned tormentingly, but then, remembering that no kind of sorcery should stop him, that stopping meant destruction, Korotkov moved toward the elevator. The roof appeared rising up the shaft on its cable. A languid beauty with glittering stones in her hair came out of the shaft, and touching Korotkov's hands tenderly she asked him, "Do you have a weak heart, comrade?"

"No, oh, no, comrade," Korotkov uttered, stunned, and stepped toward the cage, "don't hold me up."

"Comrade, go to Ivan Finogenovich then," said the beauty sadly, blocking Korotkov's path to the elevator.

"I don't want to!" cried Korotkov in a whine, "Comrade! I'm in a hurry. What are you doing?"

But the woman remained adamant and sad.

"I can't do anything, you know that yourself," she said, still holding onto Korotkov's hand. The elevator stopped, spat out a man carrying a briefcase, closed and went down again.

"Let me go!" shrieked Korotkov, and tearing his hand away, he dashed down the stairs with a curse. Hurtling past six marble flights and almost killing a tall old woman wearing a lace headpiece who crossed herself after, he found himself downstairs alongside a huge new glass wall under an inscription in silver on blue: "Preceptresses" was written above, and below was a piece of paper on which was written in ink: "Information." Dark horror overcame Korotkov. He could clearly see Underwarr flitting along on the other side of the wall. The former, terrifying Underwarr, tinged with blue from shaving. He was passing quite close to Korotkov, separated from him only by a thin layer of glass. Trying not to think about anything, Korotkov dashed toward a glittering copper door handle and shook it, but it did not give.

Gritting his teeth, he tore at the shining copper again, and only then saw in desperation the tiny inscription: "Around through entrance six."

Underwarr flitted by and vanished in a black niche on the other side of the glass.

"Where is No. 6? Where is No. 6?" he cried weakly to someone. Passers-by shied away. A small side door opened, and out of it came a lustrine little old man wearing blue glasses and carrying a huge list in his hands. Glancing at Korotkov over his glasses, he smiled and chewed his lips.

"What? You're still around?" he mumbled. "By God, there's no point. You listen to me, old fellow, forget it. I've already crossed you off anyway. He, he."

"Crossed me off what?" Korotkov turned to stone.

"He. It's obvious where—from the lists. With a pencil. Scratch—and that's all. He, he," the old man laughed voluptuously.

"Wa-ait a minute . . . Where do you know me from?"

"He. You're joking, Vasily Pavlovich."

"My name is Varfolomey," said Korotkov, touching his cold and slippery forehead with his hand, "Petrovich."

For a minute the smile left the face of the terrible old man.

He fixed his eyes on the sheet and drew his long fingernail across the lines.

"Why are you mixing me up? Here it is—Kolobkov, V. P."

"My name is Korotkov," shouted Korotkov impatiently.

"That's what I said, 'Kolobkov,'" the old man took offense. "And here's Underwarr too. They've both been transferred—and Chekushin takes Underwarr's place."

"What? . . ." shouted Korotkov, forgetting himself from joy, "Underwarr has been tossed out?"

"Precisely, sir. He managed to supervise for all of one day, and they booted him out."

"God!" Korotkov exclaimed exultantly. "I've been saved! I've been saved!" And forgetting himself, he shook the bony, sharp-nailed hand of the old man. The latter smiled. For an instant Korotkov's joy dimmed. Something strange and ominous flashed in the blue eye sockets of the old man. The smile, exposing his bluish gums, seemed strange too. But Korotkov immediately drove away the unpleasant feeling and started fussing.

"Therefore I should run over to MATMAT right now?"

"Definitely," the old man confirmed, "that's what it says here, MATMAT. Only please give me your little workbook; I'll make a notation in it with this nice little pencil."

Korotkov immediately reached in his pocket, turned pale, reached in the other, turned even paler, slapped his pants pockets, and with a choked howl rushed back up the stairs looking under his feet. Bumping into people, desperate Korotkov flew to the very top, tried to find the beauty with stones and ask her something, but saw that the beauty had been transformed into an ugly, snotty little boy.

"Nice little boy!" Korotkov rushed up to him, "My yellow wallet . . ."

"It's a lie," the kid answered viciously, "I didn't take it, they're lying."

"No, no, dear fellow, that wasn't it . . . not you . . . my documents."

The kid looked at him from under his eyebrows and suddenly howled in a bass, crying.

"Oh, my God!" cried Korotkov in desperation, and he dashed down to the old man.

But when he arrived, the old man was not there. He had vanished. Korotkov dashed to the small door, ripped at the handle. It turned out to be locked. In the half-darkness there was a faint smell of sulphur.

The thoughts spun through Korotkov's mind like a snowstorm, and one new one leapt out: "The trolley!" He suddenly remembered quite clearly how two young men had squeezed around him on the platform, one of them was skinny with a black moustache which seemed to be fake.

"Oh, trouble, now this is trouble," Korotkov muttered, "this is the trouble to end all troubles."

He ran out into the street, ran along the street to its end, turned into an alley, and found himself at the entrance of a small building of unpleasant architecture. A gloomy, one-eyed, gray man who looked not at Korotkov, but somewhere to the side, asked, "Where do you think you're going?"

"I am Comrade Korotkov, V. P., from whom the documents were just stolen . . . Every last one . . . I could be arrested . . ."

"Very simply too," the man on the porch affirmed.

"So let me . . ."

"Have Korotkov come personally."

"But *I* am Korotkov, comrade."

"Give me your identification papers."

"They were just stolen from me," moaned Korotkov, "stolen, comrade, a young man with a moustache."

"With a moustache? That must be Kolobkov. Undoubtedly him. He works our area specially. You go look for him in the tea shops now."

"Comrade, I can't," wept Korotkov, "I have to go to MATMAT to see Underwarr. Let me by."

"Give me a certificate that they were stolen."

"From whom?"

"From your house manager." [11]

Korotkov left the porch and ran down the street.

"To MATMAT or to the house manager?" he wondered. "The house manager's office hours are only mornings, so I'll go to MATMAT."

At that instant a distant clock struck four times in a rust-colored tower, and immediately people carrying briefcases started running out of every door. It was dusk, and a light, wet snow started falling from the sky.

"It's too late," thought Korotkov, "homeward."

[V I]

THE FIRST NIGHT

THERE WAS A white note sticking out of the keyhole. Korotkov read it in the twilight.

Dear neighbor!

I'm going away to mother in Zveningorod. I'm leaving you the

11. House managers or building supervisors had a number of jobs, particularly seeing that everyone was registered for his particular city and "unregistered" when he left or died. Everyone could get a theoretical number of square feet of "living space." Everyone had, and has, an internal passport.

wine as a present. Drink all you want—no one wants to buy it. They're in the corner.

> Yours,
> A. Paikova

Smiling obliquely, Korotkov rattled the lock, took twenty trips to drag all of the bottles standing in the corner of the corridor into his room, lit a light, and just as he was, in his cap and overcoat, fell onto his bed. Like someone enchanted he spent about half an hour staring at the portrait of Cromwell which dissolved in the thick twilight; then he hopped up and suddenly had an attack of manic behavior. Tearing off his cap, he tossed it into the corner, with one sweep he threw all of the packages of matches onto the floor and started to stomp on them with his feet.

"Take that! And that! And that!" howled Korotkov, and with a crunch he smashed the damned boxes, vaguely imagining that he was crushing Underwarr's head.

At the thought of his egg-shaped head, he suddenly remembered the shaven and bearded faces, and at this point Korotkov stopped.

"Now just a minute . . . how can it be?" he whispered and drew his hand across his eyes, "What is this? Why am I standing around concerned with trifles when this is all so terrifying? Can he really be a double person?"

Terror crept through the black windows into the room, and Korotkov closed their blinds trying not to look through them. But this gave him no relief. From time to time the double face—now growing a beard, now abruptly being shaved—would float out of the corners, its greenish eyes flashing. Finally, Korotkov could no longer stand it, and feeling as if his head were going to crack from the tension, he began to weep softly.

After having cried and getting some relief, he ate yesterday's slimy potatoes, and then returning to the cursed riddle again, he wept a little more.

"Come on . . ." he suddenly muttered, "why am I weeping when I have wine?"

He drank half a tea cup of wine in one gulp. The sweet fluid took effect within five minutes—his left temple began to ache painfully, and he felt a burning, nauseating desire to drink. After drinking three glasses of water, Korotkov completely forgot Underwarr from the pain in his temple, ripped off his outer clothing with a groan, and languorously, rolling back his eyes, he fell into bed. "I'd like some pyramidon . . ." he whispered for a long time, until murky sleep took pity on him.

[V I I]

THE ORGAN AND THE CAT

AT TEN O'CLOCK in the morning the next day Korotkov hastily boiled his tea, drank a quarter of a glass with no appetite, and sensing that there was a difficult, trouble-filled day ahead, he left his room and ran across the wet asphalt courtyard in the fog. On the door of the little building was written: "House Manager." Korotkov's hand had already reached toward the button when his eyes read: "Due to death no certificates are being issued."

"Oh, my Lord," Korotkov exclaimed in vexation, "what is this —failures at every step." And he added, "Well, I'll have to do the documents later and go to MATMAT now. I have to inquire what's going on. Maybe Chekushin is already back."

On foot, since all of his money had been stolen, Korotkov made his way to MATMAT and going through the vestibule he headed straight for the office. On the threshold to the office he stopped and opened his mouth. There was not a single familiar face in the crystal hall. No Starlin, no Anna Evgrafovna, in a word no one. Behind the desks, no longer reminding one of crows on a wire, but of Tsar Alexei Mikhailovich's three falcons,[12] sat three absolutely iden-

12. An allusion to a royal coat of arms.

tical shaven blond-haired men wearing light-gray checked suits and one young woman with dreamy eyes and jewelled earrings in her ears. The young men paid no attention whatever to Korotkov and continued scratching in their ledgers, but the woman made eyes at him. And when he answered by smiling perplexedly, she smiled haughtily and turned away. "Strange," thought Korotkov, and stumbling on the threshold he went out of the office. He hesitated by the door to his own room, sighed as he looked at the dear old sign: "Clerk," opened the door and went in. The light immediately went out in Korotkov's eyes, and the floor swayed lightly under his feet. At Korotkov's desk, elbows spread wide, furiously scratching away with a pen, sat Underwarr in the flesh. Shiny, crimped hair covered his chest. Korotkov caught his breath as he glanced at the lacquered bald spot over the green cloth.[13] Underwarr was first to break the silence.

"What do you want, comrade?" he cooed politely in a falsetto.

Korotkov licked his lips with a shudder, sucked a small pocket of air into his narrow chest, and said just audibly, "Ahem . . . comrade, I am the clerk here . . . That is . . . Well, if you recall the order . . ."

Amazement sharply changed the upper part of Underwarr's face. His light brows raised, and his forehead turned into an accordion.

"Excuse me," he replied politely, "*I* am the clerk here."

Temporary muteness struck Korotkov. When it had passed, he uttered these words: "But what do you mean? Yesterday, that is. Oh, I see. Excuse me, please, I got it mixed up. Please."

He backed out of the room, and in the corridor he said to himself hoarsely, "Korotkov, try to remember, what is today's date?"

And he answered himself, "Tuesday, that is, Friday. Nineteen hundred . . ."

He turned around and immediately two corridor light bulbs

13. Virtually all offices and conference rooms in the U.S.S.R. have green felt on the desks and tables.

flared up before him on a human ball of ivory, and Underwarr's shaved face blotted out the whole world.

"Good!" the pan thundered, and a shudder ran through Korotkov, "I've been waiting for you. Fine. Glad to meet you."

With these words he moved toward Korotkov and shook his hand so hard that Korotkov stood on one foot like a stork on a roof.

"I've apportioned the staff," Underwarr said quickly, jerkily, and weightily. "Three there," he indicated the door into the main office, "and Manechka, of course. You will be my assistant. Underwarr is the clerk. I gave it to all the others in the neck. And that idiot Panteleimon too. I have information that he was the doorman for the Alpine Rose. I'm going to run to another office, but meanwhile you and Underwarr write a report about all of them, especially that . . . what's his name . . . Korotkov. Incidentally, you look a little bit like that bastard. Only he has a black eye."

"Me? No," said Korotkov, weaving back and forth and with his jaw hanging open, "I'm not a bastard. All of my documents have been stolen. To the last one."

"All?" Underwarr exclaimed. "Nonsense. All the better."

He latched onto Korotkov's hand (as he was trying painfully to catch his breath), and running along the corridor he dragged him into the cherished private office and threw him on a soft leather chair, sitting down at his desk himself. Still feeling a strange waving of the floor under his feet, Korotkov shrank into a ball, and closing his eyes muttered, "Monday was the twentieth, so Tuesday was the twenty-first. No. What's wrong with me? The year is twenty-one. Reference number 0.15, place for signature dash Varfolomey Korotkov. That means me. Tuesday, Wednesday, Thursday, Friday, Saturday, Sunday, Monday. Both Tuesday and Thursday begin with "T," and Wednesday . . . esss . . . with "S," just like Saturday . . ." [14]

14. Wednesday and Saturday (*sreda* and *subbota*) both begin with "s."

Underwarr scribbled across some paper with a crackle, stamped it with a seal, and jabbed it at him. At that instant the telephone began to ring furiously. Underwarr grabbed hold of the receiver and bellowed into it, "Aha! So. So. I'm on the way this minute."

He bolted toward the coat rack, snatched his service cap from it, covered his bald head with it, and disappeared through the door with the parting words, "Wait for me at Underwarr's."

Everything went totally bleary before Korotkov's eyes when he read what had been written on the paper with the stamp:

The bearer of this document is certified as my assistant, Comrade Vasily Pavlovich Kolobkov, which I hereby certify to be true.
Underwarr.

"O-oh!" moaned Korotkov, dropping the paper and his cap on the floor, "What is going on?"

At the same moment the door sang squeakily, and Underwarr returned wearing his beard.

All the lights went out.

"A-a-a-ah . . ." Korotkov wailed, unable to bear the torture, and out of his head he leapt at Underwarr baring his teeth. Terror overcame Underwarr's face so much that it turned yellow all at once. Bumping backwards into the door, he opened it loudly, fell back into the corridor, and failing to support himself he squatted down—but he quickly straightened up and took off running with a cry, "Messenger! Messenger! Help!"

"Stop! Stop! I implore you, comrade . . ." exclaimed Korotkov, coming to his senses and rushing after him.

There was a big noise in the main office, and the falcons leapt up as if on command. The dreamy eyes of the woman at the typewriter darted up.

"They're going to shoot! They're going to shoot!" her hysterical cry burst forth.

Underwarr was first into the vestibule where he hopped onto the organ platform, hesitated for a second about where to run, tore forward, and cutting a sharp corner, he disappeared behind the organ. Korotkov dashed after him, slipped, and would probably have smashed his head against the bannister if it had not been for the huge, black, crooked handle sticking out of the yellow side of the organ. It caught the hem of Korotkov's overcoat, and rotten cheviot tore apart with a quiet ripping sound, and Korotkov sat softly down on the cold floor. The side door behind the organ slammed clangorously behind Underwarr.

"God . . ." Korotkov began and did not finish.

A strange sound, like a glass breaking, came from the grandiose organ cabinet with its dust-covered brass pipes—then a dusty, uterine rumble, a strange chromatic shriek, and a pealing of bells. Then a sonorous major chord, a galvanizing full-blooded stream of sound, and the whole three-decked yellow cabinet began to play, pouring back and forth inside the deposits of sounds which had stood interrupted too long:

The Moscow fire burned and blared . . .

Panteleimon's pale face suddenly appeared in the black square of the door. An instant and he was metamorphosed. His eyes flashed a victorious gleam, he straightened up, whipped his right hand across his left as if tossing an invisible napkin over it, bolted from where he was standing, and sideways, obliquely, like an off-horse on a troika, he swept along the stairs holding his hands as if he were carrying a tray covered with cups.

The smo-oke stretched across the river.

"What have I done?" Korotkov was horrified.

The instrument which had turned over the first long interrupted waves now went on smoothly in a thousand-headed, leonine roar and clangor, flooding the empty halls of MATMAT.

And on the walls of the Kremlin gates . . .

Through the howling and rumbling and bells an automobile horn pierced, and immediately Underwarr came back in through the main entrance—the shaven, vengeful, and menacing Underwarr. In his ominous bluish gleam he began coming smoothly up the stairs. Korotkov's hair stood on end, and soaring forward he ran out the side door, down the crooked staircase behind the organ, ran out into the courtyard covered with gravel, and then into the street. He flew along the street as if in a race, still listening to the building of the Alpine Rose rumbling hollowly behind him:

And he stood there in his grey coat . . .

At the corner a cabby was waving his whip, madly trying to move his nag from its place.

"Lord! Lord!" Korotkov wept stormily, "It's him again! What is this?"

The bearded Underwarr grew up from the pavement alongside the droshky, hopped into it, and began to pound the cabby on the back, urging him in a thin voice, "Get going! Get going, you good-for-nothing!"

The nag moved forward, started kicking its legs up, and then swept forward under the burning blows of the whip, filling the street with carriage rattling. Through his stormy tears Korotkov saw the cabby's lacquered cap fly off and under it curled-up banknotes flew off in various directions. Little boys chased after them with whistles. Turning around, the cabby yanked up the reins in desperation, but Underwarr began to pummel him insanely on the back and scream, "Drive on! Drive on! I'll pay you."

Crying out desperately, the cabby said, "Hey, Your Excellency, is this murder or what?" whipped the nag into a full gallop, and everything vanished around the corner.

Sobbing, Korotkov looked up at the grey sky quickly sweeping overhead, staggered a little, and exclaimed in pain, "Enough! I won't leave it like this! I'll have it out with him." He jumped and caught onto the trolley's arc-shaped back railing. The arc shook him for about five minutes and tossed him out in front of a nine-storey green building. Having run into the vestibule, Korotkov pushed his head through the four-sided opening in the wooden partition and asked a huge blue teakettle, "Where's the complaint bureau, comrade?"

"Eighth floor, 9th corridor, apartment 41, room 302," the teakettle answered in a female voice.

"Eighth, 9th, 41st, three hundred . . . three hundred . . . what was . . . 302," muttered Korotkov running up the broad staircase. "Eighth, 9th, 8th stop, 40 . . . no, 42 . . . no, 302," he mumbled, "Oh, God, I've forgotten . . . yes, 40th, the fortieth . . ."

On the eighth floor he passed three doors, saw the black number "40" on the fourth, and entered an immense two-lighted hall with columns in it. In the corners lay reels of rolled-up paper, and the entire floor was littered with torn-off pieces covered with writing. In this section a small table with a typewriter on it and a gold sort of woman loomed—she was softly humming a song, supporting her cheek with her fist, sitting at the table. Looking around in perplexity, Korotkov saw the massive figure of a man wearing a white *kuntush*[15] walk down from a platform behind the columns, walking heavily. A drooping greyish moustache could be seen on his marble face. Smiling an extraordinarily polite and lifeless plaster-of-Paris smile, the man approached Korotkov, shook his hand delicately, clicked his heels, and said, "Jan Sobieski." [16]

"It can't be," the dumbfounded Korotkov replied.

The man smiled pleasantly.

"Just imagine, many people are amazed," he started talking with incorrect accents, "but, comrade, don't think I have anything in common with that bandit. Oh, no. A bitter coincidence, nothing more. I have already petitioned to have my name changed to Sotsovski. That's much prettier, and not as dangerous. However, if

15. From the Hungarian *köntös*. A loose outer garment or kaftan once worn by Poles and Ukrainians.
16. King of Poland, 1674–96.

it is unpleasant for you," the man twisted his mouth touchily, "I am not foisting myself upon you. We can always find someone else. We are in demand."

"My goodness, what are you saying," Korotkov exclaimed in distress, sensing that here too something strange was starting, just as it had everywhere else. He looked back as if he were being hunted, afraid that the shaven face and the bald shell would emerge from somewhere, and then he added in a clumsy way, "I'm very glad, yes, very . . ."

A motley flush passed lightly over the marble man; raising Korotkov's hand delicately, he drew him toward a little table, reiterating, "I'm very glad, too. But here's the rub, imagine it—I don't even have a place where you can sit down. We're being kept in a pen in spite of our significance." (The man waved his hand toward the reels of paper.) "Intrigues . . . *But,* we're going to show our stuff, don't worry . . . Hm . . . What new thing have you to cheer us up?" he asked pale Korotkov affectionately. "Oh, yes, pardon, a thousand pardons, allow me to introduce . . ." he swept his arm elegantly toward the typewriter, ". . . Henrietta Potapovna Persimfans."

The woman immediately shook Korotkov's hand with her cold hand and looked at him languorously.

"And," the boss continued sweetly, "what have you brought to cheer us up? A feuilleton? Sketches?" rolling his white eyes back, he drawled on, "You cannot imagine how much we need them."

"Queen of Heaven . . . what is going on?" Korotkov thought hazily; then, gasping for breath, he started to talk.

"Something . . . eh . . . terrible has happened to me. He . . . I don't understand. For God's sake, don't think that I'm having hallucinations . . . Ahem . . . ha, ha . . ." (Korotkov tried to laugh artificially, but it didn't come off.) "He's alive. I assure you . . . but I won't understand anything—first with a beard, and a minute later without the beard. I simply can't understand . . . And his voice changes . . . beside which all of my documents down to the last one have been stolen, and the house manager, as bad luck would have it, has died. This Underwarr . . ."

"I knew it," the boss cried, "so it's them?"

"Oh, my God, well of course," the woman echoed, "Oh, it's those horrible Underwarrs."

"Do you know," the boss interrupted excitedly, "I'm sitting on the floor because of him. There, sir, what do you think of that? Now what does he know about journalism? . . ." the boss grabbed Korotkov by a button, "Be so kind as to tell me what he knows about it. He spent two days here, and it was absolute torture for me. But imagine the good fortune: I went to see Fyodor Vasilievich, and he finally got him out. I put the question pointedly: him or me. He was transferred to some MATMAT or, the devil knows where. Let him stink of those matches! But the furniture—he managed to transfer the furniture to that damned bureau. All of it! How do you like that? And what, may I inquire, am I going to write on? What are you going to write on? For I don't doubt that you will be ours, dear (the man embraced Korotkov). That rascal propelled our fine satin Louis Quatorze furniture irresponsibly off to that stupid bureau which will be shut up tighter than hell tomorrow anyway."

"What bureau?" Korotkov asked hollowly.

"Oh, those complaints or whatever they are there," the boss said with vexation.

"What?" Korotkov cried, "What? Where is it?"

"There," the boss answered surprisedly, jabbing his finger toward the floor. For the last time Korotkov cast his mad glance over the white *kuntush* and a minute later found himself in the corridor. After thinking a little, he flew to the left, looking for the down staircase. He ran for about five minutes, following the capricious twists of the corridor, and after five minutes he found himself at the very spot from which he had run. Door No. 40.

"Oh, damn!" moaned Korotkov; he stomped his feet and ran off to the right—and within five minutes he was again back at the same place. No. 40. Tearing at the door, Korotkov ran into the room and made sure that it was empty. Only the typewriter on the table smiled silently with its white teeth. Korotkov ran up to the colonnade and there he caught sight of the boss. He was standing on a pedestal, now with no smile on his offended face.

"Forgive me for not saying goodbye . . ." Korotkov began—and fell silent. The boss was standing there without an ear and with no nose, and his left arm was broken off. Falling backwards and turning cold, Korotkov again ran out into the corridor. An unnoticeable, secret door opposite suddenly opened, and from it issued a wrinkled, brown old woman carrying empty buckets on a yoke.

"Hey you! Hey you, old woman!" Korotkov shouted anxiously, "where's the bureau?"

"I don't know, sir, I don't know, kind sir," the old woman replied, "but don't run around, dearie, you won't find it anyhow. Can you really think so—there are ten floors."

"O-o-oh . . . you idiot," roared Korotkov, gnashing his teeth and dashing toward the door. It slammed behind him, and Korotkov found himself in a dead-end, nearly dark space with no exit. Throwing himself at the walls and scratching at them like someone buried in a pit, he finally fell against a white spot, and it let him out onto some sort of staircase. With staccato steps he ran down them. He could hear steps coming to meet him from below. A mournful uneasiness penetrated Korotkov's heart, and he started to stop. Another moment—and a glittering service cap appeared, a gray blanket and long beard flashed into view. Korotkov stumbled and grabbed hold of the railing with his hands. Their glances met simultaneously, and both of them started to howl in thin voices of terror and pain. Korotkov began to retreat upstairs backwards; Underwarr stepped back down, full of insuperable horror.

"Wait," Korotkov croaked, "a minute . . . you just explain . . ."

"Save me!" Underwarr roared, changing the thin voice for his first copper bass. Having retreated, he fell over backwards onto his head with a thunderous racket; and the blow did not pass in vain. Having been metamorphosed into a black cat with phosphorescent eyes, he flew back up, intersecting the landing sweepingly and with velvet softness, rolled himself into a ball, and jumping onto the sill, he disappeared through the broken glass and cobwebs. For a moment Korotkov's brain was enveloped in a white shroud, but it immediately fell off and an extraordinary moment of clarity took its place.

"Now I understand everything," Korotkov whispered, and started to laugh softly, "aha, I see. So that's it. The cats! I understand it all. Cats!"

He began to laugh louder and louder, until the whole staircase was filled with resonant rolls.

[V I I I]

THE SECOND NIGHT

SITTING ON his flannelette bed in the twilight, Comrade Korotkov had drunk three bottles of wine—so that he would forget everything and calm down. Now his head was aching all over: right and left temples, crown, and even the eyelids. A light nausea rose from the pit of his stomach, swept around in waves, and Comrade Korotkov vomited into the wash basin twice.

"This is what I'll do," Korotkov whispered weakly, hanging his head down, "tomorrow I'll try not to meet him. But since he is whirling around everywhere, I'll wait him out—either in an alley or a dead end. He'll pass right by. And if he starts chasing me, I'll run away. He'll be left behind. Go along, he'll say, wherever you want. And I do not want to go to MATMAT any more. Forget it. Be your own director and clerk, Underwarr, and I don't want any of your trolley money. I'll manage without it. Just leave me alone, please. Whether you're a cat or not a cat, with a beard or without a beard—you'll be you by yourself and I'll be me by myself. I'll find myself another little job, and I'll work quietly and peacefully. I won't bother anybody and nobody will bother me. And I'm not going to file any complaints about you. Tomorrow I'll just get my documents straightened out—and that'll be it. . . .

A clock began to strike hollowly in the distance. Bong . . . bong . . . "That's at Pestrukhiny," thought Korotkov, and he started counting. "Ten . . . eleven . . . midnight, thirteen, fourteen, fifteen . . . forty . . ."

"The little clock struck forty times," Korotkov smirked bitterly, and then he started crying again. Then the church wine nauseated him again, shudderingly and painfully.

"It's strong wine, oh, it's strong," murmured Korotkov and with a moan he fell back onto the pillow. About two hours passed, and the unextinguished lamp still illuminated the pale face and mussed hair on the pillow.

[I X]

TYPEWRITER TERROR

THE AUTUMN DAY met Comrade Korotkov dimly and strangely. Looking back down the stairs timidly, he went up to the eighth floor, turned right at random and trembled joyfully. A painted hand directed him to the sign: "Rooms 302–349." Following the finger of the rescuing hand, he reached a door with the sign: "302—Complaint Bureau." Glancing in cautiously so as not to bump into anyone he shouldn't, Korotkov entered and found himself in front of a family of women with typewriters. After having hesitated a little, he went up to the one on the end—a dusky, lusterless one—bowed, and wanted to say something, but the brunette suddenly interrupted him. The gazes of all of the women fixed on Korotkov.

"Let's go out into the corridor," the lusterless one said harshly, tremblingly fixing her hair.

"My God, again, again something . . ." flashed sadly through Korotkov's mind. Sighing heavily, he obeyed. The six who remained in the room began to whisper excitedly behind them.

The brunette led Korotkov out, and in the half-darkness of the corridor, she said, "You are terrible . . . I didn't sleep all night because of you, and I've decided. Have it your way. I will give myself to you."

Korotkov looked at the dusky face with its huge eyes, with the smell of lilies of the valley; he emitted some sort of guttural sound, and said nothing. The brunette threw her head back, bared her teeth like a martyr, grabbed Korotkov's hand, drew him to herself, and whispered, "Why don't you say something, you seducer? You have conquered me with your boldness, my serpent. Kiss me, kiss me quick—while there's no one from the control commission here."

Again the strange sound escaped from Korotkov's mouth. He staggered, felt something soft and sweet on his lips, and huge pupils appeared right in front of Korotkov's eyes.

"I will give myself to you . . ." was whispered right into Korotkov's mouth.

"I don't need it," he replied hoarsely, "my documents have been stolen."

"So-o," suddenly rang out behind him.

Korotkov turned around and saw the lustrine old man.

"O-oh!," screamed the brunette, and covering her face with her hands she ran through the door.

"He, he," said the little old man, "that's great. Wherever one goes, there you are, Mister Kolobkov. Well, you are a real lover boy. But why mention it—whether you kiss or don't kiss, you won't kiss yourself into an expense-paid business trip. They gave it to me, an old man, and I am to go. That's what they did, sir."

With these words he gave Korotkov a dried-up little finger.

"But I'll make a complaint about you," the lustrine continued maliciously, "yes, sir. You've seduced three in the main office, now, it appears, you're getting down to the lower divisions? Is it all the same to you whether the little angels are crying now? They're lamenting now, the poor little girls, but it's too late, sir. You can't give back a girl's honor. You can't give it back."

The little old man dragged out a large handkerchief covered with orange flowers, began to cry, and blew his nose.

"You want to snatch the last crumbs from the hands of an old man, Mister Kolobkov? Well then . . ." The old man started to shake and weep, dropping his briefcase. "Take them, eat up. Let an old man, a non-Party member, a sympathizer, die from hunger . . . Let him, you say. That's where his road leads, the old mongrel. But just remember, Mister Kolobkov," the old man's voice became prophetically threatening and full of a tolling of bells, "it won't do you any good, that Satanic money. It'll become a knife in your throat," and the old man dissolved in tempestuous weeping.

Hysteria overwhelmed Korotkov; abruptly and unexpectedly even for himself, he started stamping his feet rapidly.

"Dammit to hell!" he cried thinly, and his pained voice echoed through the walls. "I am not Kolobkov. Get away from me! I'm not Kolobkov. I won't go! I won't go!"

He began to tear at his collar.

The old man dried up in an instant, he began to tremble from terror.

"Next!" croaked the door. Korotkov fell silent and bolted through it, turned to the left, passed the typewriters, and turned up in front of a big, elegant blond man wearing a dark blue suit. The blond man nodded to Korotkov and said, "Be brief, comrade. All at once. Make it snappy. Poltava or Irkutsk?"

"My documents have been stolen . . . stolen!" replied the anguished Korotkov, looking around wildly, "And a cat appeared. He has no right. I have never gotten into a fight in my life, it was the matches. He has no right to persecute me. I don't care if he is Underwarr. And my documents have been sto . . ."

"Now this is nonsense," the blue one answered, "we give out uniforms, shirts, and sheets. If you're going to Irkutsk, then even a second-hand jacket. Be briefer."

He twisted a key melodically in a lock, and having pulled out the drawer and glanced into it, he said amiably, "Sergei Nikolaevich, if you please."

And instantly a pair of darting blue eyes and a neatly combed head as light haired as flax looked out of the ash drawer. Behind them came an unbending neck, like a snake's; a starched collar crunched out, a jacket, arms, and pants appeared, and within a second a completely finished and ready secretary clambered out onto the red cloth with a squeak of "Good morning." He shook himself like a dog coming out of the water, hopped down, pulled his cuffs down further, took a fountain pen out of his pocket, and immediately began to write.

Korotkov staggered back, stretched out his arm, and said querulously to the blue one, "Look, look, he crawled out of that desk. What is this? . . ."

"Naturally he did," answered the blue one, "he can't lie around in there all day. It's time. Now. Time-study."

"But how? How?" rang Korotkov's voice.

"Oh my Lord," the blue one got excited, "don't hold things up, comrade."

The brunette's head emerged from the door and shouted excitedly and joyfully, "I've already dispatched his documents to Poltava. And I'll go with him. I have an aunt in Poltava below the forty-third degree of latitude and the fifth of longitude."

"Well now, that's marvelous," replied the blond, "I'm tired of this dawdling around."

"I don't want to!" screamed Korotkov, his gaze wandering. "She is going to give herself to me, and I cannot bear that. I don't want it! Get my documents back. My holy name. Return it!"

"Comrade, that's done in the marriage bureau," squeaked the secretary, "we can do nothing."

"Oh, you idiot!" exclaimed the brunette, looking in again, "agree to it! Agree!" she shouted in a prompter's whisper. Her head kept appearing and disappearing.

"Comrade!" Korotkov started sobbing, wiping the tears across his face. "Comrade! I implore you, give me my documents. Be a friend. Be one, I beg of you with all the fibers of my soul, and I will go away into a monastery."

"Comrade! No hysterics. Concretely and abstractly set it forth in writing, quickly and secretly—Poltava or Irkutsk? Don't take time away from a busy man! No walking around in the corridors! No spitting! No smoking! No slowing down the exchange of money!" the blond thundered, losing control of himself.

"Handshaking has been abolished!" [17] crowed the secretary.

"Long live hugs!" whispered the brunette passionately, and like a piece of fluff she swept across the room leaving the smell of lilies of the valley on Korotkov's neck.

"The thirteenth commandment says: don't go in to see your neighbor without an official report," mumbled the lustrine one, and he flew through the air, flapping with the folds of his cloak . . . "And I do not go in, I do not, sir—but nevertheless I am throwing this paper down, like this—slam! . . . You'll sign anything—and in the prisoner's dock." He tossed a pack of white sheets from out of his wide black sleeve, and they flew about and scattered on the desks, like seagulls on the cliffs by the sea.

A dimness began to fill the room and the windows started to rock.

"Comrade blond!" cried the exhausted Korotkov, "Shoot me on the spot, but issue me whatever little document you have. I will kiss your hand."

In the dimness the blond started to puff up and grow larger, without stopping the frenzied signing of the old man's papers for a minute and tossing them to the secretary who caught them with joyful rumbling.

17. Right after the Revolution handshaking was discouraged, because it was regarded as a hangover of bourgeois society.

"To hell with him!" thundered the blond, "To hell with him. Typists, hey!"

He waved a huge arm, the wall fell apart before Korotkov's very eyes, and tinkling their bells thirty typewriters on desks began to play a fox-trot. Swaying their hips, wiggling their shoulders voluptuously, tossing up their creamy legs in a white foam, the thirty women set off in a can-can and circled around the desks.

White snakes of paper crawled into the maws of the typewriters, started rolling themselves in, tearing apart, and reuniting. White trousers with violent stripes came out. "The bearer of this is in fact the bearer, and not any riff-raff."

"Put 'em on!" bellowed the blond in the mist.

"Aie-e-e-e!" whimpered Korotkov thinly, and he started to pound his head against the corner of the blond's desk. This made his head feel better for a minute, and someone's face in tears dashed in front of Korotkov.

"Valerian drops!" shouted someone on the ceiling.

The winged cloak, like a black bird, blocked off the light; the old man whispered in alarm, "There's only one way out now—to Dyrkin in the fifth section. Move! Move!"

It started to smell of ether, then arms gently carried Korotkov into the half-dark corridor. The winged cloak embraced Korotkov and drew him along, whispering and giggling, "Well, I really fixed them—I scattered papers on their desks of the sort that each of them will get more than five years, and it's a defeat on the field of battle for them. Move! Move!"

The cloak flitted to the side, wind and dampness blew from the cage descending into the abyss.

[X]

DYRKIN THE TERRIBLE

THE MIRRORED BOX began to fall downward, and two Korot-
kovs fell with it. The first and main one forgot the second Korotkov
in the mirror of the box, and went out alone into the cool vestibule.
A very fat and pink man met Korotkov with the words, "Just
marvelous. I'm putting you under arrest."

"I cannot be arrested," replied Korotkov—and he laughed a
Satanic laughter, "because I am no one knows who. Of course. I
cannot be arrested or married. And I will not go to Poltava."

The fat man trembled in terror, looked into Korotkov's pupils,
and started to retreat.

"Go ahead and arrest me," Korotkov screeched, and he stuck out
a pale shaking tongue smelling of valerian drops at the fat man,
"how can you arrest me if instead of documents all there is is a
fig? Maybe I'm a Hohenzollern."

"Lord Jesus," said the fat man; and he crossed himself with a
quaking hand and turned from pink to yellow.

"Was Underwarr caught?" asked Korotkov abruptly, looking back
at him. "Answer me, tubby."

"Not at all," replied the fat man, changing the pink shade for a
grayish one.

"And what are we going to do now? Eh?"

"To Dyrkin, there's no other way," babbled the fat man, "it's
best of all to go to him. Only he's terrifying. Oy, terrifying! And
don't go close to him. Two have already flown out of his office up
there. He smashed his telephone today."

"All right," replied Korotkov, and he spit in a devil-may-care way,
"it makes no difference now. Let's go up!"

"Don't stub your toe, comrade authorized assistant," said the fat man tenderly, escorting Korotkov into the elevator.

On the upper landing they met a lad of about sixteen who shouted menacingly, "Where are you going? Stop!"

"Don't hit me, fellow," said the fat man, curling up like a hedgehog and covering his head with his arms, "to Dyrkin himself."

"Pass on," shouted the lad.

The fat man whispered, "You just go on, Your Radiance, and I'll wait for you here on this little bench. I feel awfully sick . . ."

Korotkov landed in a dark anteroom, from there went into a large empty room in which a worn blue carpet was stretched out.

Korotkov hesitated a little before the door with the sign "Dyrkin," but then he went in and found himself in a cozily furnished office with a huge crimson desk and a clock on the wall. Dyrkin, small and puffy, shot up like a spring from behind the desk, and making his moustaches stand on end, roared, "Shut up!"—even though Korotkov had said absolutely nothing so far.

At the moment a pale youth carrying a briefcase appeared in the office. Dyrkin's face was instantly covered with smiling wrinkles.

"A-ah!" he exclaimed sweetly, "Arthur Arthurovich. My respects to you."

"Listen, Dyrkin," the youth began in a metallic voice, "you wrote Puzyrev to the effect that I, supposedly, had established my personal dictatorship in the pension fund office and filched the May pension money. Did you? Answer me, you mangy bastard."

"Me?" muttered Dyrkin, magically turning from Dyrkin the Terrible into Dyrkin the Good. "Me, Arthur Dictaturych . . . Of course, I . . . There's no reason for you to . . ."

"Oh, you scum, you scum," said the youth distinctly; he shook his head, and swinging his briefcase, he banged Dyrkin in the ear with it, as if putting a pancake onto a plate.

Dyrkin moaned mechanically and froze.

"That's what you and any other good-for-nothings will get if they allow themselves to stick their noses into my business," the youth said premonishingly, and threatening Korotkov with a red fist in parting, he went out.

For two minutes or so there was silence in the office, with only the pendants on the candelabra tinkling from a truck passing by somewhere.

"There, young man," said the good and humiliated Dyrkin, smiling bitterly, "that's the reward for diligence. You don't get enough sleep at night, you don't get to eat enough, you don't drink enough, and there is always one result—a punch in the mug. Maybe you came to do the same thing? Why not? . . . Go ahead, hit Dyrkin, hit him. His mug is obviously state property. Maybe your hand is sore? Then you just take the candelabra."

And Dyrkin stuck his puffy cheeks out from behind the desk temptingly. Understanding nothing, Korotkov—after smiling crookedly and bashfully—took the candelabra by the base and with a crunch he smashed Dyrkin on the head with the candles. Blood started to drip from his nose onto the cloth, and he ran out through the inner door shouting, "Guard!"

"Coo-coo!" cried the forest cuckoo joyfully, hopping out of the little, decorated Nuremburg house on the wall.

"Coo-Clux-Clan?" it shouted; and it turned into a bald head, "we'll make a note of how you clobber workers."

Fury overwhelmed Korotkov. He brandished the candelabra and struck the clock with it. It replied with a crash and a shattering of golden hands. Underwarr jumped out of the clock, turned into a white cock on which there was the inscription "Reference," and whisked out the door. Immediately Dyrkin's howl rang out behind the inner doors: "Catch him, the bandit!" And heavy footsteps flew in every direction. Korotkov spun around and took off running.

[X I]

A CINEMA-STYLE CHASE
AND THE ABYSS

THE FAT MAN galloped into the elevator from the landing, slammed the cage doors, and plunged downward. And down the huge dilapidated staircase, in the following order, rushed: first, the fat man's top hat, behind it—the white reference cock, behind the cock—the candelabra, which flew past one inch over the pointed white head, then Korotkov, the sixteen-year-old with a revolver in his hand, and some other people as well, stomping along in hob-nailed boots. The staircase groaned with a bronze ringing sound, and on each landing doors kept closing in alarm.

Someone hung over from the top floor and shouted down through a megaphone, "What section is being moved? You forgot the safe!"

A woman's voice below answered, "Bandits!" Having overtaken the top hat and candelabra, Korotkov jumped through the huge doors into the street first, and sucking in a huge quantity of super-heated air, he flew along the street. The white cock was swallowed up by the earth, leaving a sulphurous odor; the black-winged cloak materialized out of thin air and plodded alongside Korotkov with a high-pitched, drawn-out cry, "They're beating up working people, comrades!"

Passers-by in Korotkov's path turned off to the sides and stood in gateways; short whistles kept bursting and then dissolving. Someone halloed furiously, hooted, and hoarse alarmed shouts of "stop him" began to break out. Iron shutters were lowered with staccato thunder, and some cripple sitting by the trolley tracks screeched, "They're off!"

Now shots were flying after Korotkov, frequent, merry ones, like Christmas crackers, and the bullets ricocheted now to the side, now overhead. Puffing like a bellows, Korotkov headed for a giant—an eleven-storey building with its side to the main street and its facade on a narrow side street. On the very corner a glass sign with the words "Restaurant and Beer" exploded in a starburst, and a middle-aged cabby fell from the seat of his carriage to the pavement with a languid expression on his face and the words: "Nice going! What's wrong with you, brothers, are you shooting anyone who's around?"

A man who had run out of the side street made an attempt to grab Korotkov by the bottom of his jacket, and he was left with it in his hands. Korotkov turned the corner, flew a few more yards, and ran into the mirrored expanse of the vestibule. A small boy wearing galoons and gilded buttons hopped away from the elevator and started to cry.

"Get in, mister, get in!" he howled. "Just don't hit an orphan!"

Korotkov tore into the cabin of the elevator, sat down on the green divan opposite another Korotkov, and gasped like a fish on the sand. The poor boy, sobbing, got in behind him, closed the door, pulled the rope, and the elevator went up. And immediately, in the vestibule below, shots thundered and glass doors started spinning around.

The elevator moved up softly and nauseatingly; the boy, calming down, wiped his nose with one hand and managed the rope with the other.

"Did you steal money, mister?" he asked with curiosity, examining the tormented Korotkov.

"Underwarr . . . we'll attack . . ." Korotkov replied, gasping for breath, "and now he's gone on the offensive . . ."

"Mister, you'd be best off on the very top, where the billiard room is," the boy advised, "there on the roof you can sit it out, if you've got a Mauser."

"All right, the top . . ." Korotkov agreed.

In a minute the elevator stopped smoothly, the boy threw open the doors, and snuffing his nose, said, "Get out, mister, climb onto the roof."

Korotkov hopped out, looked around, and listened. From below there was a growing, rising roar; from the side the click of hard balls through a glass partition behind which alarmed faces flitted. The boy darted into the elevator, locked himself in, and tumbled downward.

Surveying the position with an eagle eye, Korotkov hesitated for an instant, and then ran into the billiard room with the war cry, "Forward!" Green tables with shiny white balls and pale faces flashed here and there. Very close below a shot cracked with a deafening echo and somewhere glass shattered with a crash. As if on signal, the gamblers tossed away their cues, and single file, with a stomping of feet, they bolted through the side doors. Dashing about, Korotkov bolted the doors behind them; with a clatter he locked the main glass entrance door which led from the stairs into the billiard room, and in a flash he armed himself with balls. A few seconds passed and the first head grew up beside the elevator on the other side of the glass. A ball flew from Korotkov's hands, went through the glass with a whistle, and the head immediately disappeared. A pale fire flashed in its place, and a second head grew up, followed by a third. The balls flew one after the other, and the glass in the partition kept smashing. A rolling, pounding sound filled the staircase, and in answer to it, like a deafening Singer sewing machine, a machine gun began to roar and shake the entire building. The glass and frames were cut out of the upper part of the partition as if by a knife, and plaster flew all over the billiard room in a cloud of dust.

Korotkov realized that it was impossible to hold this position. Covering his head with his arms, he ran over and kicked at the third glass wall—beyond which the flat asphalt roof of the huge building began. The glass cracked and fell to pieces. Under tumultuous fire, Korotkov managed to throw five pyramids out onto the roof, and they rolled all over the asphalt like lopped-off heads. Korotkov hopped out after them, and just in time because the machine gun was aimed lower, and it cut out the entire lower part of the frame.

"Surrender!" he heard vaguely.

Before Korotkov were the sickly looking sun right over his head, a grayish sky, a slight wind, and the frozen asphalt. From below and outside the city made itself known with an alarmed, muffled roar. Jumping onto the asphalt and looking around, Korotkov picked up three balls, skipped over to the parapet, climbed onto it, and looked down. His heart sank. Before him he saw the roofs of the buildings which seemed flattened and small, a square across which trolleys and beetle-people were crawling—and immediately Korotkov made out gray figures dancing up to the entrance along the fissure which was the side street; and behind them he saw a heavy toy, speckled with shiny, golden little heads.

"They've surrounded me!" Korotkov moaned. "Firemen."

Leaning across the parapet, he took aim and let the three balls go, one after the other. They whizzed up, then described an arc, and plunged downward. Korotkov grabbed up another three, again climbed up, and winding up, released them too. The balls flashed like silver, then when they got lower they turned to black, then they again flashed and disappeared. It seemed to Korotkov that the beetles started to run across the sun-drenched square in distress. Korotkov bent over to pick up another round of ammunition, but he did not succeed. People appeared in the break into the billiard room with an unceasing crunch and crackle of glass. They poured out onto the roof like peas. Out flew gray service caps, gray overcoats, and then—out through the upper glass, without touching the ground—flew the lustrine little old man. Then the wall fell completely apart, and the terrible, shaven Underwarr rolled out menacingly on his rollers with an ancient musket in his hands.

"Surrender!" was howled from in front, behind, and above, and all of these shouts were drowned out by an unbearable, deafening, pan-like bass.

"Of course," Korotkov shouted weakly, "of course. The battle is lost. *Ta-ta-ta*," he played a bugle retreat on his lips.

The courage of death streamed into his soul. Taking hold and balancing himself, Korotkov climbed up onto the parapet ledge, stumbled a bit, pulled himself up to his full height, and shouted, "Better death than shame!"

The pursuers were two steps away. Korotkov already saw the outstretched arms; already the flame was leaping out of Underwarr's mouth. The sunny abyss beckoned Korotkov so much that his breath caught. With a piercing victory cry he vaulted off and flew up. In an instant his breath was cut off. Unclearly, very unclearly, he saw the gray fly upwards past him, full of black holes as if from an explosion. Then, very clearly, he saw the gray fall downward, and he himself rose upward toward the narrow fissure of the side street—which turned out to be above him. Then the incarnadine sun cracked resoundingly in his head, and he saw nothing more.

The Fatal Eggs

A Tale[1]

[I]

PROFESSOR PERSIKOV'S
CURRICULUM VITAE

ON APRIL 16, 1928, in the evening, Persikov,[2] professor of Zoology at the Fourth State University and director of the Zoological Institute in Moscow, entered his office at the Zoological Institute on Herzen Street. The professor switched on the frosted globe overhead and looked around.

The beginning of the terrifying catastrophe must be set precisely on that ill-fated evening, and just as precisely, Professor Vladimir Ipatievich Persikov must be considered the prime cause of this catastrophe.

He was exactly fifty-eight-years-old. A remarkable head shaped like a pestle, bald, with tufts of yellowish hair standing out on the

---

1. "The Fatal Eggs" was first published in *Nedra*, No. 6 (Moscow, 1925), pp. 79–148. A slightly censored version (with descriptions which might be seen as anti-religious cut) was published in Riga and later by the Chekhov Publishing House in M. Bulgakov, *Sbornik rasskazov* (New York, 1952). Readers of Russian should be aware that the émigré editions are incomplete. The events of the story, according to Mayakovsky, were reported as true in a New York newspaper in the twenties, and he used this as one of his many attacks on Bulgakov.

2. Persikov derives from *persik*, "peach."

sides. A smooth-shaven face with a protruding lower lip. Because of this Persikov always had a somewhat pouting expression on his face. Small, old-fashioned spectacles in a silver frame on a red nose; small, glittering eyes; tall, stoop shouldered. He spoke in a high, squeaky voice, and among his other idiosyncracies was this: whenever he spoke of anything emphatically and with assurance, he screwed up his eyes and curled the index finger of his right hand into a hook. And since he always spoke with assurance, for his erudition in his field was utterly phenomenal, the hook appeared very often before the eyes of Professor Persikov's listeners. As for any topics outside his field, i.e., zoology, embryology, anatomy, botany, and geography, Professor Persikov almost never spoke of them.

The professor did not read newspapers and did not go to the theater, and the professor's wife ran away from him in 1913 with a tenor from the Zimin Opera, leaving him the following note: "Your frogs make me shudder with intolerable loathing. I will be unhappy for the rest of my life because of them."

The professor never remarried and had no children. He was very short-tempered, but he cooled off quickly; he liked tea with raspberries; and he lived on Prechistenka in a five-room apartment, one room of which was occupied by his housekeeper Marya Stepanovna, a shriveled little old woman who looked after the professor like a nanny.

In 1919 the government requisitioned three of his five rooms. Then he declared to Marya Stepanovna: "If they don't cease these outrages, Marya Stepanovna, I will emigrate."

There is no doubt that had the professor realized this plan, he could easily have got settled in the department of zoology at any university in the world, since he was an absolutely first-rate scientist; and with the exception of Professors William Weccle of Cambridge and Giacomo Bartolommeo Beccari of Rome, he had no equals in the field bearing in one way or another on amphibians. Professor Persikov could lecture in four languages besides Russian, and he spoke French and German as fluently as Russian. Persikov did not carry out his intention to emigrate, and 1920 turned out to be even worse than 1919. Events kept happening one after the other. Great Nikitskaya was renamed Herzen Street. Then the clock built into the building on the corner of Herzen and Mokhovaya stopped at a quarter past eleven, and finally, in the terraria at the Zoological Institute, unable to endure the perturbations of that famous year, first eight splendid specimens of the tree frog died, then fifteen ordinary toads, followed, finally, by a most remarkable specimen of the Surinam toad.

Immediately after the toads, whose deaths decimated the population of the first order of amphibians, which is properly known as tailless, the institute's permanent watchman, old Vlas, who did not belong to the class of amphibians, moved on into a better world. The cause of his death, however, was the same as that of the poor animals, and Persikov diagnosed it at once: "Lack of feed."

The scientist was absolutely right: Vlas had to be fed with flour, and the toads with mealworms, but since the former had disappeared, the latter had also vanished. Persikov tried to shift the remaining twenty specimens of the tree frog to a diet of cockroaches, but the cockroaches had also disappeared somewhere, thus demonstrating their malicious attitude toward War Communism. And so, even the last specimens had to be tossed out into the garbage pits in the institute's courtyard.

The effect of the deaths, especially that of the Surinam toad, on Persikov is beyond description. For some reason he put the whole blame for the deaths on the current People's Commissar of Education.

Standing in his hat and galoshes in the corridor of the chilly institute, Persikov spoke to his assistant, Ivanov, a most elegant gentleman with a pointed blond beard. "Why killing him is not enough for this, Peter Stepanovich! Just what are they doing? Why, they'll ruin the institute! Eh? A singular male, an extraordinary specimen of *Pipa americana,* thirteen centimeters long . . ."

As time went on things got worse. After Vlas died, the windows of the institute froze right through, and patterned ice covered the inner surface of the glass. The rabbits died, then the foxes, wolves, fish, and every last one of the garter snakes. Persikov started going around in silence for whole days through; then he caught pneumonia, but did not die. When he recovered he went to the institute twice a week, and in the amphitheater, where the temperature for some reason never changed from its constant five degrees below freezing regardless of the temperature outside, wearing his galoshes, a hat with earflaps, and a woolen muffler, exhaling clouds of white steam, he read a series of lectures on "The Reptilia of the Torrid Zone" to eight students. Persikov spent the rest of his time at his place on Prechistenka, covered with a plaid shawl, lying on the sofa in his room, which was crammed to the ceiling with books, coughing, staring into the open maw of the fiery stove which Marya Stepanovna fed gilded chairs, and thinking about the Surinam toad.

But everything in this world comes to an end. Nineteen twenty and 1921 ended, and in 1922 a kind of reverse trend began. First, Pankrat appeared, to replace the late Vlas; he was still young for a zoological guard, but he showed great promise; the institute building was now beginning to be heated a little. And in the summer Persikov managed, with Pankrat's help, to catch fourteen specimens of the common toad in the Klyazma River. The terraria once again teemed with life . . . In 1923 Persikov was already lecturing eight times a week—three at the institute and five at the university; in 1924 it was thirteen times a week, including the workers' schools, and in the spring of 1925 he gained notoriety by flunking seventy-six students, all of them on amphibians.

"What? How is it you don't know how amphibians differ from reptiles?" Persikov would ask. "It's simply ridiculous, young man. Amphibians have no pelvic buds. None. So, sir, you ought to be ashamed. You are a Marxist, probably?"

"Yes, a Marxist," the flunked student would answer, wilting.

"Very well, come back in the fall, please," Persikov would say politely, and then shout briskly to Pankrat, "Give me the next one!"

As amphibians come back to life after the first heavy rain following a long drought, so Professor Persikov came back to life in 1926 when the united Russo-American Company built fifteen fifteen-storey houses in the center of Moscow, starting at the corner of Gazetny Lane and Tverskaya, and 300 eight-apartment cottages for workers on the outskirts of town, ending once and for all the terrible and ridiculous housing crisis which had so tormented Muscovites in the years 1919 to 1925.

In general, it was a remarkable summer in Persikov's life, and sometimes he rubbed his hands with a quiet and contented chuckle, recalling how he and Marya Stepanovna had been squeezed into two rooms. Now the professor had gotten all five rooms back; he had spread out, arranged his 2,500 books, his stuffed animals, diagrams, and specimens in their places, and lit the green lamp on the desk in his study.

The institute was unrecognizable too: it had been covered with a coat of cream-colored paint, water was conducted to the reptile room by a special pipeline, all ordinary glass was replaced by plate glass, five new microscopes had been sent to the institute, as had glass-topped dissecting tables, 2,000-watt lamps with indirect lighting, reflectors, and cases for the museum.

Persikov came to life, and the whole world unexpectedly learned of it in December 1926, with the publication of his pamphlet: *More on the Problem of the Propagation of the Gastropods*, 126 pp., "Bulletin of the Fourth University."

And in the fall of 1927 his major opus, 350 pages long, later translated into six languages, including Japanese: *The Embryology of the Pipidae, Spadefoot Toads, and Frogs*, State Publishing House: price, three rubles.

But in the summer of 1928 the incredible, horrible events took place . . .

[I I]

THE COLORED SPIRAL

AND SO, the professor turned on the bulb and looked around. He switched on the reflector on the long experiment table, donned a white smock, and tinkled with some instruments on the table . . .

Many of the thirty thousand mechanical vehicles which sped through Moscow in 1928 darted along Herzen Street, wheels humming on the smooth paving stones; and every few minutes a trolley marked 16 or 22 or 48 or 53 rolled, grinding and clattering, from Herzen Street toward Mokhovaya. Reflections of varicolored lights were thrown on the plate-glass windows of the office, and far and high above, next to the dark, heavy cap of the Cathedral of Christ, one could see the misty, pale lunar sickle.

But neither the moon nor Moscow's springtime noises interested Professor Persikov in the slightest. He sat on a three-legged revolving stool and with fingers stained brown from tobacco, he turned the adjustment screw of the magnificent Zeiss microscope under which an ordinary undyed culture of fresh amoebas had been placed. At the moment that Persikov was shifting the magnification from five to ten thousand, the door opened slightly, a pointed little beard and a leather apron appeared, and his assistant called, "Vladimir Ipatievich, the mesentery is set up—would you like to take a look?"

Persikov nimbly slid off the stool, leaving the adjustment screw turned halfway, and slowly turning a cigarette in his fingers, he went into his assistant's office. There, on a glass table, a semi-chloroformed frog, fainting with terror and pain, was crucified on a cork plate, its translucent viscera pulled out of its bloody abdomen into the microscope.

"Very good," said Persikov, bending down to the eyepiece of the microscope.

Apparently one could see something very interesting in the frog's mesentery, where as clearly as if on one's hand living blood corpuscles were running briskly along the rivers of the vessels. Persikov forgot his amoebas and for the next hour and a half took turns with Ivanov at the microscope lens. As they were doing this both scientists kept exchanging animated comments incomprehensible to ordinary mortals.

Finally, Persikov leaned back from the microscope, announcing, "The blood is clotting, that's all there is to that."

The frog moved its head heavily, and its dimming eyes were clearly saying, "You're rotten bastards, that's what . . ."

Stretching his benumbed legs, Persikov rose, returned to his office, yawned, rubbed his permanently inflamed eyelids with his fingers, and sitting down on his stool, he glanced into the microscope, put his fingers on the adjustment screw intending to turn it—but did not turn it. With his right eye Persikov saw a blurred white disk, and in it some faint, pale amoebas—but in the middle of the disk there was a colored spiral resembling a woman's curl. Persikov himself and hundreds of his students had seen this spiral very many times, and no one had ever taken any interest in it, nor, indeed, was there any reason to. The colored swirl of light merely interfered with observation and showed that the culture was not in focus. Therefore it was ruthlessly eliminated with a single turn of the knob, illuminating the whole field with an even white light.

The zoologist's long fingers already lay firmly on the knob, but suddenly they quivered and fell off. The reason for this was Persikov's right eye; it had suddenly become intent, amazed, and flooded with excitement. To the woe of the Republic, this was no talentless mediocrity sitting at the microscope. No, this was Professor Persikov! His entire life, all of his intellect became concentrated in his right eye. For some five minutes of stony silence the higher creature observed the lower one, tormenting and straining his eye over the part of the culture which was outside of focus. Everything around was silent. Pankrat had already fallen asleep in his room off the vestibule, and only once the glass doors of the cabinets rang musically and delicately in the distance: that was Ivanov locking his office as he left. The front door groaned behind him. And it was only later that the professor's voice was heard. He was asking, no one knows whom, "What is this? I simply don't understand."

A last truck passed by on Herzen Street, shaking the old walls of the institute. The flat glass bowl with forceps in it tinkled on the table. The professor turned pale and raised his hands over the microscope like a mother over an infant who is being threatened by danger. Now there could be no question of Persikov turning the knob, oh no, he was afraid that some outside force might push what he had seen out of the field of vision.

It was bright morning with a gold strip slanting across the cream-colored entrance to the institute when the professor left the microscope and walked up to the window on his numb feet. With trembling fingers he pressed a button, and the thick black shades shut out the morning, and the wise, learned night came back to life in the study. The sallow and inspired Persikov spread his feet wide apart, and staring at the parquet with tearing eyes, he started talking: "But how can this be? Why, it's monstrous! . . . It's monstrous, gentlemen," he repeated, addressing the toads in the terrarium—but the toads were sleeping and did not answer.

He was silent for a moment, then walked to the switch, raised the shades, turned off all the lights, and peered into the microscope. His face got tense, and his bushy yellow eyebrows came together. "Uhmmm, uhmmm," he muttered. "Gone. I see. I see-e-e-e," he drawled, looking at the extinguished globe overhead madly and inspiredly. "It's very simple." And he again lowered the swishing shades, and again he lit the globe. Having glanced into the microscope, he grinned gleefully, and almost rapaciously. "I'll catch it," he said solemnly and gravely, raising his finger in the air. "I'll catch it. Maybe it's from the sun."

Again the shades rolled up. Now the sun was out. It poured across the institute walls and lay in slanting planes across the paving stones of Herzen Street. The professor looked out the window, calculating what the position of the sun would be during the day. He stepped away and returned again and again, dancing slightly, and finally he leaned over the windowsill on his stomach.

He got started on some important and mysterious work. He covered the microscope with a glass bell. Melting a chunk of sealing wax over the bluish flame of a Bunsen burner, he sealed the edges of the bell to the table, pressing down the lumps of wax with his thumb. He turned off the gas and went out, and he locked the office door with an English lock.

The institute corridors were in semidarkness. The professor made his way to Pankrat's room and knocked for a long time with no result. At last there was a sound behind the door something like the growling of a chained dog, hoarse coughing and muttering, and Pankrat appeared in a spot of light wearing striped underpants tied at his ankles. His eyes fixed wildly on the scientist; he was still groaning somewhat from sleep.

"Pankrat," said the professor, looking at him over his spectacles. "Forgive me for waking you up. Listen, my friend, don't go into my office this morning. I left some work out which must not be moved. Understand?"

"U-hm-m, I understand," Pankrat replied, understanding nothing. He was swaying back and forth and grumbling.

"No, listen, wake up, Pankrat," said the zoologist, and he poked Pankrat lightly in the ribs, which brought a frightened look into his face and a certain shadow of awareness into his eyes. "I locked the office," continued Persikov. "So you shouldn't clean up before my return. Understand?"

"Yes, sir-r," gurgled Pankrat.

"Now that's excellent, go back to bed."

Pankrat turned, vanished behind the door, and immediately

crashed back into bed, while the professor began to put his things on in the vestibule. He put on his gray summer coat and floppy hat. Then, recalling the picture in the microscope, he fixed his eyes on his galoshes and stared at them for several seconds, as if he were seeing them for the first time. Then he put on the left galosh and tried to put the right one over it, but it would not go on.

"What a fantastic accident it was that he called me," said the scientist, "otherwise I would never have noticed it. But what does it lead to? . . . Why, the devil only knows what it can lead to!"

The professor grinned, frowned at his galoshes, removed the left galosh, and put on the right one. "My God! Why, one can't even imagine all the consequences." The professor contemptuously kicked away the left galosh, which annoyed him by refusing to fit over the right, and went to the exit wearing one galosh. At that point he dropped his handkerchief and walked out, slamming the heavy door. On the stairs he took a long time looking for matches in his pockets, patting his sides; then he found them and headed down the street with an unlit cigarette in his lips.

Not a single person did the scientist meet all the way to the cathedral. There the professor tilted his head back and gaped at the golden cupola. The sun was sweetly licking it on one side.

"How is it I have never seen it before, such a coincidence? . . . Phooey, what an idiot." The professor bent down and fell into thought, looking at his differently shod feet. "Hm . . . what should I do? Return to Pankrat? No, there's no waking him up. It'd be a shame to throw it away, the vile thing. I'll have to carry it." He took off the galosh and carried it in his hand with disgust.

Three people in an ancient automobile turned the corner from Prechistenka. Two tipsy men with a garishly painted woman in silk pajamas of the latest 1928 style sitting on their knees.

"Hey, popsy!" she cried in a low, rather hoarse voice. "Did 'ja drink up the other galosh!"

"The old boy must have loaded up at the Alcazar," howled the drunk on the left, while the one on the right leaned out of the car and shouted, "Is the all-night tavern on Volkhonka open, buddy? We're headed there!"

The professor looked at them sternly above his spectacles, dropped the cigarette from his lips, and immediately forgot their existence. Slanting rays of sunshine appeared, cutting across Prechistensky Boulevard, and the helmet on the Cathedral of Christ began to flame. The sun had risen.

[III]

PERSIKOV CAPTURED IT

THE FACTS OF THE MATTER were as follows. When the professor had brought his eye of genius to that eyepiece, for the first time in his life he had paid attention to the fact that one particularly vivid and thick ray stood out in the multicolored spiral. This ray was a bright red color and it emerged from the spiral in a little sharp point, like a needle, let us say.

It is simply very bad luck that this ray fixed the skilful eye of the virtuoso for several seconds.

In it, in this ray, the professor caught sight of something which was a thousand times more significant and important than the ray itself, that fragile off-shoot born accidentally of the movement of the microscope's lens and mirror. Thanks to the fact that his assistant had called the professor away, the amoebas lay about for an hour and a half subject to the action of the ray, and the result was this: while the granular amoebas outside the ray lay about limp and helpless, strange phenomena were taking place within the area where the pointed red sword lay. The red strip teemed with life. The gray amoebas, stretching out their pseudopods, strove with all their might toward the red strip, and in it they would come to life as if by sorcery. Some force infused them with the spirit of life. They crawled in flocks and fought each other for a place in the ray. Within it a frenzied (no other word can properly describe it) process of multiplication went on. Smashing and overturning all the laws that Persikov knew as well as he knew his own five fingers, the amoebas budded before his eyes with lightning speed. In the ray they split apart, and two seconds later each part became a new, fresh organism. In a few seconds these organisms attained full growth and maturity, only to immediately produce new generations in their turn. The red strip and the entire disk quickly became overcrowded, and the inevitable struggle began. The newborn ones attacked each other furiously, tearing each other to shreds and swallowing them up. Among the newly born lay corpses of those which had perished in the battle for existence. The best and strongest were victorious. And these best ones were terrifying. First, they were approximately twice the size of ordinary amoebas, and second, they were distinguished by some sort of special viciousness and motility. Their movements were speedy, their pseudopods much longer than normal, and they used them, without exaggeration, as an octopus uses its tentacles.

The next evening, the professor, drawn and pale, studied the new generation of amoebas—without eating, keeping himself going only by smoking thick, roll-your-own cigarettes. On the third day, he shifted to the prime source—the red ray.

The gas hissed softly in the burner, again the traffic whizzed along the street, and the professor, poisoned by his hundredth cigarette, his eyes half-shut, threw himself back in his revolving chair. "Yes, everything is clear now. The ray brought them to life. It is a new ray, unresearched by anyone, undiscovered by anyone. The first thing to be clarified is whether it is produced only by electric light or by the sun as well," Persikov muttered to himself.

In the course of one more night this was clarified. He captured three rays in three microscopes, he obtained none from the sun, and he expressed himself thus: "We must hypothesize that it does not exist in the sun's spectrum . . . hmmm . . . in short, we must hypothesize that it can be obtained only from electric light." He looked lovingly at the frosted globe above him, thought for a moment, inspired, and invited Ivanov into his office. He told him everything and showed him the amoebas.

Assistant Professor Ivanov was astounded, completely crushed; how was it that such a simple thing as this slender arrow had never been noticed before! By anyone, dammit. You wish, even by himself, Ivanov, and this really was monstrous! "You just look! . . . Just look, Vladimir Ipatievich!" cried Ivanov, his eye gluing itself to the eyepiece in horror. "What is happening? . . . They're growing before my very eyes . . . Look, look!"

"I have been watching them for three days," Persikov replied animatedly.

Then there was a conversation between the two scientists, the idea of which may be summed up as follows: Assistant Professor Ivanov undertakes to construct a chamber with the aid of lenses and mirrors in which this ray will be produced in magnified form—and outside the microscope. Ivanov hopes—indeed, he is absolutely sure that this is quite simple. He will produce the ray, Vladimir Ipatievich cannot doubt that. Here there was a slight pause.

"When I publish my work, Peter Stepanovich, I will write that the chambers were constructed by you," Persikov put in, feeling that the pause needed to be resolved.

"Oh, that's not important . . . Still, of course . . ."

And the pause was instantly resolved. From that moment on, the ray utterly absorbed Ivanov too. While Persikov, losing weight and getting exhausted, was sitting all day and half the nights over the microscope, Ivanov bustled around the brilliantly lit physics laboratory combining lenses and mirrors. A technician assisted him.

After a request was sent through the Commissariat of Education, Persikov received from Germany three parcels containing mirrors and polished lenses—biconvex, biconcave, and even convex-concave. This all ended with Ivanov finishing the construction of a chamber and actually capturing the red ray in it. And in all justice, it was an expert job: the ray came out thick,—almost four centimeters in diameter—sharp and powerful.

On the first of June, the chamber was installed in Persikov's office, and he avidly began experiments with frog roe exposed to the ray. The results of these experiments were staggering. Within two days thousands of tadpoles hatched from the roe. But that is the least of it—within twenty-four hours, growing at a fantastic rate, the tadpoles developed into frogs, and they were so vicious and voracious that half of them immediately devoured the other half. Then the survivors began to spawn, ignoring all normal time rules, and in another two days they had produced a new generation, this time without the ray, which was absolutely numberless. The devil only knows what had started in the scientist's office: the tadpoles were crawling out of the office and spreading all over the institute, in the terraria, and on the floor, from every nook and cranny, stentorian choruses began to croak as if this were a bog. Pankrat, who had always feared Persikov like fire anyway, was now experiencing one single feeling for him—mortal terror. After a week, the scientist himself began to feel he was going crazy. The institute was pervaded with the odors of ether and prussic acid, which almost poisoned Pankrat who had taken off his mask at the wrong time. They finally managed to exterminate the teeming swamp population with poisons, and the rooms were thoroughly aired out.

Persikov said the following to Ivanov: "You know, Peter Stepanovich, the ray's effect on the deutoplasm and the ovum in general is quite remarkable."

Ivanov, who was a cool and reserved gentleman, interrupted the professor in an unusual tone. "Vladimir Ipatych, why are you discussing petty details, deutoplasm? Let's be frank—you have discovered something unprecedented!" Though it cost him obvious great effort, still Ivanov squeezed out the words: "Professor Persikov, you have discovered the ray of life!"

A faint color appeared on Persikov's pale, unshaven cheekbones. "Now, now, now," he muttered.

"You," continued Ivanov, "you will make such a name . . . It makes my head spin. Do you understand," he continued passionately, "Vladimir Ipatych, the heroes of H. G. Wells are simply nonsense compared to you . . . And I had always thought his stories were fairy tales. . . . Do you remember his *The Food of the Gods?*" [3]

"Oh, a novel," replied Persikov.

"Why yes, good Lord, a famous one!"

"I have forgotten it," said Persikov. "I remember now, I did read it, but I've forgotten it."

"How can you not remember, why just look . . ." From the glass-topped table Ivanov picked up a dead frog of incredible size with a bloated belly and held it up by the leg. Even after death it had a malevolent expression on its face. "Why, this is monstrous!"

[IV]

DEACONESS DROZDOVA

GOD KNOWS how it happened, whether Ivanov was to blame for it or sensational news transmits itself through the air, but everyone in gigantic, seething Moscow suddenly started talking about the ray of Professor Persikov. True, this talk was casual and very vague. The news of the miraculous discovery hopped through the glittering capital like a wounded bird, sometimes disappearing, sometimes fluttering up again, until the middle of July when a brief notice treating the ray appeared on the twentieth page of the newspaper *Izvestia,* under the heading: "News of Science and Technology." It was said distantly that a well-known professor of the Fourth State University had invented a ray which greatly accelerated the vital

3. H. G. Wells' *The Food of the Gods* was written in 1904.

processes of lower organisms and that this ray required further study. The name, of course, was garbled and printed as "Pepsikov."

Ivanov brought in the newspaper and showed the notice to Persikov.

"Pepsikov," grumbled Persikov, puttering around with the chamber in his office, "where do these blabbermouths learn everything?"

Alas, the garbled name did not save the professor from events, and they began the very next day, immediately upsetting Persikov's whole life.

After a preliminary knock, Pankrat entered the office and handed Persikov a magnificent satiny calling card. "He's out there," Pankrat added timidly.

Printed on the card in exquisite type was:

ALFRED ARKADIEVICH
BRONSKY

Contributor to the Moscow
Journals *Red Spark*, *Red Pepper*, and
Red Projector and the newspaper
Red Evening Moscow

"Tell him to go to hell," Persikov said in a monotone, and he threw the card under the table.

Pankrat turned, walked out, and five minutes later he came back with a suffering face and a second specimen of the same card.

"Are you making fun of me, or what?" Persikov croaked, and he looked terrifying.

"From the GPU,[4] the man says," Pankrat answered, turning pale.

Persikov grabbed the card with one hand, almost tearing it in half, and with the other hand he threw a pair of pincers onto the table. On the card there was a note written in curlicued handwriting: "I beg sincerely, with apologies, most esteemed professor, for you to receive me for three minutes in connection with a public matter of

4. *Gosudarstvennoe Politicheskoe Upravlenie*—"State Political Administration," one of the many names over the years for the secret police.

the press; I am also a contributor to the satirical journal *The Red Raven,* published by the GPU."

"Call him in," said Persikov, and he breathed out heavily.

Immediately a young man with a smooth-shaven, oily face bobbed up behind Pankrat's back. The face struck one with its permanently raised eyebrows, like a Chinaman's, and the little agate eyes beneath them, which never for a second met the eyes of his interlocutor. The young man was dressed quite impeccably and fashionably: a long narrow jacket down to the knees, the widest of bell-bottomed trousers, and preternaturally wide patent-leather shoes with toes like hooves. In his hands the young man held a cane, a hat with a sharply pointed crown, and a notebook.

"What do you want?" asked Persikov in a voice that made Pankrat step back behind the door immediately. "You *were* told I am busy."

Instead of answering, the young man bowed to the professor twice, once to the left and once to the right—and then his eyes wheeled all over the room, and immediately the young man made a mark in his notebook.

"I'm busy," said the professor, looking with revulsion into the guest's little eyes, but he made no effect, since the eyes were impossible to catch.

"A thousand apologies, esteemed professor," the young man began in a high-pitched voice, "for breaking in on you and taking up your precious time, but the news of your earth-shaking discovery— which has created a sensation all over the world—compels our journal to ask you for whatever explanations . . ."

"What kind of explanations all over the world?" Persikov whined squeakily, turning yellow. "I am not obliged to give you any explanations or anything of the sort . . . I'm busy . . . terribly busy."

"What exactly is it you are working on?" the young man asked sweetly, making another mark in his notebook.

"Oh, I . . . why do you ask? Do you intend to publish something?"

"Yes," answered the young man, and suddenly he started scribbling furiously in his notebook.

"First of all, I have no intention of publishing anything until I complete my work—particularly in these papers of yours . . . Secondly, how do you know all this?" And Persikov suddenly felt that he was losing control.

"Is the news that you have invented a ray of new life accurate?"

"What new life?" the professor snapped angrily. "What kind of rubbish are you babbling? The ray I am working on has not yet been investigated very much, and generally nothing is known about it as yet! It is possible that it may accelerate the vital processes of protoplasm."

"How much?" the young man inquired quickly.

Persikov completely lost control. What a character! The devil only knows what this means! "What sort of philistine questions are these? Suppose I said, oh, a thousand times . . ."

Rapacious joy flashed through the little eyes of the young man. "It produces giant organisms?"

"Nothing of the sort! Well, true, the organisms I have obtained are larger than normal . . . Well, they do possess certain new characteristics . . . But, of course, the main thing is not the size, but the incredible speed of reproduction," said Persikov to his misfortune, and he was immediately horrified by what he had said. The young man covered a page with his writing, turned it, and scribbled on.

"But don't you write that!" Persikov said hoarsely, in desperation, already surrendering and feeling that he was in the young man's hands. "What are you writing there?"

"Is it true that in forty-eight hours you can obtain two million tadpoles from frog roe?"

"What quantity of roe?" Persikov shouted, again infuriated. "Have you ever seen a grain of roe . . . well, let's say, of a tree frog?"

"From half a pound?" the young man asked, undaunted.

Persikov turned purple.

"Who measures it like that? Tfui! What are you talking about? Well of course if you took half a pound of frog roe, then . . . perhaps . . . well, hell, perhaps about that number or maybe even many more."

Diamonds began to sparkle in the young man's eyes, and in a single swoop he scratched up another page. "Is it true that this will cause a world revolution in animal husbandry?"

"What kind of newspaper question is that?" howled Persikov. "And, generally, I'm not giving you permission to write rubbish. I can see by your face that you're writing some sort of rotten trash!"

"Your photograph, professor, I beg you urgently," the young man said, slamming his notebook shut.

"What? My photograph? For your stupid little journals? To go with that devilish garbage you're scribbling there? No, no, no! . . . And I'm busy. I'll ask you to . . ."

"Even if it's an old one. And we'll return it to you instantly."

"Pankrat!" the professor shouted in a rage.

"My compliments," the young man said and vanished.

Instead of Pankrat, Persikov heard the strange rhythmic creaking of some machine behind the door, a metallic tapping across the floor, and in his office appeared a man of extraordinary bulk, dressed in a blouse and trousers made of blanket material. His left leg, a mechanical one, screaked and scropped, and in his hands he held a briefcase. His round shaven face, filled with yellowish gelatine, offered an amiable smile. He bowed to the professor in military fashion and straightened up, causing his leg to twang like a spring. Persikov went numb.

"Mr. Professor," began the stranger in a pleasant, somewhat husky voice, "forgive an ordinary mortal for breaking in on your privacy."

"Are you a reporter?" asked Persikov. "Pankrat!"

"Not at all, Mr. Professor," replied the fat man. "Permit me to introduce myself: sea captain and contributor to the newspaper

Industrial News, published by the Council of People's Commissars."

"Pankrat!" Persikov shouted hysterically, and at that instant the telephone in the corner flashed a red signal and rang softly. "Pankrat!" repeated the professor. "Hello, what is it?"

"Verzeihen Sie, bitte, Herr Professor," croaked the telephone in German,*"dass ich störe. Ich bin ein Mitarbeiter des Berliner Tageblatts."*

"Pankrat!" The professor shouted into the receiver, *"Bin momentan sehr beschäftigt und kann Sie deshalb jetzt nicht empfangen! . . .* Pankrat!"

And in the meantime the bell at the front entrance of the institute was starting to ring constantly.

"Nightmarish murder on Bronny Street!" howled unnatural hoarse voices twisting in and out of the thicket of lights among wheels and flashing headlights on the warm June pavement. "Nightmarish outbreak of chicken plague in the yard of Deacon Drozdov's widow, with her portrait! . . . Nightmarish discovery of Professor Persikov's ray of life!"

Persikov jumped so violently that he nearly fell under the wheels of a car on Mokhovaya, and he furiously grabbed the newspaper.

"Three kopeks, citizen!" shrieked the boy, and squeezing himself into the crowd on the sidewalk, he again started howling, *"Red Evening Moscow,* discovery of x-ray."

The stunned Persikov opened the newspaper and leaned against a lamppost. From a smudged frame in the left corner of the second page there stared at him a bald-headed man with mad, unseeing eyes and a drooping jaw—the fruit of Alfred Bronsky's artistic endeavors. "V. I. Persikov, who discovered the mysterious red ray," announced the caption under the drawing. Below it, under the heading, "World Riddle," the article began with the words: " 'Sit down, please,' the venerable scientist Persikov said to us amiably . . ."

Under the article was a prominent signature: "Alfred Bronsky (Alonso)."

A greenish light flared up over the roof of the university, the fiery words SPEAKING NEWSPAPER leapt across the sky, and a crowd immediately jammed Mokhovaya.

" 'Sit down, please!!!' " a most unpleasant high-pitched voice, exactly like the voice of Alfred Bronsky, magnified a thousand times, suddenly boomed from the roof across the way, "the venerable scientist Persikov said to us amiably. 'I have long desired to acquaint the proletariat of Moscow with the results of my discovery! . . .' "

Persikov heard a quiet mechanical screaking behind his back, and someone tugged at his sleeve. Turning around, he saw the round yellow face of the mechanical leg's owner. His eyes were wet with tears and his lips were shaking. "Me, Mr. Professor, me you refused to acquaint with the results of your amazing discovery, professor," he said sadly, and he sighed heavily, "you made me lose two smackers."

He looked gloomily at the roof of the university where the invisible Alfred was ranting in the black maw of the speaker. For some reason, Persikov suddenly felt sorry for the fat man. "I didn't say any 'sit down please' to him!" he muttered, catching the words from the sky with hatred. He is simply a brazen scalawag, an extraordinary type! Forgive me, please, but really now—when you're working and people break in . . . I don't mean you, of course . . ."

"Perhaps, Mr. Professor, you would give me at least a description of your chamber?" the mechanical man said ingratiatingly and mournfully. "After all, it makes no difference to you now . . ."

"In three days, such a quantity of tadpoles hatches out of half a pound of roe that it's utterly impossible to count them!" roared the invisible man in the loudspeaker.

"Too-too," shouted the cars on Mokhovaya hollowly.

"Ho, ho, ho . . . How about that! Ho, ho, ho," murmured the crowd, heads tilted back.

"What a scoundrel! Eh?" Persikov hissed to the mechanical man, trembling with indignation. "How do you like that? Why, I'm going to lodge a complaint against him!"

"Outrageous," agreed the fat man.

A most dazzling violent ray struck the professor's eyes, and everything around flared up—the lamppost, a strip of block pavement, a yellow wall, curious faces.

"It's for you, professor," the fat man whispered ecstatically and hung himself on to the professor's sleeve like a lead weight. Something clicked rapidly in the air.

"To the devil with all of them!" Persikov exclaimed despondently, ripping through the crowd with his lead weight. "Hey, taxi! To Prechistenka!"

The beat-up old car, vintage 1924, clattered to a halt at the curb, and the professor began to climb into the landau while trying to shake loose from the fat man. "You're in my way," he hissed, covering his face with his fists against the violet light.

"Did you read it? What are they yelling about? . . . Professor Persikov and his children were found on Little Bronnaya with their throats slit! . . ." voices shouted around the crowd.

"I haven't got *any* children, the sons of bitches," Persikov bellowed and suddenly found himself in the focus of a black camera, which was shooting him in profile with an open mouth and furious eyes.

"Krch . . . too . . . krch . . . too," shrieked the taxi, and it lanced into the thicket of traffic.

The fat man was already sitting in the landau warming the professor's side.

[V]

A CHICKEN TALE

In a tiny provincial town, formerly called Troitsk and currently Steklovsk, in the Steklov district of the Kostroma province, onto the steps of a little house on the street formerly[5] called Cathedral, and currently Personal, a woman wearing a kerchief and a gray dress with calico bouquets on it—and she began to sob. This woman, the widow of the former Archpriest Drozdov of the former cathedral, sobbed so loudly that soon another woman's head, in a downy woolen shawl, was stuck out the window of the house across the street, and it cried out, "What is it, Stepanovna? Another one?"

"The seventeenth!" dissolving in sobs the former Drozdova answered.

"Oh, deary, oh dear," the woman in the shawl whimpered, and she shook her head. "Why what is this anyway. Truly, it's the Lord in His wrath! Is she dead?"

"Just look, look, Matryona," muttered the deaconess, sobbing loudly and heavily. "Look what's happening to her!"

The gray, tilting gate slammed, a woman's bare feet padded across the dusty bumps in the street, and the deaconess, wet with tears, led Matryona to her poultry yard.

It must be said that the widow of Father Savvaty Drozdov, who had passed away in 1926 of antireligious woes did not give up, but started some most remarkable chicken breeding. As soon as the widow's affairs started to go uphill, such a tax was slapped on her that her chicken breeding was on the verge of terminating, had it

5. After the Revolution one's "former" position became all-important. It could determine job, living quarters, and food ration. Streets, professions, and even people became "former."

not been for kind people. They advised the widow to inform the local authorities that she was founding a workers' cooperative chicken farm. The membership of the cooperative consisted of Drozdova herself, her faithful servant Matryoshka, and the widow's deaf niece. The widow's tax was revoked, and the chicken breeding flourished so much that by 1928 the population of the widow's dusty yard, flanked by rows of chicken coops, had increased to 250 hens, including some Cochin Chinas. The widow's eggs appeared in the Steklovsk market every Sunday; the widow's eggs were sold in Tambov, and sometimes they even appeared in the glass showcases of the store that was formerly known as "Chichkin's Cheese and Butter, Moscow."

And now a precious Brahmaputra, by count the seventeenth that morning, her tufted baby, was walking around the yard vomiting. "Er . . . rr . . . url . . . url . . . ho-ho-ho," the tufted hen glugged, rolling her melancholy eyes to the sun as if she were seeing it for the last time. Cooperative member Matryoshka, was dancing before the hen in a squatting position, a cup of water in her hand.

"Here, tufted baby . . . cheep-cheep-cheep . . . drink a little water," Matryoshka pleaded, chasing the hen's beak with her cup; but the hen did not want to drink. She opened her beak wide and stretched her neck toward the sky. Then she began to vomit blood.

"Holy Jesus!" cried the guest, slapping herself on the thighs. "What's going on? Nothing but gushing blood! I've *never,* may I drop on the spot, I've never seen a chicken with a stomach ache like a human."

And these were the last words heard by the departing tufted baby. She suddenly keeled over on her side, helplessly pecked the dust a few times, and turned up her eyes. Then she rolled over on her back, lifted both feet upwards, and remained motionless. Spilling the water in the cup, Matryoshka burst into a baritone wail, as did the deaconess herself, the chairman of the cooperative, and the guest leaned over to her ear and whispered, "Stepanovna, may I eat dirt, but someone's ruined your chickens. Who's ever seen anything like it before? Why, this ain't no chicken sickness! It's that somebody's bewitched your chickens."

"The enemies of my life!" the deaconess cried out to the heavens. "Do they want to run me out of this world?"

A loud roosterish crow answered her words, after which a wiry bedraggled rooster tore out of a chicken coop sort of sideways like a boisterous drunk out of a tavern. He rolled his eyes back wildly at them, stamped up and down in place, spread his wings like an eagle, but did not fly off anywhere—he began to run in circles around the yard like a horse on a rope. On the third circle he stopped, overwhelmed by nausea, because he then began to cough and croak, spat bloody spots all around him, fell over, and his claws aimed toward the sun like masts. Feminine wailing filled the yard. And it was echoed by a troubled clucking, flapping, and fussing in the chicken coops.

"Well, ain't it the evil eye?" the guest asked victoriously. "Call Father Sergei; let him hold a service."

At six in the evening, when the sun lay low like a fiery face among the faces of the young sunflowers, Father Sergei, the prior of the Cathedral Church, was climbing out of his vestments after finishing the prayer service at the chicken coops. People's curious heads were stuck out over the ancient collapsing fence and peering through the cracks. The sorrowful deaconess, kissing the cross, soaked the torn canary-yellow ruble note with tears and handed it to Father Sergei, in response to which, sighing, he remarked something about, well, see how the Lord's shown us His wrath. As he was saying this Father Sergei wore an expression which indicated that he knew very well precisely why the Lord had shown His wrath, but that he was just not saying.

After that, the crowd dispersed from the street, and since hens retire early, nobody knew that three hens and a rooster had died at the same time in the hen house of Drozdova's next-door neighbor. They vomited just like the Drozdov hens, and the only difference was that their deaths took place quietly in a locked hen house. The rooster tumbled off his perch head down and died in that position. As for the widow's hens, they died off immediately after the prayer service, and by evening her hen houses were deadly quiet—the birds lay around in heaps, stiff and cold.

When the town got up the next morning, it was stunned as if by thunder, for the affair had assumed strange and monstrous proportions. By noon only three hens were still alive on Personal Street, and those were in the last house, where the district financial inspector lived, but even they were dead by one o'clock. And by evening the town of Steklovsk was humming and buzzing like a beehive, and the dread word "plague" was sweeping through it. Drozdova's name landed in the local newspaper, *The Red Warrior,* in an article headlined "Can It Be Chicken Plague?" and from there it was carried to Moscow.

Professor Persikov's life took on a strange, restless, and disturbing character. In a word, working under such circumstances was simply impossible. The day after he had gotten rid of Alfred Bronsky, he had to disconnect his office telephone at the institute by taking the receiver off the hook, and in the evening, as he was riding the trolley home along Okhotny Row, the professor beheld himself on the roof of a huge building with a black sign on it: WORKERS' GAZETTE. Crumbling and turning green and flickering, he, the professor, climbed into a landau, and behind him, clutching at his sleeve, climbed a mechanical ball wearing a blanket. The professor on the white screen on the roof covered his face with his fists against a violet ray. Then a golden legend leaped out: "Professor Persikov in a car explaining his discovery to our famous reporter Captain Stepanov." And, indeed, the wavering car flicked past the Cathedral of Christ along Volkhonka, and in it the professor struggled helplessly, his physiognomy like that of a wolf at bay.

"They are some sort of devils, not men," the zoologist muttered through his teeth as he rode past.

That same day, in the evening, when he returned to his place on

Prechistenka, the housekeeper, Marya Stepanovna, handed the zoologist seventeen notes with telephone numbers that had called while he was gone, along with Marya Stepanovna's verbal declaration that she was exhausted. The professor was getting ready to tear up the notes, but stopped, because opposite one of the numbers he saw the notation "People's Commissar of Public Health."

"What's this?" the learned eccentric asked in honest bewilderment. "What has happened to them?"

At a quarter past ten the same evening the doorbell rang, and the professor was obliged to converse with a certain citizen in dazzling attire. The professor had received him because of a calling card, which stated (without first name or surname), "Plenipotentiary Chief of the Trade Departments of Foreign Embassies to the Soviet Republic."

"Why doesn't he go to hell?" growled Persikov, throwing down his magnifying glass and some diagrams on the green cloth of the table and saying to Marya Stepanovna, "Ask him here into the study, this plenipotentiary."

"What can I do for you?" Persikov asked in a tone that made the Chief wince a bit. Persikov transferred his spectacles to his forehead from the bridge of his nose, then back, and he peered at his visitor. He glittered all over with patent leather and precious stones, and a monocle rested in his right eye. "What a vile mug," Persikov thought to himself for some reason.

The guest began in a roundabout way, asked specific permission to light his cigar, in consequence of which Persikov with the greatest of reluctance invited him to sit down. The guest proceeded to make extended apologies for coming so late.

"But . . . the professor is quite impossible to catch . . . hee-hee . . . pardon . . . to find during the day," (when laughing the guest cachinnated like a hyena).

"Yes, I'm busy!" Persikov answered so abruptly that the guest twitched a second time.

"Nevertheless, he permitted himself to disturb the famous scientist. Time is money, as they say . . . Is the cigar annoying the professor?"

"Mur-mur-mur," answered Persikov, "he permitted? . . ."

"The professor *has* discovered the ray of life, hasn't he?"

"For goodness sake, what sort of life! It's all the fantasies of cheap reporters!" Persikov got excited.

"Oh no, hee-hee-hee. . . . He understands perfectly the modesty which is the true adornment of all real scientists . . . But why fool around . . . There were telegrams today . . . In world capitals such as Warsaw and Riga everything about the ray is already known. Professor Persikov's name is being repeated all over the world. The world is watching Professor Persikov's work with bated breath . . . But everybody knows perfectly well the difficult position of scientists in Soviet Russia. *Entre nous soit dit* . . . There are no strangers here? . . . Alas, in this country they do not know how to appreciate scientific work, and so he would like to talk things over with the professor . . . A certain foreign state is quite unselfishly offering Professor Persikov help with his laboratory work. Why cast pearls here, as the Holy Scripture says? The said state knows how hard it was for the professor during 1919 and 1920, during this . . . hee-hee . . . revolution. Well, of course, in the strictest secrecy . . . the professor would acquaint this state with the results of his work, and in exchange it would finance the professor. For example, he constructed a chamber—now it would be interesting to become acquainted with the blueprints for this chamber . . ."

At this point the visitor drew from the inside pocket of his jacket a snow-white stack of banknotes.

"The professor can have a trifling advance, say, five thousand rubles, at this very moment . . . and there is no need to mention a receipt . . . the Plenipotentiary Trade Chief would even feel offended if the professor so much as mentioned a receipt."

"Out!!" Persikov suddenly roared so terrifyingly that the piano in the living room made a sound with its high keys.

The visitor vanished so quickly that Persikov, shaking with rage, himself began to doubt whether he had been there, or if it had been a hallucination.

"His galoshes?" Persikov howled a minute later from the hallway.

"The gentleman forgot them," replied the trembling Marya Stepanovna.

"Throw them out!"

"Where can I throw them? He'll come back for them."

"Take them to the house committee. Get a receipt. I don't want a trace of those galoshes! To the committee! Let them have the spy's galoshes! . . ."

Crossing herself, Marya Stepanovna picked up the magnificent leather galoshes and carried them out to the back stairs. There she stood behind the door for a few moments, and then hid the galoshes in the pantry.

"Did you turn them in?" Persikov raged.

"I did."

"Give me the receipt!"

"But, Vladimir Ipatych. But the chairman is illiterate!"

"This. Very Instant. I. Want. The. Receipt. Here! Let some literate son of a bitch sign for him!"

Marya Stepanovna just shook her head, went out, and came back fifteen minutes later with a note: "Received from Prof. Persikov 1 (one) pair galo. Kolesov."

"And what's this?"

"A tag, sir."

Persikov stomped all over the tag, and hid the receipt under the blotter. Then some idea darkened his sloping forehead. He rushed to the telephone, roused Pankrat at the institute, and asked him: "Is everything in order." Pankrat growled something into the receiver, from which one could conclude that everything, in his opinion, was in order.

But Persikov calmed down only for a minute. Frowning, he clutched the telephone and jabbered into the receiver: "Give me . . .

oh, whatever you call it . . . Lubyanka[6] . . . *Merci* . . . Which of you there should be told about this? . . . I have suspicious characters hanging around here in galoshes, yes . . . Professor Persikov of the Fourth University . . ."

Suddenly the conversation was abruptly disconnected and Persikov walked away, muttering some sort of swear words through his teeth.

"Are you going to have some tea, Vladimir Ipatych?" Marya Stepanovna inquired timidly, looking into the study.

"I'm not going to have any tea . . . mur-mur-mur . . . and to hell with them all . . . they've gone mad . . . I don't care."

Exactly ten minutes later the professor was receiving new guests in his study. One of them, amiable, rotund, and very polite, was wearing a modest khaki military field jacket and riding breeches. On his nose, like a crystal butterfly, perched a pince-nez. Generally, he looked like an angel in patent leather boots. The second, short and terribly gloomy, was wearing civilian clothes, but they fit in such a way that they seemed to constrain him. The third guest behaved in a peculiar manner; he did not enter the professor's study but remained in the semidark hallway. From there he had a full view of the well-lit study which was filled with billows of tobacco smoke. The face of this third visitor, who was also wearing civilian clothes, was graced with a dark pince-nez.

The two in the study wore Persikov out completely, carefully examining the calling card and interrogating him about the five thousand, and making him keep describing the earlier visitor.

"The devil only knows," grumbled Persikov. "A repulsive physiognomy. A degenerate."

"He didn't have a glass eye, did he?" the short one asked hoarsely.

"The devil only knows. But no, it isn't glass; his eyes keep darting around."

6. Moscow's most notorious political prison.

"Rubenstein?" the angel said to the short civilian softly and interrogatively. But the latter shook his head darkly.

"Rubenstein wouldn't give any money without a receipt, never," he mumbled. "This is not Rubenstein's work. This is someone bigger."

The story of the galoshes provoked a burst of the keenest interest from the guests. The angel uttered a few words into the telephone of the house office: "The State Political Administration invites the secretary of the house committee Kolesov to report at Professor Persikov's apartment with the galoshes," and Kolesov appeared in the study instantly, pale, holding the galoshes in his hands.

"Vasenka!" the angel called softly to the man who was sitting in the hall. The latter rose limply and moved into the study like an unwinding toy. His smoky glasses swallowed up his eyes.

"Well?" he asked tersely and sleepily.

"The galoshes."

The smoky eyes slid over the galoshes, and as this happened it seemed to Persikov that they were not at all sleepy; on the contrary, the eyes that flashed askance for a moment from behind the glasses were amazingly sharp. But they immediately faded out.

"Well, Vasenka?"

The man they addressed as Vasenka replied in a languid voice, "Well, what's the problem? They're Pelenzhkovsky's galoshes."

The house committee instantly lost Professor Persikov's gift. The galoshes disappeared into a newspaper. The extremely overjoyed angel in the military jacket got up, began to shake the professor's hand, and even made a little speech, the content of which boiled down to the following: "This does the professor honor. . . . The professor may rest assured . . . no one will bother him again, either at the institute or at home . . . steps will be taken . . . his chambers are quite safe."

"Could you shoot the reporters while you're at it?" Persikov asked, looking at him over his spectacles.

His question provoked a burst of merriment among his guests.

Not only the gloomy short one, but even the smoky one smiled in the hall. The angel, sparkling and glowing, explained that this was not possible.

"And who was that scalawag who came here?"

At this everyone stopped smiling, and the angel answered evasively that it was nobody, a petty swindler, not worth any attention . . . but nevertheless, he urged citizen professor to keep the evening's events in strictest secrecy, and the guests departed.

Persikov returned to his study and diagrams, but he still did not get to do any work. A fiery dot appeared on the telephone, and a female voice offered the professor a seven-room apartment if he would like to marry an interesting and hot-blooded widow. Persikov bawled into the receiver, "I advise you to go to Professor Rossolimo for treatment!" and then the telephone rang a second time.

Here Persikov was somewhat abashed because a rather well-known personage from the Kremlin was calling; he questioned Persikov sympathetically and at great length about his work and made known his wish to visit the laboratory. As he started to leave the phone, Persikov mopped his forehead, and took the receiver off the hook. At that moment there was a sudden blare of trumpets in the upstairs apartment, followed by the shrieking of the Valkyries: the director of the Woolen Fabrics Trust had tuned his radio to a Wagner concert from the Bolshoi Theater. Over the howling and crashing pouring down from the ceiling, Persikov shouted to Marya Stepanovna that he was going to take the director to court, that he was going to smash that radio, that he was going to get the hell out of Moscow, because obviously people had made it their goal to drive him out of there. He broke his magnifying glass and went to bed on the couch in his study, and he fell asleep to the gentle runs of a famous pianist that came wafting from the Bolshoi.

The surprises continued the next day too. When he got to the institute on the trolley, Persikov found an unknown citizen in a stylish green derby waiting at the entrance. He looked Persikov over closely, but addressed no questions to him, and therefore Persikov ignored him. But in the foyer, Persikov, besides the bewildered Pankrat, was met by a second derby which rose and greeted him courteously. "Hello there, Citizen Professor."

"What do you want?" Persikov asked menacingly, pulling off his overcoat with Pankrat's help. But the derby quickly pacified Persikov, whispering in the tenderest voice that the professor had no cause to be upset. He, the derby, was there for precisely the purpose of protecting the professor for any importunate visitors; the professor could set his mind at ease with regard not only to the doors of his study, but even to the windows. Upon which the stranger turned over the lapel of his suit coat for a moment and showed the professor a certain badge.

"Hm . . . how about that, you've really got things well set up," Persikov mumbled, and added naively, "and what will you eat here?"

To this the derby grinned and explained that he would be relieved.

The three days after this went by splendidly. The professor had two visits from the Kremlin, and one from students whom he gave examinations. Every last one of the students flunked, and from their faces it was clear that Persikov now inspired only superstitious awe in them.

"Go get jobs as trolleycar conductors! You aren't fit to study zoology," came from the office.

"Strict, eh?" the derby asked Pankrat.

"Ooh, a holy terror," answered Pankrat, "even if someone passes, he comes out reeling, poor soul. He'll be dripping with sweat. And he heads straight for a beer hall . . ."

Engrossed in these minor chores, the professor did not notice the three days pass; but on the fourth day he was recalled to reality again, and the cause of this was a thin, squeaky voice from the street.

"Vladimir Ipatievich!" the voice screeched from Herzen Street into the open window of the office.

The voice was in luck: the last few days had exhausted Persikov. Just at the moment he was resting in his armchair, smoking, and staring languidly and feebly with his red-circled eyes. He could not go on. And therefore it was even with some curiosity that he looked out the window and saw Alfred Bronsky on the sidewalk. The professor immediately recognized the titled owner of the calling card by his pointed hat and notebook. Bronsky bowed to the window tenderly and deferentially.

"Oh, is it you?" the professor asked. He did not have enough energy left to get angry, and he was even curious to see what would happen next. Protected by the window, he felt safe from Alfred. The ever-present derby in the street instantly cocked an ear toward Bronsky. A most disarming smile blossomed on the latter's face.

"Just a pair of minutes, dear professor," Bronsky said, straining his voice from the sidewalk. "Only one small question, a purely zoological one. May I ask it?"

"Ask it," Persikov replied laconically and ironically, and he thought to himself, "After all, there is something American in this rascal."

"What do you have to say as for the hens, dear professor?" shouted Bronsky, folding his hands into a trumpet.

Persikov was nonplussed. He sat down on the windowsill, then got up, pressed a button, and shouted, poking his finger toward the window, "Pankrat, let that fellow on the sidewalk in."

When Bronsky appeared in the office Persikov extended his amiability to the extent of barking, "Sit down!" at him.

And Bronsky, smiling ecstatically, sat down on the revolving stool.

"Please explain something to me," began Persikov. "Do you write there—for those papers of yours?"

"Yes, sir," Alfred replied deferentially.

"Well, it's incomprehensible to me, how you can write when you don't even know how to speak Russian correctly. What is this 'a pair of minutes' and 'as for the hens'? You probably meant to ask 'about the hens'?"

Bronsky burst out into a thin and respectful laugh. "Valentin Petrovich corrects it."

"Who's this Valentin Petrovich?"

"The head of the literary department."

"Well, all right! Besides, I am not a philologist. Let's forget your Petrovich. What is it specifically that you wish to know about hens?"

"In general everything you have to tell, professor."

Here Bronsky armed himself with a pencil. Triumphant sparks flickered in Persikov's eyes.

"You come to me in vain; I am not a specialist on the feathered beasts. You would be best off to go to Emelyan Ivanovich Portugalov of the First University. I myself know extremely little."

Bronsky smiled ecstatically, giving him to understand that he understood the dear professor's joke. "Joke: little," he jotted in his notebook.

"However, if it interests you, very well. Hens, or pectinates . . . Order, *Gallinae*. Of the pheasant family . . ." Persikov began in a loud voice, looking not at Bronsky, but somewhere beyond him, where a thousand people were presumably listening, "Of the pheasant family, *Phasianidae*. They are birds with fleshy combs and two lobes under the lower jaw . . . hm . . . although sometimes there is only one in the center of the chin . . . Well, what else? Wings, short and rounded. Tails of medium length, somewhat serrated, even, I would say, denticulated, the middle feathers crescent shaped . . . Pankrat, bring me Model No. 705 from the model cabinet—a cock in cross section . . . but no, you have no need of that? Pankrat, don't bring the model . . . I reiterate to you, I am not a specialist —go to Portugalov. Well, I personally am acquainted with six species of wild hens—hm . . . Portugalov knows more—in India and the Malay Archipelago. For example, the Banki rooster, or Kazintu, found in the foothills of the Himalayas, all over India, in

Assam and Burma . . . Then there's the swallow-tailed rooster, or *Gallus varius*, of Lombok, Sumbawa, and Flores. On the island of Java there is a remarkable rooster, *Gallus eneus*; in southeast India, I can recommend the very beautiful *Gallus souneratti* to you. As for Ceylon, there we meet the Stanley rooster, not found anywhere else."

Bronsky sat there, his eyes bulging, scribbling.

"Anything else I can tell you?"

"I would like to know something about chicken diseases," Alfred whispered very softly.

"Hm, I'm not a specialist, you ask Portugalov . . . Still, and all . . . well, there are tapeworms, flukes, scab mites, red mange, chicken mites, poultry lice or *Mallophaga*, fleas, chicken cholera, croupous-diphtheritic inflammation of the mucous membranes . . . pneumonomycosis, tuberculosis, chicken mange—there are all sorts of diseases." There were sparks leaping in Persikov's eyes. "There can be poisoning, tumors, rickets, jaundice, rheumatism, the *Achorion schoenleinii* fungus . . . a quite interesting disease. When it breaks out little spots resembling mold form on the comb."

Bronsky wiped the sweat from his forehead with a colored handkerchief. "And what, professor, in your opinion is the cause of the present catastrophe?"

"What catastrophe?"

"What, do you mean you haven't read, professor?" Bronsky cried with surprise, and pulled out a crumpled page of *Izvestia* from his briefcase.

"I don't read newspapers," answered Persikov, grimacing.

"But why, professor?" Alfred asked tenderly.

"Because they write gibberish," Persikov answered, without thinking.

"But how about this, professor?" Bronsky whispered softly, and he unfolded the newspaper.

"What's this?" asked Persikov, and he got up from his place. Now the sparks began to leap in Bronsky's eyes. With a pointed lacquered nail he underlined a headline of incredible magnitude across the entire page:

CHICKEN PLAGUE IN THE REPUBLIC

"What?" Persikov asked, pushing his spectacles onto his forehead.

[V I]

MOSCOW IN JUNE OF 1928

SHE GLEAMED BRIGHTLY, her lights danced, blinked, and flared on again. The white headlights of buses and the green lights of trolleys circled around Theater Square; over the former Muir and Merilis, above the tenth floor built up over it, a multicolored electric woman was jumping up and down making up multicolored words letter by letter: WORKERS' CREDIT. In the square opposite the Bolshoi, around the multicolored fountain shooting up sprays all night, a crowd was milling and rumbling. And over the Bolshoi a giant loudspeaker was booming: "The anti-chicken vaccinations at the Lefort Veterinary Institute have produced excellent results. The number . . . of chicken deaths for the day declined by half."

Then the loudspeaker changed its timbre, something rumbled in it; over the theater a green stream flashed on and off, and the loudspeaker complained in a deep bass: "Special commission set up to combat chicken plague, consisting of the People's Commissar of Public Health; the People's Commissar of Agriculture, the Chief of Animal Husbandry, Comrade Avis-Hamska, Professors Persikov and Portugalov, and Comrade Rabinovich! . . . New attempts at intervention," the speaker cachinnated and wept like a jackal, "in connection with the chicken plague!"

Theater Lane, Neglinny Prospect, and the Lubyanka flamed with white and violet streaks, spraying shafts of light, howling with horns, and whirling with dust. Crowds of people pressed against the wall by the huge pages of advertisements lit by garish red reflectors.

"Under threat of the most severe penalties, the populace is forbidden to employ chicken meat or eggs as food. Private tradesmen who attempt to sell these in the markets will be subject to criminal prosecution and confiscation of all property. All citizens who own eggs must immediately surrender them at their local police precincts."

On the roof of *The Worker's Gazette* chickens were piled sky-high on the screen, and greenish firemen, quivering and sparkling, were pouring kerosene on them with long hoses. Then red waves swept across the screen; unreal smoke billowed, tossed about like rags, and crept along in streams, and fiery words leaped out: "BURNING OF CHICKEN CORPSES ON THE KHODYNKA."

Among the wildly blazing show windows of the stores which worked until three in the morning (with breaks for lunch and supper) gaped the blind holes of windows boarded up under their signs; "Egg Store. Quality Guaranteed." Very often, screaming alarmingly, passing lumbering buses, hissing cars marked "MOSHEALDEPART FIRST AID" swept past the traffic policemen.

"Someone else has stuffed himself with rotten eggs," the crowd murmured.

On the Petrovsky Lines the world-renowned Empire Restaurant glittered with its green and orange lights, and on its tables, next to the portable telephones, stood cardboard signs stained with liqueurs: "By decree—no omelettes. Fresh oysters have been received."

At the Ermitage, where tiny Chinese lanterns, like beads, glowed mournfully amid the artificial, cozy greenery, the singers Shrams and Karmanchikov on the eye-shattering, dazzling stage sang ditties composed by the poets Ardo and Arguiev:

Oh, Mamma, what will I do without eggs?

while their feet thundered out a tap dance.

Over the theater of the late Vsevolod Meyerhold, who died, as everyone knows, in 1927, during the staging of Pushkin's *Boris Godunov*[7] when a platform full of naked boyars collapsed on him, there flashed a moving multicolored neon sign promulgating the writer Erendorg's play, *Chicken Croak*, produced by Meyerhold's disciple, Honored Director of the Republic Kukhterman. Next door, at the Aquarium Restaurant, scintillating with neon signs and flashing with half-naked female bodies to thunderous applause, the writer Lazer's review entitled *The Hen's Children* was being played amid the greenery of the stage. And down Tverskaya, with lanterns on either side of their heads, marched a procession of circus donkeys carrying gleaming placards. Rostand's *Chantecler* being revived at the Korsh Theater.

Little newsboys were howling and screaming among the wheels of the automobiles: "Nightmarish discovery in a cave! Poland preparing for nightmarish war! Professor Persikov's nightmarish experiments!"

At the circus of the former Nikitin, in the greasy brown arena that smelled pleasantly of manure, the dead-white clown Bom was saying to Bim, who was dressed in a huge checkered sack, "I know why you are so sad!"

"Vhy-y?" squeaked Bim.

"You buried your eggs in the ground, and the police from the fifteenth precinct found them."

"Ha, ha, ha, ha," the circus laughed, so that the blood stopped in the veins joyfully and anguishingly—and the trapezes and the cobwebs under the shabby cupola swayed dizzily.

"Oop!" the clowns cried piercingly, and a sleek white horse

---

7. Vsevolod Meyerhold, who was still quite alive when this story was written, was already famous for his unorthodox, "futuristic" productions of Russian classics. He and Bulgakov, who was a more traditional playwright, were enemies for years, partly because of the friction between Bulgakov and Mayakovsky, Meyerhold's close collaborator.

carried out on its back a woman of incredible beauty, with shapely legs in scarlet tights.

Looking at no one, noticing no one, not responding to the nudging and soft and tender enticements of prostitutes, Persikov, inspired and lonely, crowned with sudden fame, was making his way along Mokhovaya toward the fiery clock at the Manège. Here, without looking around at all, engrossed in his thoughts, he bumped into a strange, old-fashioned man, painfully jamming his fingers directly against the wooden holster of a revolver hanging from the man's belt.

"Oh, damn!" squeaked Persikov. "Excuse me."

"Of course," answered the stranger in an unpleasant voice, and somehow they disentangled themselves in the middle of this human logjam. And heading for Prechistenka the professor instantly forgot the collision.

[V I I]

FEYT

IT IS NOT KNOWN whether the Lefort Veterinary Institute's inoculations really were any good, whether the Samara roadblock detachments were skillful, whether the stringent measures taken with regard to the egg salesmen in Kaluga and Voronezh were successful, or whether the Extraordinary Commission in Moscow worked efficiently, but it is well known that two weeks after Persikov's last interview with Alfred, in a chicken way things had already been completely cleaned up in the Union of Republics. Here and there forlorn feathers still lay about in the backyards of district towns, bringing tears to the eyes of the onlookers, and in hospitals the last of the greedy people were still finishing the last spasms of bloody diarrhea and vomiting. Fortunately, human deaths were no more than a thousand in the entire Republic. Nor did any serious disorders ensue. True, a prophet had appeared briefly in Volokolamsk, proclaiming that the chicken plague had been caused by none other than the commissars, but he had no special success. In the Volokolamsk marketplace several policemen who had been confiscating chickens from the market women were beaten up, and some windows were broken in the local post and telegraph office. Luckily, the efficient Volokolamsk authorities quickly took the necessary measures as a result of which, first, the prophet ceased his activities, and second, the post office's broken windows were replaced.

Having reached Archangel and Syumkin village in the North, the plague stopped by itself, for the reason that there was nowhere for it to go—as everybody knows, there are no hens in the White Sea. It also stopped at Vladivostok, for there only the ocean is beyond that. In the far South it disappeared, petering out somewhere in the parched expanses of Ordubat, Dzhulfa, and Karabulak; and in the West it halted in an astonishing way exactly on the Polish and Rumanian borders. Perhaps the climate of these countries is different or perhaps the quarantine measures taken by the neighboring governments worked, but the fact remains that the plague went no further. The foreign press noisily and avidly discussed the unprecedented losses, while the government of the Soviet Republics, without any noise, was working tirelessly. The Special Commission to Fight the Chicken Plague was renamed the Special Commission for the Revival and Reestablishment of Chicken Breeding in the Republic and was augmented by a new Special Troika, made up of sixteen members. A "Goodpoul" office was set up, with Persikov and Portugalov as honorary assistants to the chairman. Their pictures appeared in the newspapers over titles such as "Mass Purchase of Eggs Abroad" and "Mr. Hughes Wants to Undermine the Egg Campaign." All Moscow read the stinging feuilleton by the journalist

Kolechkin, which closed with the words, "Don't whet your teeth on our eggs, Mr. Hughes—you have your own!"

Professor Persikov was completely exhausted from overworking himself for the last three weeks. The chicken events disrupted his routine and put a double burden upon him. Every evening he had to work at conferences of chicken commissions, and from time to time he was obliged to endure long interviews either with Alfred Bronsky or with the mechanical fat man. He had to work with Professor Portugalov and Assistant Professors Ivanov and Bornhart, dissecting and microscoping chickens in search of the plague bacillus, and he even had to write up a hasty pamphlet "On the Changes in Chicken Kidneys as a Result of the Plague" in three evenings.

Persikov worked in the chicken field with no special enthusiasm, and understandably so—his whole mind was filled with something else which was most basic and important—the problem from which he had been diverted by the chicken catastrophe, i.e. the red ray. Straining still further his already shaken health, stealing hours from sleep and meals, sometimes falling asleep on the oilcloth couch in his institute office, instead of going home to Prechistenka, Persikov spent whole nights puttering with his chamber and his microscope.

By the end of July the race let up a little. The work of the re-named commission fell into a normal groove, and Persikov returned to his interrupted work. The microscopes were loaded with new cultures, and under the ray in the chamber fish and frog roe matured with fantastic speed. Specially ordered glass was brought from Königsberg by plane, and during the last days of July mechanics laboring under Ivanov's supervision constructed two large new chambers in which the ray reached the width of a cigarette pack at its source and at its widest point—a full meter. Persikov joyfully rubbed his hands and started to prepare for some sort of mysterious and complicated experiments. To start with he talked to the People's Commission of Education on the telephone, and the receiver quacked out the warmest assurances of all possible cooperation, and then Persikov telephoned Comrade Avis-Hamska, the director of the Animal Husbandry Department of the Supreme Commission. Persikov received Avis-Hamska's warmest attention. The matter involved a large order abroad for Professor Persikov. Avis said into the telephone that he would immediately wire Berlin and New York. After this there was an inquiry from the Kremlin about how Persikov's work was progressing, and an important and affable voice asked whether Persikov needed an automobile.

"No, thank you, I prefer to ride the trolley," replied Persikov.

"But why?" the mysterious voice asked, laughing condescendingly.

In general everybody spoke to Persikov either with respect and terror, or laughing indulgently, as though he were a small, though overgrown, child.

"It's faster," Persikov replied, to which the resonant bass replied into the telephone, "Well, as you wish."

Another week passed, during which Persikov, withdrawing still further from the receding chicken problems, engrossed himself completely in the study of the ray. From the sleepless nights and over-exertion his head felt light, as if it were transparent and weightless. The red circles never left his eyes now, and Persikov spent almost every night at the institute. Once he abandoned his zoological retreat to give a lecture at the huge Tsekubu Hall on Prechistenka—about his ray and its effect on the egg cell. It was a tremendous triumph for the eccentric zoologist. The applause was so thunderous that something crumbled and dropped down from the ceilings of the colonnaded hall; hissing arc lights poured light over the black dinner jackets of the Tsekubu members and the white gowns of the ladies. On the stage, on a glass-topped table next to the lectern, a moist frog as big as a cat sat on a platter, gray and breathing heavily. Many notes were thrown onto the stage. They included seven declarations of love, and Persikov tore them up. The Tsekubu chairman dragged him forcibly onto the stage to bow to the audience. Persikov bowed irritably; his hands were sweaty, and the knot of his black tie rested not beneath his chin, but behind his left ear. There amid the sounds of respiration and the mist before him were hundreds of yellow faces and white shirtfronts, and suddenly the yellow holster of a revolver flashed and disappeared somewhere behind a white column. Persikov dimly perceived it, and forgot it. But as he was departing after the lecture, walking down the raspberry-colored carpet of the staircase, he suddenly felt sick. For a moment the dazzling chandelier in the vestibule turned black, and Persikov felt faint and nauseous . . . He thought he smelled something burning; it seemed to him that blood was dripping, sticky and hot, down his neck . . . And with a shaky hand the professor caught at the handrail.

"Are you sick, Vladimir Ipatych?" anxious voices flew at him from all sides.

"No, no," replied Persikov, recovering. "I am just overtired . . . yes . . . May I have a glass of water?"

It was a very sunny August day. That bothered the professor, so the shades were lowered. A reflector on a flexible stand threw a sharp beam of light onto a glass table piled with instruments and slides. Leaning against the backrest of the revolving chair in exhaustion, Persikov smoked, and his eyes, dead tired but satisfied, looked through the billows of smoke at the partly open door of the chamber where, faintly warming the already close and impure air of the office, the red sheaf of his ray lay quietly.

Someone knocked on the door.

"Well?" asked Persikov.

The door creaked softly, and Pankrat entered. He put his arms stiffly at his sides, and blanching with fear before the divinity, he said, "Mr. Professor, out there Feyt has come to you."

A semblance of a smile appeared on the scientist's cheeks. He narrowed his eyes and said, "That's interesting. But I'm busy."

"He says he has an official paper from the Kremlin."

"Fate with a paper? A rare combination," uttered Persikov, adding, "oh, well, get him in here."

"Yes, sir," said Pankrat, and he disappeared through the door like an eel.

A minute later it creaked again and a man appeared on the threshold. Persikov squeaked around on his swivel chair, and, above his spectacles, fixed his eyes on the visitor over his shoulder. Persikov was very remote from life—he was not interested in it—but even Persikov was struck by the predominant, the salient characteristic of the man who had entered: he was peculiarly old-fashioned. In 1919 the man would have been entirely in place in the streets of the capital; he would have passed in 1924, in the beginning of the year—but in 1928 he was odd. At a time when even the most backward section of the proletariat—the bakers—wore ordinary jackets, and the military service jacket was a rarity in Moscow—an old-fashioned outfit irrevocably discarded by the end of 1924—the man who had entered was wearing a double-breasted leather coat, olive-green trousers, puttees, and gaiters on his legs, and at his hip a huge Mauser of antiquated make in a cracked yellow holster. His face produced the same kind of impression on Persikov that it did on everyone else—an extremely unpleasant impression. His little eyes looked at the whole world with surprise, but at the same time with assurance; there was something bumptious in the short legs with their flat feet. His face was blue from close shaving. Persikov immediately frowned. He squeaked the screw of his chair mercilessly, and looking at the man no longer over his spectacles but through them, he asked, "You have some paper? Where is it?"

The visitor was apparently overwhelmed by what he saw. Generally he had little capacity for being taken aback, but here he was taken aback. Judging by his tiny eyes, he was struck most of all by the twelve-shelved bookcase, which reached to the ceiling and was crammed with books. Then, of course, there were the chambers, in which—as though in hell—the scarlet ray flickered, diffused and magnified through the glass. And Persikov himself in the penumbra beside the sharp needle of light emitted by the reflector was sufficiently strange and majestic in his revolving chair. The visitor fixed on the professor a glance in which sparks of deference were clearly leaping through the self-assurance. He presented no paper, but said, "I am Alexander Semyonovich Feyt!"[8]

"Well? So what?"

"I have been appointed director of the model Sovkhoz[9]—the 'Red Ray' Sovkhoz," explained the visitor.

"And?"

"And so I've come to see you, comrade, with a secret memorandum."

"Interesting to learn. Make it short, if you can."

The visitor unbuttoned the lapel of his coat and pulled out an order printed on magnificent thick paper. He held it out to Persikov. Then, without invitation, he sat down on a revolving stool.

"Don't jiggle the table," Persikov said with hatred.

The visitor looked around at the table in fright—at the far end, in a moist dark aperture, some sort of eyes gleamed lifelessly like emeralds. They exuded a chill.

No sooner had Persikov read the paper than he rose from his stool and rushed to the telephone. Within a few seconds he was already speaking hurriedly and with an extreme degree of irritation. "Excuse me . . . I cannot understand . . . How can this be? I . . . without my consent or advice . . . Why the devil only knows what he'll do with it!"

Here the stranger turned on his stool, extremely insulted. "Pardon me," he began, "I am the direc . . ."

But Persikov waved him away with his hooked index finger and continued. "Excuse me, I can't understand . . . And finally, I categorically refuse. I will not sanction any experiments with eggs . . . Until I try them myself . . ."

Something squawked and clicked in the receiver, and even from

8. In Russian his name is Rokk, and *rok* means "fate."
9. A state collective farm.

a distance one could understand that the condescending voice in the receiver was speaking to a small child. It ended with crimson Persikov slamming down the receiver and saying past it into the wall, "I wash my hands of this!"

He returned to the table, took the paper from it, read it once from top to bottom above his spectacles, then from bottom to top through them, and suddenly he yelled, "Pankrat!"

Pankrat appeared in the door as though rising up through a trap door at the opera. Persikov glanced at him and ejaculated, "Get out, Pankrat!"

And without showing the least surprise, Pankrat disappeared.

Then Persikov turned to his guest and began, "All right, sir . . . I submit. It's none of my business. And I'm not even interested."

The professor not so much offended as amazed his guest. "But pardon me," he began, "you *are* a comrade? . . ."

"Comrade . . . comrade. . . . Is that all you know how to say?" Persikov grumbled, and fell silent.

"Well!" was written on Feyt's face.

"Pard . . ."

"Now, sir, if you please," interrupted Persikov. "This is the arc light. From it you obtain, by manipulating the ocular," Persikov snapped the lid of the chamber, which resembled a camera, "a cluster which you can gather by adjusting object-lens No. 1, here, and mirror No. 2." Persikov turned off the ray, turned it on again—aimed at the floor of the asbestos chamber. "And on the floor you can place whatever you please in the ray and conduct experiments. Extremely simple, don't you think?"

Persikov meant to show irony and contempt, but his visitor did not notice, peering intently into the chamber with his glittering little eyes.

"But I warn you," Persikov went on, "one should not put one's hands in the ray, because, according to my observations, it causes growth of the epithelium—and I unfortunately have not yet been able to establish whether it is malignant or not."

Here the visitor nimbly hid his hands behind his back, dropping his leather cap, and he looked at the professor's hands. They were covered with iodine stains, and his right wrist was bandaged.

"And how do you do it, professor?"

"You can buy rubber gloves at Schwab's on Kuznetsky," the professor replied irritably. "I'm not obliged to worry about that."

Here Persikov looked up at his visitor, as though studying him through a magnifying glass. "Where are you from? Why you? In general, why you?"

Feyt was finally deeply offended, "Pard . . ."

"After all, one has to know what it's all about . . . Why have you latched on to my ray? . . ."

"Because it's a matter of utmost importance."

"Oh. The utmost? In that case—Pankrat!"

And when Pankrat appeared: "Wait, I'll think it over."

And Pankrat obediently disappeared.

"I cannot understand one thing," said Persikov. "Why is such rushing and secrecy necessary?"

"You have already got me muddled, professor," Feyt answered. "You know that every last chicken has died off?"

"Well, what about it?" shrieked Persikov. "Do you want to resurrect them instantly, or what? And why use a ray that has still been insufficiently studied?"

"Comrade Professor," replied Feyt, "I must say, you do mix me up. I am telling you that it is essential for us to reestablish chicken breeding, because they're writing all kinds of nasty things about us abroad. Yes."

"Let them write."

"Well, you know!" Feyt responded mysteriously, shaking his head.

"I'd like to know who got the idea of breeding chickens from eggs . . ."

"I did," answered Feyt.

"Uhmmm . . . So . . . And why, may I inquire? Where did you hear about the characteristics of this ray?"

"I attended your lecture, professor."

"I haven't done anything with eggs yet! I am just getting ready to!"

"It'll work, I swear it will," Feyt said suddenly with conviction and enthusiasm. "Your ray is so famous, you could hatch elephants with it, let alone chickens."

"Tell me," uttered Persikov. "You aren't a zoologist, are you? No? A pity . . . you'd make a very bold experimenter . . . Yes, but you are risking failure. And you are just taking up my time . . ."

"We'll return your chambers."

"When?"

"Well, as soon as I breed the first group."

"How confidently you say that! Very well, sir. Pankrat!"

"I have men with me," said Feyt. "And guards . . ."

By that evening Persikov's office had been desolated . . . The tables were bare. Feyt's men had carried off the three large chambers, leaving the professor only the first, his own little one with which he had begun the experiments.

July twilight was settling over the institute; grayness filled it and flowed along the corridors. From the study came the sound of monotonous footsteps—this was Persikov pacing the large room from window to door without turning on the light. It was a strange thing: that evening an inexplicably dismal mood overcame both the people who inhabited the institute and the animals. The toads for some reason raised a particularly dismal concert, twittering ominously, premonishingly. Pankrat had to chase along the corridors after a garter snake that had escaped from its cage, and when he caught it, the snake looked as though it had decided to flee wherever its eyes would lead it, if only to get away.

In the deep twilight the bell rang from Persikov's office. Pankrat appeared on the threshold and he saw a strange sight. The scientist was standing solitarily in the center of the room, looking at the tables. Pankrat coughed once and stood still.

"There, Pankrat," said Persikov, and he pointed to the bare table.

Pankrat was horrified. It seemed to him that the professor's eyes were tear-stained in the twilight. It was so extraordinary and so terrible.

"Yes, sir," Pankrat answered lugubriously, thinking, "It'd be better if you'd yell at me."

"There," repeated Persikov, and his lips quivered like a child's when his favorite toy has suddenly, for no reason, been taken away from it. "You know, my good Pankrat," Persikov went on, turning away to the window, "my wife . . . who left me fifteen years ago—she joined an operetta . . . and now it turns out she is dead . . . What a story, my dear Pankrat . . . I was sent a letter."

The toads screamed plaintively, and twilight enveloped the professor. There it is . . . night. Moscow . . . here and there outside the windows some sort of white globes began to light up . . . Pankrat, confused and in anguish, held his hands straight down his sides, stiff with fear . . .

"Go, Pankrat," the professor murmured heavily, waving his hand. "Go to bed, my dear, kind Pankrat."

And night came. For some reason Pankrat ran out of the office on his tiptoes, hurried to his cranny, rummaged through the rags in the corner, pulled out a half-full bottle of Russian vodka, and gulped down almost a regular glassful in one breath. He chased it with some bread and salt, and his eyes cheered up a bit.

Later in the evening, close to midnight now, Pankrat was sitting barefoot on a bench in the dimly lit vestibule, talking to the sleepless derby on duty, and scratching his chest under the calico shirt. "It'd be better if he'd kill me, I swear . . ."

"He really was crying?" the derby inquired with curiosity.

"I swear . . ." Pankrat assured him.

"A great scientist," agreed the derby. "Obviously no frog can take the place of a wife."

"Absolutely," Pankrat agreed. Then he thought a bit and added, "I'm thinking of getting my woman permission to come out here[10] . . . why should she sit there in the village? Only she can't stand them snakes no how . . ."

"Sure, they're terribly nasty," agreed the derby.

From the scientist's office not a sound could be heard. And there was no light in it. No strip under the door.

[V I I I]

EVENTS AT THE SOVKHOZ

THERE IS ABSOLUTELY no time of year more beautiful than mid-August in, let us say, the Smolensk province. The summer of 1928, as is well known, was one of the finest ever, with spring rains which had come at precisely the right time, a full hot sun, and a fine harvest . . . The apples were ripening in the former Sheremetiev estate . . . the woods stood green, the fields lay in yellow squares. A man becomes better in the bosom of nature. And Alexander Semyonovich would not have seemed as unpleasant here as in the city. And he no longer wore that obnoxious coat. His face had a coppery tan, his unbuttoned calico shirt betrayed a chest overgrown with the thickest black hair, his legs were clad in canvas trousers. And his eyes had grown calmer and kinder.

Alexander Semyonovich ran briskly down the stairs from the becolumned porch over which a sign was nailed, under a star: THE "RED RAY" SOVKHOZ. And he went straight to meet the pickup truck which had brought him three black chambers under guard.

All day Alexander Semyonovich bustled around with his helpers, setting up the chambers in the former winter garden—the Sheremetiev greenhouse . . . By evening all was in readiness. A frosted white globe glowed under the glass ceiling, the chambers were

10. One had to get police permission for changes of residence.

arranged on bricks, and the mechanic who had come with the chambers, clicking and turning the shiny knobs, turned the mysterious red ray onto the asbestos floor of the black boxes.

Alexander Semyonovich bustled around, and had climbed the ladder himself to check out the wiring.

On the following day, the same pickup returned from the station and disgorged three crates made of magnificent smooth plywood and plastered all over with labels and warnings in white letters on black backgrounds: "*Vorsicht: Eier!* Handle with care: Eggs."

"But why did they send so few?" wondered Alexander Semyonovich—however, he immediately started bustling around and unpacking the eggs. The unpacking was done in the same greenhouse with the participation of: Alexander Semyonovich himself; his wife Manya, a woman of extraordinary bulk; the one-eyed former gardener of the former Sheremetievs, currently working on the sovkhoz in the universal capacity of watchman; the guard, now condemned to life on the sovkhoz; and Dunya, the cleaning woman. This was not Moscow, and so the nature of everything here was simpler, friendlier, and more homely. Alexander Semyonovich supervised, glancing affectionately at the crates, which looked like such a sturdy, compact present under the soft sunset light coming through the upper windows of the greenhouse. The guard, whose rifle rested peacefully by the door, broke open the clamps and metal bindings with a pair of pliers. Crackling filled the room. Dust flew. Flopping along in his sandals, Alexander Semyonovich fussed around the crates.

"Take it easy," he said to the guard. "Careful. Don't you see it's eggs?"

"Don't worry," the provincial warrior grunted, drilling away. "Just a second." T-r-r-r . . . and the dust flew.

The eggs turned out to be exceedingly well packed: under the wooden lid there was a layer of wax paper, then absorbent paper, then a solid layer of wood shavings, and then sawdust, in which the white tips of the eggs gleamed.

"Foreign packing," Alexander Semyonovich said lovingly digging into the sawdust. "Not the way we do things here. Manya, careful, you'll break them."

"You've gotten silly, Alexander Semyonovich," replied his wife. "Imagine, such gold. Do you think I've never seen eggs before? . . . Oy! What big ones!"

"Europe," said Alexander Semyonovich, "Did you expect our crummy little Russian peasant eggs? . . . They must all be Brahmaputras, the devil take 'em! German . . ."

"Sure they are," confirmed the guard, admiring the eggs.

"Only I don't understand why they're dirty," Alexander Semyonovich said reflectively . . . "Manya, you look after things. Have them go on with the unloading, and I'm going to make a telephone call."

And Alexander Semyonovich set off for the telephone in the sovkhoz office across the yard.

That evening the telephone cracked in the office of the Zoological Institute. Professor Persikov ruffled his hair and went to the phone. "Well?" he asked.

"The provinces calling, just a minute," the receiver replied with a soft hiss in a woman's voice.

"Well, I'm listening," Persikov said fastidiously into the black mouth of the phone.

Something clicked in it, and then a distant masculine voice anxiously spoke in his ear. "Should the eggs be washed, professor?"

"What? What is it? What are you asking?" Persikov got irritated. "Where are you calling from?"

"From Nikolsky, Smolensk province," the receiver answered.

"I don't understand any of this. I don't know any Nikolsky. Who is this?"

"Feyt," said the receiver sternly.

"What Feyt? Oh, yes . . . it's you . . . so what is it you're asking?"

"Should they be washed? . . . I was sent a batch of chicken eggs from abroad . . ."

"Well?"

"They seem slimy somehow . . ."

"You're mixing something up . . . How can they be 'slimy' as you put it? Well, of course, there can be a little . . . perhaps some droppings stuck on . . . or something else . . ."

"So they shouldn't be washed?"

"Of course not . . . What are you doing—are you all ready to load the chambers with the eggs?"

"I am. Yes," replied the receiver.

"Harumpf," Persikov snorted.

"So long," the receiver clicked and went silent.

"So long," Persikov repeated with hatred to Assistant Professor Ivanov. "How do you like that character, Peter Stepanovich?"

Ivanov laughed. "Was that him? I can imagine what he'll cook up with those eggs out there."

"The id . . . id . . . idiot," Persikov stuttered furiously. "Just imagine, Peter Stepanovich. Fine, it is quite possible that the ray will have the same effect on the deutoplasm of the chicken egg that it did on the plasm of the amphibians. It is quite possible that the hens will hatch. But neither you nor I can say what sort of hens they will be . . . Maybe they won't be good for a damned thing. Maybe they'll die in a day or two. Maybe they'll be inedible! Can I guarantee that they'll be able to stand on their feet? Maybe their bones will be brittle." Persikov got all excited and waved his hands, crooking his index fingers.

"Absolutely right," agreed Ivanov.

"Can you guarantee, Peter Stepanovich, that they'll produce another generation? Maybe this character will breed sterile hens. He'll drive them up to the size of a dog, and then you can wait until the second coming before they'll have any progeny."

"No one can guarantee it," agreed Ivanov.

"And what bumptiousness!" Persikov got himself even more distraught. "What insolence! And, note this, I have been ordered to instruct this scoundrel." Persikov pointed to the paper delivered by Feyt (it lay on the experiment table). "How am I to instruct this ignoramus, when I myself cannot say anything on the problem?"

"But was it impossible to refuse?" asked Ivanov.

Persikov turned crimson, picked up the paper, and showed it to Ivanov. The latter read it and smiled ironically.

"Um, yes," he said very significantly.

"And then, note this . . . I've been waiting for my order for two months—and there's neither hide nor hair of it. While that one is sent the eggs instantly, and generally gets all kinds of cooperation."

"He won't get a damned thing out of it, Vladimir Ipatych. And it will just end by their returning the chambers to you."

"If only they don't take too long doing it, otherwise they're holding up my experiments."

"That's what's really rotten. I have everything ready."

"Did you get the diving suits?"

"Yes, today."

Persikov calmed down somewhat, and livened up. "Hhmmm . . . I think we'll do it this way. We can seal the doors of the operating room tight and open the window . . ."

"Of course," agreed Ivanov.

"Three helmets?"

"Three. Yes."

"Well, so . . . That means you, I, and possibly one of the students. We'll give him the third helmet."

"Greenmut's possible."

"The one who's working on the salamanders with you now? Hmmm, he's not bad . . . although, wait, last spring he couldn't describe the structure of the air bladder of the Gymnodontes," Persikov added rancorously.

"No, he's not bad . . . He's a good student," interceded Ivanov.

"We will have to go without sleep for one night," Persikov went on. "And one more thing, Peter Stepanovich, you check the gas— otherwise the devil only knows about these so-called Goodchems— they'll send some sort of trash."

"No, no," Ivanov waved his hands. "I already tested it yesterday. We must give them their due, Vladimir Ipatych, it's excellent gas."

"On whom did you try it?"

"On ordinary toads. You let out a little stream and they die instantly. Oh, yes, Vladimir Ipatych, we'll also do this—you write a request to the GPU, asking them to send an electric revolver."

"But I don't know how to use it."

"I'll take that on myself," answered Ivanov. "We used to practice with one on the Klyazma, just for fun . . . there was a GPU man living next door to me. A remarkable thing. Quite extraordinary. Noiseless, kills outright from a hundred paces. We used to shoot crows . . . I don't think we even need the gas."

"Hmmm, that's a clever idea . . . Very." Persikov went to the corner of the room, picked up the receiver, and croaked, "Let me have that, oh, what d'you call it . . . Lubyanka . . ."

The days got unbearably hot. One could clearly see the dense transparent heat shimmering over the fields. But the nights were marvelous, deceptive, green. The moon shone brightly, casting such beauty on the former Sheremetiev estate that it is impossible to express it in words. The sovkhoz palace gleamed as though made of sugar, the shadows trembled in the park, and the ponds were cleft into two colors—a slanting shaft of moonlight across it, and the rest, bottomless darkness. In the patches of moonlight you could easily read *Izvestia,* except for the chess column, which is printed in tiny nonpareil. But, naturally, nobody read *Izvestia* on nights like these . . . Dunya, the cleaning woman, turned up in the copse behind the sovkhoz, and as a result of some coincidence, the red-moustachioed driver of a battered sovkhoz pickup turned up there too.

What they did there—remains unknown. They took shelter in the melting shadow of an elm, right on the driver's outspread leather jacket. A lamp burned in the kitchen where two gardeners were having their supper, and Madame Feyt, wearing a white robe, was sitting on the becolumned veranda and dreaming as she gazed at the beautiful moon.

At ten in the evening when all of the sounds had subsided in the village of Kontsovka, situated behind the sovkhoz, the idyllic landscape was filled with the charming, delicate sounds of a flute. It is unthinkable to try to express how this suited the copses and former columns of the Sheremetiev palace. Fragile Liza from *The Queen of Spades*[11] mingled her voice in a duet with the voice of the passionate Polina, and the melody swept up into the moonlit heights like the ghost of an old regime—old, but infinitely lovely, enchanting to the point of tears.

"Waning . . . waning . . ." the flute sang, warbling and sighing.

The copses fell silent, and Dunya, fatal as a wood nymph, listened, her cheek pressed to the prickly, reddish masculine cheek of the driver.

"He blows good, the son of a bitch," said the driver, encircling Dunya's waist with his manly arm.

Playing the flute was none other than the sovkhoz director himself, Alexander Semyonovich Feyt, and we must give him his due, he played extremely well. The fact is that at one time the flute had been Alexander Semyonovich's specialty. Right up until 1917 he had been a member of Maestro Petukhov's well-known concert ensemble, whose harmonic sounds rang out every night in the lobby of the cozy Magic Dreams Cinema in the city of Yekaterinoslav. The great year of 1917, which had broken the careers of many people, had turned Alexander Semyonovich onto new roads too. He abandoned the Magic Dreams and the dusty star-spangled satin in the lobby and dove into the open sea of war and revolution, ex-

11. Tchaikovsky's romantic opera based on Pushkin's short story of the same title.

changing his flute for a deadly Mauser. For a long time he was tossed on the waves, which cast him up now in the Crimea, now in Moscow, now in Turkestan, and even in Vladivostok. It took a revolution to bring Alexander Semyonovich fully into his own. The man's true greatness was revealed, and naturally he was not meant to sit around the lobby of the Dreams. Without getting into great detail, let us say that late 1927 and early 1928 found Alexander Semyonovich in Turkestan where he had, first, edited a huge newspaper and, next, as the local member of the Supreme Agricultural Commission, covered himself with glory through his remarkable work in irrigating the Turkestan territory. In 1928 Feyt arrived in Moscow and got a well-deserved rest. The highest committee of the organization whose card the provincial-looking, old-fashioned man carried in his pocket with honor showed its appreciation and appointed him to a quiet and honorable post. Alas! Alas! To the misfortune of the Republic, the seething brain of Alexander Semyonovich was not cooled off; in Moscow Feyt ran across Persikov's discovery, and in his room at the Red Paris Hotel on Tverskaya, Alexander Semyonovich conceived the idea of using Persikov's ray to replenish the chicken population of the Republic in one month. Feyt's plan was heard out by the Commission on Animal Husbandry, they agreed with him, and Feyt went with the thick sheet of paper to the eccentric zoologist.

The concert over the glassy waters and copses and park was already drawing to a close when suddenly something happened that interrupted it ahead of time. Namely, the dogs in Kontsovka, who should have been asleep at that hour, suddenly burst out into an incredible fit of barking which gradually turned into a general and very anguished howling. The howling, increasing in volume, flew across the fields, and this howling was suddenly answered by a chattering, million-voiced concert of frogs in all the ponds. All of this was so uncanny that for a minute it even seemed that the mysterious, witching night had grown dim.

Alexander Semyonovich lay down his flute and went out onto

the veranda, "Manya! Do you hear that? Those damned dogs . . . What do you think is making them so wild?"

"How should I know?" replied Manya, staring at the moon.

"You know what, Manechka, let's go and take a look at the eggs," suggested Alexander Semyonovich.

"By God, Alexander Semyonovich, you've gone completely nuts with your eggs and chickens. Take a little rest!"

"No, Manechka, let's go."

A bright bulb was burning in the greenhouse. Dunya also came in, face flushed and eyes flashing. Alexander Semyonovich gently opened the observation panes, and everyone started peering inside the chambers. On the white asbestos floor the spotted bright-red eggs lay in even rows; the chambers were silent, and the 15,000 watt bulb overhead was hissing quietly.

"Oh, what chicks I'll hatch out of here!" Alexander Semyonovich said enthusiastically, looking now into the observation slits in the side walls of the chambers, now into the wide air vents above. "You'll see. What? I won't?"

"You know, Alexander Semyonovich," said Dunya, smiling, "the peasants in Kontsovka are saying you're the Anti-Christ. Them are devilish eggs, they say. It's a sin to hatch eggs by machine. They wanted to murder you."

Alexander Semyonovich shuddered and turned to his wife. His face had turned yellow. "Well, how do you like that? Such people! What can you do with people like that? Eh? Manechka, we'll have to arrange a meeting for them. Tomorrow I'll call some Party workers from the district. I'll make a speech myself. In general we'll have to do some work here . . . It's some sort of bear's den, a wild place . . ."

"Dark minds," said the guard, reposing on his coat at the greenhouse door.

The next day was marked by the strangest and most inexplicable events. In the morning, at the first flash of the sun, the copses which usually greeted the luminary with a mighty and ceaseless twittering of birds, met it in total silence. This was noticed by absolutely everyone. As though before a storm. But there was not the slightest hint of a storm. Conversations in the sovkhoz assumed a strange, ambiguous tone, very disturbing to Alexander Semyono-vich, especially because from the words of the old Kontsovka peasant nicknamed Goat's Goiter, a notorious troublemaker and smart aleck, it got spread around that, supposedly, all the birds had gathered into flocks and cleared out of Sheremetievka at dawn, heading north—which was all simply stupid. Alexander Semyonovich was very upset and wasted the whole day telephoning the town of Grachevka. From there he was promised two speakers would be sent to the sovkhoz in a day or two with two topics—the international situation and the question of the "Goodpoul" Trust.

Neither was the evening without its surprises. Whether or not in the morning the woods had gone silent, demonstrating with utmost clarity how unpleasant and ominous absence of sound is in a forest, and whether or not all of the sparrows had cleared out of the sov-khoz yards by midday heading somewhere else—by evening the pond in Sheremetievka *had* gone silent. This was truly astounding, since the famous croaking of the Sheremetievka frogs was quite well known to everyone for forty versts around. But now all of the frogs seemed to have died out. Not a single voice came from the pond, and the sedge was soundless. It must be admitted that Alexander Semyonovich completely lost his composure. All of these events began to cause talk, and talk of a very unpleasant kind, i.e. it was behind Alexander Semyonovich's back.

"It's really strange," Alexander Semyonovich said to his wife at lunch. "I can't understand why those birds had to fly away."

"How should I know?" answered Manya. "Maybe from your ray?"

"Manya, you're just a plain fool," said Alexander Semyonovich, throwing down his spoon. "You're like the peasants. What has the ray got to do with it?"

"Well, I don't know. Leave me alone."

That evening the third surprise happened—the dogs at Kontsovka again started howling—and how they howled! The moonlit fields were filled with the ceaseless wailing, anguished, angry moans.

To some extent Alexander Semyonovich felt rewarded by yet another surprise—a pleasant one in the greenhouse. An uninterrupted tapping began to come from the red eggs in the chambers. "Tap . . . tap . . . tap . . . tap". . . came tapping from first one egg, then another, then yet another.

The tapping in the eggs was a triumphant tapping for Alexander Semyonovich. The strange events in the woods and the pond were instantly forgotten. Everyone gathered in the greenhouse: Manya, Dunya, the watchman, and the guard, who left his rifle at the door.

"Well? What do you have to say about that?" Alexander Semyonovich asked victoriously. They all pressed their ears curiously to the doors of the first chamber. "It's the chicks—tapping, with their beaks," Alexander Semyonovich continued, beaming. "You say I won't hatch any chicks? Not so, my friends." And in an excess of emotion he slapped the guard on the back. "I'll hatch out such chicks you'll ooh and ah. Now I have to look sharp," he added sternly. "As soon as they begin to break through, let me know immediately."

"Right," the watchman, Dunya, and the guard answered in chorus.

"Tap . . . tap . . . tap." The tapping started again, now in one, now in another egg in the first chamber. Indeed, the picture of new life being born before your eyes within the thin, translucent casings was so interesting that this whole society sat on for a long while on the empty overturned crates, watching the raspberry-colored eggs ripen in the mysterious flickering light. They broke up to go to bed rather late, after the greenish night had poured light over the sovkhoz and the surrounding countryside. It was an eerie night, one might even say terrifying, perhaps because its utter silence was broken now and then by outbursts of causeless, plaintive, and heart-rending howling from the dogs in Kontsovka. What made those damned dogs go mad was absolutely unknown.

In the morning a new unpleasantness awaited Alexander Semyonovich. The guard was extremely embarrassed, put his hand over his heart, swore and made God his witness that he had not fallen asleep, but that he had noticed nothing. "It's a queer thing," the guard insisted. "I'm not to blame, Comrade Feyt."

"Thank you, my heartfelt thanks," Alexander Semyonovich began the roasting, "What are you thinking about, comrade? Why were you put here? To watch! So you tell me where they've disappeared to! They've hatched, haven't they? That means they've escaped. That means you left the door open and went away to your room. I want those chicks back here—or else!"

"There's no where for me to go. Don't I know my job?" The warrior finally took offense. "You're blaming me for nothing, Comrade Feyt!"

"Where've they gone to?"

"Well how should I know?" the warrior got infuriated at last. "Am I supposed to be guarding them? Why am I posted here? To see that nobody filches the chambers, and I'm doing my job. Here are your chambers. But I'm not obliged by the law to go chasing after your chickens. Who knows what kind of chicks you'll hatch out of there; you probably couldn't catch them on a bicycle, maybe!"

Alexander Semyonovich was somewhat taken aback, grumbled a bit more, then fell into a state of astonishment. It was indeed a strange thing. In the first chamber, which had been loaded before the others, the two eggs lying closest to the base of the ray turned out to be broken. And one of them had even rolled off to the side. The shell was scattered on the asbestos floor under the ray.

"What the devil?" muttered Alexander Semyonovich. "The windows are shut—they couldn't have flown out through the roof!" He tilted his head back and looked up where there were several wide holes in the glass transom of the roof.

"What's wrong with you, Alexander Semyonovich," Dunya cried extremely surprised. "All we need is flying chicks. They're here somewhere. Cheep . . . cheep . . . cheep," she began to call, looking in the corners of the greenhouse where there were dusty flowerpots, boards, and other rubbish. But no chicks responded anywhere.

All of the personnel ran about the sovkhoz yard for two hours, searching for the nimble chicks, but no one found anything anywhere. The day went by in extreme agitation. The guard over the chambers was increased by one watchman, and he had been given the strictest order to look through the windows of the chambers every fifteen minutes and call Alexander Semyonovich the second anything happened. The guard sat by the door, sulking, holding his rifle between his knees. Alexander Semyonovich was snowed under with chores, and he did not have his lunch until almost two in the afternoon. After lunch he took an hour-long nap in the cool shade on the former ottoman of Prince Sheremetiev, drank some sovkhoz kvass, dropped by the greenhouse and made sure that everything was in perfect order there now. The old watchman was sprawled on his belly on a piece of burlap and staring, blinking, into the observation window of the first chamber. The guard was sitting alertly without leaving the door.

But there was also something new: the eggs in the third chamber, loaded last of all, began to do a sort of gulping and clucking, as if someone were sobbing inside.

"Oh, they're ripening," said Alexander Semyonovich. "Getting ripe and now I see. Did you see?" he addressed the watchman . . .

"Yes, it's a marvel," the latter replied in a completely ambiguous tone, shaking his head.

Alexander Semyonovich sat by the chambers for a while, but nothing hatched in his presence; he got up, stretched, and declared that he would not leave the estate that day, he would just go down to the pond for a swim, and if anything started to happen, he was to be called immediately. He ran over to the palace to his bedroom, where two narrow spring beds with crumpled linen stood, and on the floor there was a pile of green apples and heaps of millet, prepared for the coming fledglings. He armed himself with a shaggy towel, and after a moment's thought he picked up his flute, intending to play at leisure over the unruffled waters. He walked out of the palace briskly, cut across the sovkhoz yard, and headed down the small willow avenue toward the pond. He strode along briskly, swinging the towel and carrying the flute under his arm. The sky was pouring down heat through the willows, and his body ached and begged for water. On his right hand began a thicket of burdocks, into which he spat as he passed by; and immediately there was a rustling in the tangle of broad leaves, as though someone had started dragging a log. Feeling an unpleasant fleeting twinge in his heart, Alexander Semyonovich turned his head toward the thicket and looked at it with wonder. The pond had reverberated with no sounds of any kind for two days now. The rustling ceased; the unruffled surface of the pond and the gray roof of the bathhouse flashed invitingly beyond the burdocks. Several dragonflies darted past in front of Alexander Semyonovich. He was just about to turn to the wooden planks leading down to the water when the rustle in the greenery was repeated, and it was accompanied by a short hiss, as if a locomotive were discharging steam and oil. Alexander Semyonovich got on guard and peered into the dense wall of weeds.

"Alexander Semyonovich," his wife's voice called at that moment, and her white blouse flashed, disappeared, and flashed again in the raspberry patch. "Wait, I'll go for a swim too."

His wife hastened toward the pond, but Alexander Semyonovich made no answer, all attention was riveted on the burdocks. A grayish and olive-colored log began to rise from the thicket, growing up before his eyes. The log, it seemed to Alexander Semyonovich, was splotched with some sort of moist yellowish spots. It began to stretch, flexing and undulating, and it stretched so high that it was above the scrubby little willow . . . Then the top of the log broke, leaned over somewhat, and over Alexander Semyonovich was something resembling in height a Moscow electric pole. But this something was about three times thicker than a pole and far more beautiful, thanks to the scaly tattoo. Still comprehending nothing, but his blood running cold, Alexander Semyonovich looked at the summit of the terrifying pole, and his heart stopped beating for several seconds. It seemed to him that a frost had suddenly struck the August day, and it turned dim, as though he were looking at the sun through a pair of summer pants.

There turned out to be a head on the upper end of the log. It was flat, pointed, and adorned with a spherical yellow spot on an olive-green background. Lidless, open, icy, narrow eyes sat on the top of the head, and in these eyes gleamed utterly infinite malice. The head made a movement, as though pecking the air, then the pole plunged back into the burdock, and only the eyes remained, staring unblinkingly at Alexander Semyonovich. The latter, bathed in sticky sweat, uttered four completely incredulous words and caused only by terror bordering on insanity. So beautiful those eyes among the leaves were!

"What sort of joke . . ."

Then he recalled that the fakirs . . . yes . . . yes . . . India . . . a woven basket and a picture . . . They charm . . .

The head arched up again, and the body began to emerge too. Alexander Semyonovich lifted the flute to his lips, squeaked hoarsely, and gasping for breath every second, he began to play the waltz from *Eugene Onegin*.[12] The eyes in the foliage instantly began to smolder with implacable hate for the opera.

"Have you lost your mind, playing in this heat?" Manya's merry voice resounded, and out of the corner of his eye Alexander Semyonovich caught sight of a white spot.

Then a sickening scream pierced through the whole sovkhoz, expanded and flew up into the sky, while the waltz hopped up and down as if it had a broken leg. The head in the thicket shot forward

12. Tchaikovsky's romantic opera based on Pushkin's novel in verse of the same title.

—its eyes left Alexander Semyonovich, abandoning his soul to repentance. A snake approximately fifteen yards long and as thick as a man leaped out of the burdock like a steel spring. A cloud of dust whirled from the road and the waltz was over. The snake swept past the sovkhoz manager straight toward the white blouse down the road. Feyt saw it all quite distinctly: Manya turned yellow-white, and her long hair stood up like wire a half-yard over her head. Before Feyt's eyes the snake opened its maw for a moment, something like a fork flicked out of it, and as she was sinking to the dust its teeth caught Manya by the shoulder and jerked her a yard above the earth. Manya repeated her piercing death scream. The snake coiled itself into a huge screw, its tail churning up a sandstorm, and it began to crush Manya. She did not utter another sound, and Feyt just heard her bones snapping. Manya's head swept up high over the earth, tenderly pressed to the snake's cheek. Blood splashed from Manya's mouth, a broken arm flipped out, and little fountains of blood spurted from under her fingernails. Then, dislocating its jaws, the snake opened its maw, slipped its head over Manya's all at once, and began to pull itself over her like a glove over a finger. Such hot breath spread all around the snake that it touched Feyt's face, and its tail almost swept him off the road in the acrid dust. It was then that Feyt turned gray. First the left, then the right half of his jet-black hair was covered with silver. In mortal nausea he finally tore away from the road, and seeing and hearing nothing, making the countryside resound with wild howls, he took off running . . .

[IX]

A LIVING MASS

SHCHUKIN, the agent of the State Political Administration (GPU) at the Dugino Station, was a very brave man. He said thoughtfully to his assistant, redheaded Polaitis, "Oh, well, let's go. Eh? Get the motorcycle." Then he was silent for a moment, and added, turning to the man who was sitting on the bench, "Put down the flute."

But the trembling, gray-haired man on the bench in the office of the Dugino GPU did not put his flute down—he began to cry and mumble. Then Shchukin and Polaitis realized that the flute would have to be taken from him. His fingers seemed frozen to it. Shchukin, who possessed enormous strength, almost that of a circus performer, began to unbend one finger after the other, and he unbent them all. Then he put the flute on the table.

This was in the early, sunny morning the day following Manya's death.

"You will come with us," said Shchukin, addressing Alexander Semyonovich. "You will show us what happened where." But Feyt moved away from him in horror and covered his face with his hands in defense against a terrible vision.

"You must show us," Polaitis added sternly.

"No, let him alone. Don't you see, that man is not himself."

"Send me to Moscow," Alexander Semyonovich begged, crying.

"You mean you won't return to the sovkhoz at all?"

But instead of an answer, Feyt again put out his hands as if to ward them off, and horror poured from his eyes.

"Well, all right," decided Shchukin. "You really aren't up to it . . . I see. The express will be arriving soon, you go ahead and take it."

Then, while the station guard was plying Alexander Semyonovich with water, and the latter's teeth chattered on the blue, cracked cup, Shchukin and Polaitis held a conference. Polaitis felt that, generally, none of this had happened, and that Feyt was simply mentally ill and had had a terrifying hallucination. But Shchukin tended to think that a boa constrictor had escaped from the circus which was currently performing in the town of Grachevka. Hearing their skeptical whispers, Alexander Semyonovich stood up. He came to his senses somewhat, and stretching out his arms like a Biblical prophet, he said, "Listen to me. Listen. Why don't you believe me? It was there. Where do you think my wife is?"

Shchukin became silent and serious and immediately sent some sort of telegram to Grachevka. At Shchukin's order a third agent was to stay with Alexander Semyonovich constantly and had to accompany him to Moscow. Meanwhile, Shchukin and Polaitis started getting ready for the expedition. All they had was one electric revolver, but just that was quite good protection. The 1927 fifty-round model, the pride of French technology, for close-range fighting, had a range of only one hundred paces, but it covered a field two meters in diameter and killed everything alive in this field. It was hard to miss. Shchukin strapped on the shiny electric toy, and Polaitis armed himself with an ordinary, twenty-five-round submachine gun, took some cartridge belts, and on a single motorcycle they rolled off toward the sovkhoz through the morning dew and chill. The motorcycle clattered off the twenty versts between the station and the sovkhoz in fifteen minutes (Feyt had walked all night, crouching now and then in the roadside shrubbery in spasms of mortal terror) and the sun was really beginning to bake when the sugar-white becolumned palace flashed through the greenery on the rise—at the bottom of which the Top River meandered along. Dead silence reigned all around. Near the entrance to the sovkhoz the agents passed a peasant in a cart. He was ambling slowly along, loaded with sacks, and soon he was left behind. The motorcycle swept across the bridge, and Polaitis blew the horn to call someone out. But no one responded anywhere, except for the frenzied Kontsovka dogs in the distance. Slowing down, the motorcycle drove up to the gates with their green lions. The dust-covered agents in yellow leggings jumped off, fastened the machine to the iron railing with a chain lock, and entered the yard. They were struck by the silence.

"Hey, anyone here?" Shchukin called loudly.

No one responded to his bass. The agents walked around the

yard, getting more and more astonished. Polaitis frowned. Shchukin began to look more and more serious, knitting his fair eyebrows more and more. They looked through the closed window into the kitchen and saw that no one was there, but that the entire floor was strewn with white fragments of broken china.

"You know, something really has happened here. I see that now. A catastrophe," said Polaitis.

"Hey, another in there? Hey!" called Shchukin, but the only response was an echo from under the kitchen eaves. "What the hell," grumbled Shchukin, "it couldn't have gobbled all of them up at once. Unless they ran off. Let's go into the house."

The door to the palace with the columned porch was wide open, and inside it was completely empty. The agents even went up to the mezzanine, knocking on and opening all of the doors, but they found absolutely nothing, and they went back out to the courtyard across the deserted porch.

"Let's walk around back. To the greenhouses," decided Shchukin. "We'll go over the whole place, and we can telephone from there."

The agents walked down the brick path past the flowerbeds to the backyard, crossed it, and saw the gleaming windows of the greenhouse.

"Wait just a minute," Shchukin noted in a whisper, unsnapping the pistol from his belt. Polaitis got on his guard and unslung his submachine gun. A strange and very resonant sound came from the greenhouse and from behind it. It was like the hissing of a locomotive somewhere. "Z-zau-zau . . . z-zau-zau . . . ss-s-s-s-s," the greenhouse hissed.

"Careful now," whispered Shchukin, and trying not to make noise with their heels, the agents tiptoed right up to the windows and peered into the greenhouse.

Polaitis instantly jumped back, and his face turned pale. Shchukin opened his mouth and froze with the pistol in his hand.

The whole greenhouse was alive like a pile of worms. Coiling and uncoiling in knots, hissing and stretching, slithering and swaying their heads, huge snakes were crawling all over the greenhouse floor. Broken eggshells were strewn across the floor, crunching under their bodies. Overhead burned an electric bulb of huge wattage, illuminating the entire interior of the greenhouse in an eery cinematic light. On the floor lay three dark boxes that looked like huge cameras; two of them, leaning askew, had gone out, but in the third a small, densely scarlet spot of light was still burning. Snakes of all sizes were crawling along the cables, climbing up the window frames, and twisting out through the openings in the roof. From the electric bulb itself hung a jet-black spotted snake several yards long, its head swaying near the bulb like a pendulum. Some sort of rattling clicked through the hissing sound; the greenhouse diffused a weird and rotten smell, like a pond. And the agents could just barely make out the piles of white eggs scattered in the dusty corners, and the terrible, giant, long-legged bird lying motionless near the chambers, and the corpse of a man in gray near the door, beside a rifle.

"Get back," cried Shchukin, and he started to retreat, pushing Polaitis back with his left hand and raising the pistol with his right. He managed to fire about nine times, his gun hissing and flicking greenish lightnings around the greenhouse. The sounds within rose terribly in answer to Shchukin's fire; the whole greenhouse became a mass of frenzied movement, and flat heads darted through every aperture. Thunderclaps immediately began to crash over the whole sovkhoz, flashes playing on the walls. "Chakh-chakh-chakh-takh," Polaitis fired, backing away. A strange quadruped was heard behind him, and Polaitis suddenly gave a terrified scream and tumbled backwards. A creature with splayed paws, a brownish-green color, a massive pointed snout, and a ridged tail resembling a lizard of terrifying dimensions, had slithered around the corner of the barn, and viciously biting through Polaitis' foot, it threw him to the ground.

"Help!" cried Polaitis, and immediately his left hand was crunched in the maw. Vainly attempting to raise his right hand, he dragged his gun along the ground. Shchukin whirled around and started dashing from side to side. He managed to fire once, but aimed wide of the mark, because he was afraid of killing his comrade. The second time he fired in the direction of the greenhouse, because a huge olive-colored snake head had appeared there among the small ones, and its body sprang straight in his direction. The shot killed the gigantic snake, and again, jumping and circling around Polaitis, already half-dead in the crocodile's maw, Shchukin was trying to aim so as to kill the terrible reptile without hitting the agent. Finally he succeeded. The electric pistol fired twice, throwing a greenish light on everything around, and the crocodile leaped, stretched out, stiffened, and released Polaitis. Blood was flowing from his sleeve, flowing from his mouth, and leaning on his sound right arm, he dragged his broken left leg along. His eyes were going dim. "Run . . . Shchukin," he murmured, sobbing.

Shchukin fired several times in the direction of the greenhouse, and several of its windows flew out. But a huge spring, olive-colored and sinuous, sprang from the basement window behind him, slithered across the yard, filling it with its enormous body, and in an instant coiled around Shchukin's legs. He was knocked to the ground, and the shiny pistol bounced to one side. Shchukin cried out mightily, then gasped for air, and then the rings covered him completely except for his head. A coil passed over his head once, tearing off his scalp, and his head cracked. No more shots were heard in the sovkhoz. Everything was drowned out by an overlying hissing sound. And in reply to it, the wind brought in the distant howling from Kontsovka, but now it was no longer possible to tell what kind of howling it was—canine or human.

[X]

CATASTROPHE

BULBS WERE BURNING brightly in the office of *Izvestia,* and the fat editor at the stone table was making up the second page, using dispatch-telegrams "Around the Union of Republics." One galley caught his eye; he examined it through his pince-nez and burst out laughing. He called the proofreaders from the proof room and the makeup man and he showed them all the galley. On the narrow strip of paper was printed:

> Grachevka, Smolensk province.
> A hen which is as large as a
> horse and kicks like a stallion
> has been seen in the district.
> Instead of a tail, it has a
> bourgeois lady's feathers.

The compositors roared with laughter.

"In my day," said the editor, guffawing expansively, "when I was working for Vanya Sytin on *Russkoe Slovo,*[13] some of the men would get so smashed they'd see elephants. That's the truth. But now, it seems, they're seeing ostriches."

The proofreaders roared.

"That's probably right, it's an ostrich," said the makeup man. "Should we use it, Ivan Vonifatievich?"

"Are you crazy?" answered the editor. "I'm amazed that the secretary let it past—it's simply a drunken telegram."

"It must have been quite a bender," the compositors agreed, and the makeup man removed the communication about the ostrich from the table.

13. A prerevolutionary newspaper, *The Russian Word.*

Therefore *Izvestia* came out the next day containing, as usual, a mass of interesting material, but not a hint of the Grachevka ostrich.

Assistant Professor Ivanov, who read *Izvestia* quite punctiliously, folded the paper in his office, yawned, commented, "Nothing interesting," and started putting his white smock on. A bit later the burners went on in his office and the frogs began to croak. But Professor Persikov's office was in confusion. The frightened Pankrat was standing at attention.

"I understand . . . Yes, sir," he said.

Persikov handed him an envelope sealed with wax and said, "You go directly to the Department of Animal Husbandry to that director Avis, and you tell him right out that he is a swine. Tell him that I, Professor Persikov, said so. And give him the envelope."

A fine thing, thought the pale Pankrat, and he took off with the envelope.

Persikov was raging.

"The devil only knows what's going on," he whimpered, pacing the office and rubbing his gloved hands. "It's unprecedented mockery of me and of zoology. They've been bringing piles of these damned chicken eggs, but I haven't been able to get anything essential for two months. As if it were so far to America! Eternal confusion, eternal outrage!" He began to count on his fingers: "Let's say, ten days at most to locate them . . . very well, fifteen . . . even twenty . . . then two days for air freight across the ocean, a day from London to Berlin . . . From Berlin to us . . . six hours. It's some kind of outrageous bungling!"

He attacked the telephone furiously and started to call someone. In his office everything was ready for some mysterious and highly dangerous experiments; on the table lay strips of cut paper prepared for sealing the doors, diving helmets with air hoses, and several cylinders, shiny as quicksilver, labeled: "Goodchem Trust" and "Do Not Touch." And with drawings of a skull and crossbones.

It took at least three hours for the professor to calm down and get to some minor tasks. That is what he did. He worked at the institute until eleven in the evening, and therefore he did not know anything about what was happening outside the cream-colored walls. Neither the absurd rumor that had spread through Moscow about some strange snakes, nor the strange dispatch in the evening papers, shouted by newsboys, had reached him, because Assistant Professor Ivanov was at the Art Theater watching *Tsar Fyodor Ioannovich*,[14] and therefore, there was no one to inform the professor of the news.

Around midnight Persikov came home to Prechistenka and went to bed. Before going to sleep he read in bed an English article in the magazine *News of Zoology* which he received from London. He slept and all of Moscow, which seethes until late at night, slept —and only the huge gray building in a courtyard off Tverskaya Boulevard did not sleep. The whole building was shaken by the terrific roaring and humming of *Izvestia*'s printing presses. The editor's office was in a state of incredible pandemonium. The editor, quite furious, red eyed, rushed about not knowing what to do and sending everyone to the devil's mother. The makeup man was following him around, breathing wine fumes, and saying, "Oh, well, it's not so bad, Ivan Vonifatievich, let's publish a special supplement tomorrow. We can't pull the whole issue out of the presses, you know!"

The compositors did not go home, but walked around in bunches, gathered in groups and read the telegrams that were now coming in every fifteen minutes all night long, each more peculiar and terrifying than the last. Alfred Bronsky's peaked hat flicked about in the blinding pink light flooding the press room, and the mechanical fat man screaked and limped, appearing here, there, and everywhere. The entrance doors slammed incessantly, and reporters kept appearing all night long. All twelve telephones in the press room rang constantly, and the switchboard almost automati-

14. Stanislavsky's Moscow Art Theater doing A. K. Tolstoy's verse drama *Tsar Fyodor Ioannovich* (1868).

cally answered every mysterious call with "busy, busy," and the signal horns sang and sang before the unslumbering young ladies at the switchboard.

The compositors clustered around the mechanical fat man, and the sea captain was saying to them, "They'll have to send in airplanes with gas."

"No other way," answered the compositors. "God knows what's going on out there."

Then terrible Oedipal oaths shook the air, and someone's squeaky voice screamed, "That Persikov should be shot!"

"What has Persikov to do with it?" someone answered in the crowd. "That son of a bitch on the sovkhoz—he's the one should be shot!"

"They should have posted a guard!" someone exclaimed.

"But maybe it's not the eggs at all!"

The whole building shook and hummed from the rolling presses, and the impression was created that the unprepossessing gray edifice was blazing with an electric fire.

The new day did not stop it. On the contrary, it only intensified it, even though the electricity went out. Motorcycles rolled into the asphalt yard one after the other, alternating with cars. All Moscow had awakened, and the white sheets of newspaper spread over it like birds. The sheets rustled in everyone's hands, and by eleven in the morning the newsboys had run out of papers, in spite of the fact that *Izvestia* was coming out in editions of one and a half million that month. Professor Persikov left Prechistenka by bus and arrived at the institute. There something new awaited him. In the vestibule stood wooden boxes, three in number, neatly bound with metal straps and plastered with foreign labels in German— and the labels were dominated by a single Russian inscription in chalk: "Careful—Eggs."

The professor was overwhelmed with joy. "At last!" he exclaimed. "Pankrat, break open the crates immediately and carefully, so none are crushed. They go into my office."

Pankrat immediately carried out the order, and within fifteen minutes the professor's voice began to rage in his office, which was strewn with sawdust and scraps of paper.

"What are they up to? Making fun of me, or what?" the professor howled, shaking his fists and turning the eggs in his hands. "He's some kind of animal, not an Avis. I won't allow him to laugh at me. What is this, Pankrat?"

"Eggs, sir," Pankrat answered dolefully.

"Chicken eggs, you understand, chicken eggs, the devil take them! What to hell do I need them for? Let them send them to that scalawag on his sovkhoz!"

Persikov rushed to the telephone in the corner, but he did not have time to call.

"Vladimir Ipatych! Vladimir Ipatych!" Ivanov's voice thundered from the institute corridor.

Persikov tore himself away from the phone, and Pankrat dashed aside, making way for the assistant professor. The latter ran into the room without, contrary to his gentlemanly custom, removing his gray hat, which was sitting on the back of his head. He had a newspaper in his hands.

"Do you know what happened, Vladimir Ipatych?" he cried, waving in front of Persikov's face a sheet of paper headed *Special Supplement* and graced in the center with a brightly colored picture.

"No, but listen to what they've done!" Persikov shouted in reply, without listening. "They've decided to surprise me with chicken eggs. This Avis is an utter idiot, just look!"

Ivanov was completely dumbfounded. He stared at the opened crates in horror, then at the newspaper, and his eyes almost jumped out of his head. "So that's it!" he muttered, gasping. "Now I see . . . No, Vladimir Ipatych, just take a look." He unfolded the newspaper in a flash and pointed to the colored picture with trembling fingers. It showed an olive-colored, yellow-spotted snake, coiling like a terrifying fire hose against a strange green background. It had been taken from above, from a light plane which had cautiously dived over the snake. "What would you say that is, Vladimir Ipatych?"

Persikov pushed his spectacles up onto his forehead, then slipped them over his eyes, studied the picture, and said with extreme astonishment, "What the devil! It's . . . why, it's an anaconda, a water boa!"

Ivanov threw down his hat, sat down heavily on a chair, and said, punctuating every word with a bang of his fist on the table, "Vladimir Ipatych, this anaconda is from the Smolensk province. It's something monstrous! Do you understand, that good-for-nothing has hatched snakes instead of chickens, and, do you understand, they have had progeny at the same phenomenal rate as the frogs!"

"What?" Persikov screamed, and his face turned purple. "You're joking, Peter Stepanovich . . . Where from?"

Ivanov was speechless for a moment, then he recovered his voice, and jabbing his finger at the open crate, where the tips of the white eggs gleamed in the yellow sawdust, he said, "That's where from."

"Wha-a-t!" howled Persikov, beginning to understand.

Ivanov shook both of his clenched fists quite confidently and exclaimed, "You can be sure. They sent your order for snake and ostrich eggs to the sovkhoz and the chicken eggs to you by mistake."

"My God . . . my God," Persikov repeated, and turning green in the face he began to sink onto the revolving stool.

Pankrat stood utterly dumbfounded at the door, turned pale, and speechless.

Ivanov jumped up, grabbed the paper, and underscoring a line with a sharp nail, he shouted into the professor's ears, "Well, they're going to have fun now. Vladimir Ipatych, you look." And he bellowed out loud, reading the first passage that caught his eye on the crumpled page, " 'The snakes are moving in hordes toward Mozhaisk . . . laying incredible quantities of eggs. Eggs have been seen in the Dukhovsk district . . . Crocodiles and ostriches have appeared. Special troop units . . . and detachments of the GPU halted the panic in Vyazma after setting fire to the woods outside the town to stop the onslaught of the reptiles . . .' "

Persikov, turning all colors, bluish-white, with insane eyes, rose from his stool and began to scream, gasping for breath, "Anaconda . . . anaconda . . . water boa! My God!" Neither Ivanov nor Pankrat had ever seen him in such a state.

The professor tore off his tie in one swoop, ripped the buttons from his shirt, turned a terrible livid purple like a man having a stroke, and staggering, with utterly glazed, glassy eyes, he dashed out somewhere. His shouts resounded under the stone archways of the institute. "Anaconda . . . anaconda," thundered the echo.

"Catch the professor!" Ivanov shrieked to Pankrat, who was dancing up and down in place with terror. "Get him some water! He's having a stroke!"

[XI]

BATTLE AND DEATH

THE FRENZIED electric night was ablaze in Moscow. Every light was on, and there was not a place in any apartment where there were no lamps on with their shades removed. No one single person slept in a single apartment anywhere in Moscow, which had a population of four million, except the youngest children. In every apartment people ate and drank whatever was at hand; in every apartment people were crying out; and every minute distorted faces looked out the windows from all floors, gazing up at the sky which was crisscrossed from all directions with search lights. Every now and then white lights flared up in the sky, casting pale, melting cones over Moscow, and they would fade and vanish. The sky hummed steadily with the hum of low-flying planes. It was especially terrible on Tverskaya-Yamskaya Street. Every ten minutes trains arrived at the Alexander Station, made up helter-skelter of freight and passenger cars of every class and even of tank cars, all clustered with fear-crazed people who then rushed down Tverskaya-Yamskaya in a dense mass, riding buses, riding on the roofs of trolleys, crushing one another, and falling under the wheels. At the station, rattling, disquieting bursts of gunfire banged out every now and then over the heads of the crowd: the troops were trying to stop the panic of the demented running along the railway tracks from the Smolensk province to Moscow. Now and then the station windows flew out with a crazy light gulping sound, and all the locomotives were howling. All of the streets were strewn with discarded and trampled placards, and the same placards—under fiery red reflectors—stared down from the walls. All of them were already known to everyone, so nobody read them. They proclaimed martial law in Moscow. They threatened penalties for panic and reported that unit after unit of the Red army, armed with gas, was departing for Smolensk province. But the placards could not stop the howling night. In their apartments people were dropping and breaking dishes and flowerpots; they were running around, knocking against corners; they were packing and unpacking bundles and valises in the vain hope of making their way to Kalancha Square, to the Yaroslavl or Nikolaev stations. Alas, all stations leading to the north and east had been cordoned off by the heaviest line of infantry, and huge trucks with rocking and clanging chains, loaded to the top with crates on which sat soldiers in peaked helmets, with bayonets bristling in all directions, were carrying off the gold reserves from the cellars of the People's Commissariat of Finance and huge boxes marked "Handle with Care. Tretyakov Art Gallery." Automobiles were barking and running all over Moscow.

Far on the horizon the sky trembled with the reflection of fires, and the thick August blackness was shaken by the continuous booming of howitzers.

Toward morning a serpent of cavalry passed through utterly

sleepless Moscow, which had not put out a single light. Its thousands of hooves clattered on the pavement as it moved up Tverskaya, sweeping everything out of its path, squeezing everything else into doorways and show windows, breaking out the windows as they did so. The ends of its scarlet cowls dangled on the gray backs, and the tips of its lances pierced the sky. The milling, screaming crowd seemed to recover immediately at the sight of the serried ranks pushing forward, splitting apart the seething ocean of madness. People in the crowds on the sidewalks began to roar encouragingly:

"Long live the cavalry!" cried frenzied female voices.

"Long live!" echoed the men.

"They'll crush me! They are crushing me! . . ." someone howled somewhere.

"Help!" was shouted from the sidewalks.

Packs of cigarettes, silver coins, and watches began to fly into the ranks from the sidewalks; some women hopped down onto the pavement and risking their bones they trudged along beside the mounted columns, clutching at the stirrups and kissing them. Occasionally the voices of platoon leaders rose over the continuous clatter of hooves: "Shorten up on the reins!"

Somewhere someone began a gay and rollicking song, and the faces under the dashing scarlet caps swayed over the horses in the flickering light of neon signs. Now and then, interrupting the columns of horsemen with their uncovered faces, came strange mounted figures in strange hooded helmets, with hoses flung over their shoulders and cylinders fastened to straps across their backs. Behind them crept huge tank trucks with the longest sleeves and hoses, like fire engines, and heavy, pavement-crushing caterpillar tanks, hermetically sealed and their narrow firing slits gleaming. Also interrupting the mounted columns were cars which rolled along solidly encased in gray armor, with the same kind of tubes protruding and with white skulls painted on their sides, inscribed: "Gas" and "Goodchem."

"Save us, brother!" the people cried from the sidewalks.

"Beat the snakes! . . . Save Moscow!"

"The mothers . . . The mothers . . ." curses rippled through the ranks. Cigarette packs leaped through the illuminated night air, and white teeth grinned at the demented people from atop the horses. A hollow, heart-rending song began to spread through the ranks:

> . . . no ace, no queen, no jack,
> We'll beat the reptiles; without doubt,
> Four cards are plenty . . .

Rolling peals of "hurrah" rose up over this whole mass, because the rumor had spread that at the head of all the columns, on a horse, rode the aging, graying commander of the huge cavalry who had become legendary ten years before. The crowd howled and the roars of "hurrah!" "hurrah!" swept up into the sky, somewhat calming frantic hearts.

The institute was stingily lit. Events reached it only as vague, fragmentary, distant echoes. Once a volley of shots burst fanlike under the fiery clock near the Manège: soldiers were shooting on the spot some looters who had tried to rob an apartment on Volkhonka. There was little automobile traffic on this street—it was all massing toward the railway stations. In the professor's study where a single lamp burned dimly, casting light on the table, Persikov sat with his head in his hands, silent. Layers of smoke were floating around him. The ray in the box had gone dark. The frogs in the terraria were silent because they were already asleep. The professor was not reading or working. At one side, on a narrow strip of paper under his left elbow, lay the evening edition of news dispatches reporting that all of Smolensk was in flames, and that the artillery was shelling the Mozhaisk forest all over, sector by sector, to destroy the heaps of crocodile eggs piled in all the damp ravines. It was reported that a squadron of planes had been extremely successful near Vyazma, flooding almost the entire district with gas, but that the number of human victims in the area was incalculable, because instead of abandoning the district following the rules for orderly evacuation, the people had panicked and rushed around in divided groups in all directions, at their own risk and terror. It was reported that a separate Caucasus cavalry division near Mozhaisk had won a brilliant victory over flocks of ostriches, hacking them all to pieces and destroying huge caches of ostrich eggs. In doing this the division itself had sustained insignificant losses. It was reported by the government that in case it proved impossible to halt the reptiles within two hundred versts of the capital, the latter would be evacuated in complete order. Workers and employees should maintain complete calm. The government would take the sternest measures to prevent a repetition of the Smolensk events. There, thanks to panic caused by the unexpected attack of rattlesnakes—several thousand of which appeared—the people had started hopeless, wholesale exit, leaving burning stoves—and the city began to catch fire everywhere. It was reported that Moscow had enough provisions to last for at least six months and that the Council of the Commander-in-Chief was undertaking prompt measures to fortify all apartments in order to conduct the battle with the snakes in the very streets of the capital in the event that the Red armies and air forces failed to halt the advance of the reptiles.

The professor read none of this; he stared ahead, glassy eyed, and smoked. Besides him, there were only two other people at the institute—Pankrat and the housekeeper, Marya Stepanovna, who every now and then would break into tears. The old woman had not slept for three nights, spending them in the professor's office where he adamantly refused to leave his only remaining, now extinguished chamber. Now Marya Stepanovna was huddled on the oilcloth couch in a shadow in the corner, and she was keeping silent in sorrowful meditation, watching the kettle with some tea for the professor coming to a boil on the tripod over the gas burner. The institute was silent, and everything happened abruptly.

From the sidewalk there was suddenly such an outburst of rancorous shouts that Marya Stepanovna started and cried out. Flashlights flickered in the street, and Pankrat's voice was heard in the vestibule. The professor was hardly aware of this noise. He raised his head for a second and muttered, "Ooh . . . they're going crazy . . . What can I do now?" And he again fell into his stupor. But it was rudely broken. The iron doors of the institute on Herzen Street began a terrible clangor, and all of the walls began to shake. Then the solid mirrored wall in the adjoining office crashed. The glass in the professor's office began to tinkle and fly to pieces, and a gray brick bounced through the window smashing the glass table. The frogs scuttled around in their terraria and set up a cry. Marya Stepanovna ran around shrieking, rushed to the professor, seized him by the hands, and shouted, "Run, Vladimir Ipatych, run!"

The professor rose from his revolving stool, straightened himself up, and curled his index finger into a little hook, his eyes recovering for an instant the old sharp glitter reminiscent of the old, inspired Persikov. "I'm not going anywhere," he pronounced. "This is simply stupidity. They are rushing around like lunatics . . . And if all Moscow has gone insane, then where can I go? And please stop screaming. What do I have to do with this? Pankrat!" he called, pressing a button.

He probably wanted Pankrat to stop all the commotion, something which generally he had never liked. But Pankrat could no longer do anything. The banging had ended with the institute doors flying open and a distant popping of shots; and then the whole stone institute shook with the thunder of running feet, shouts, and crashing windows. Marya Stepanovna clutched at Persikov's sleeve and began to drag him back; but he pushed her away, drew himself up to his full height, and just as he was, in his white lab coat, he walked out into the corridor. "Well?" he asked. The doors swung open, and the first thing to appear in them was the back of a military uniform with a red chevron and a star on the left sleeve. He was retreating from the door, through which a furious mob was surging forward, and he was firing his revolver. Then he started to run past Persikov, shouting to him, "Save yourself, professor! I can't do anything else!"

His words were answered by a shriek from Marya Stepanovna. The officer shot past Persikov, who was standing there like a white statue, and vanished in the darkness of the winding corridors at the opposite end.

People flew through the door, howling.

"Beat him! Kill him!"

"Public enemy!"

"You let the snakes loose!"

Distorted faces and ripped clothing jumped through the corridors, and someone fired a shot. Sticks flashed. Persikov stepped back a little, barring the door to his office, where Marya Stepanovna was kneeling on the floor in terror; and he spread out his arms, as one crucified . . . he did not want to let the mob in, and he yelled irascibly, "This is utter lunacy . . . You are absolute wild animals. What do you want?" And he bellowed, "Get out of here!" and completed his speech with a shrill, familiar cry, "Pankrat, throw them out!"

But Pankrat could no longer throw anyone out. Pankrat, trampled and torn, his skull crushed, lay motionless in the vestibule, while more and more crowds tore past him, paying no attention to the fire of the police in the street.

A short man with crooked, apelike legs, wearing a torn jacket and a torn shirt twisted to one side, dashed out ahead of the others, leaped toward Persikov, and with a terrible blow from his stick he split open Persikov's skull. Persikov tottered and began to collapse sideways. His last words were, "Pankrat . . . Pankrat . . ."

Marya Stepanovna, who was guilty of nothing, was killed and torn to pieces in the office; the chamber in which the ray had gone out was smashed to bits, the terraria were smashed to bits, and the crazed frogs were flailed with sticks and trampled underfoot. The glass tables were dashed to pieces, the reflectors were dashed to pieces, and an hour later the institute was a mass of flames. Corpses were strewn around, cordoned off by a line of troops armed with electric pistols; and fire engines, pumping water from the hydrants, were pouring streams through all the windows, from which long, roaring tongues of flame were bursting.

[X I I]

A FROSTY DEUS EX MACHINA

ON THE NIGHT of August 19 to 20 an unprecedented frost fell on the country, unlike anything any of its oldest inhabitants had ever seen. It came and lasted two days and two nights, bringing the thermometer down to eleven degrees below zero. Frenzied Moscow locked all doors, all windows. Only toward the end of the third day did the populace realize that the frost had saved the capital, and the boundless expanses which it governed, and on which the terrible catastrophe of 1928 had fallen. The cavalry at Mozhaisk had lost three quarters of its complement and was near prostration, and the gas squadrons had not been able to stop the onslaught of the vile reptiles, which were moving toward Moscow in a semicircle from the West, Southwest, and South.

The frost killed them. Two days and two nights at eleven below zero had proved too much for the abominable herds, and when the frost lifted after the 20th of August, leaving nothing but damp-ness and wetness, leaving the air dank, leaving all the greenery blasted by the unexpected cold, there was no longer anything left to fight. The calamity was over. Woods, fields, and infinite bogs were still piled high with multicolored eggs, often covered with the strange, unearthly, unique pattern that Feyt—who had vanished without a trace—had once mistaken for mud, but now these eggs were quite harmless. They were dead, the embryos within lifeless.

For a long time the infinite expanses of land were still putrescent with numberless corpses of crocodiles and snakes which had been called to life by the mysterious ray born under the eyes of genius on Herzen Street—but they were no longer dangerous; the fragile creatures of the putrescent, hot, tropical bogs had perished in two days, leaving a terrible stench, disintegration, and decay throughout the territory of three provinces.

There were long epidemics; there were widespread diseases for a long time, caused by the corpses of snakes and men; and for a long time the army combed the land, no longer equipped with gases, but with sapper gear, kerosene tanks and hoses, clearing the earth. It cleared the earth, and everything was over toward the spring of 1929.

And in the spring of 1929 Moscow again began to dance, glitter, and flash lights; and again, as before, the mechanical carriages rolled through the traffic, and the lunar sickle hung, as if on a fine thread, over the helmet of the Cathedral of Christ; and on the site of the two-storey institute that had burned down in August 1928, a new zoological palace rose, and Assistant Professor Ivanov directed it, but Persikov was no longer there. Never again did the persuasively hooked index finger rise before anyone's eyes, and never again was the squeaking, croaking voice heard by anyone. The ray and the catastrophe of 1928 were long talked and written about by the whole world, but then the name of Professor Vladimir Ipatievich Persikov was shrouded in mist and sank into darkness, as did the red ray he had discovered on that April night. The ray itself was never again captured, although the elegant gentleman and now full professor, Peter Stepanovich Ivanov, had occasionally made attempts. The raging mob had smashed the first chamber on the night of Persikov's murder. Three chambers were burned up in the Nikolsky sovkhoz, the "Red Ray," during the first battle of an air squadron with the reptiles, and no one succeeded in reconstructing them. No matter how simple the combination of lenses and mirrored clusters of light had been, the combination was never achieved again, in spite of Ivanov's efforts. Evidently this required something special, besides knowledge, something which was possessed by only one man in the world—the late Professor Vladimir Ipatievich Persikov.

Moscow, October 1924.

No. 13. The Elpit— Rabkommun Building[1]

I**T WAS LIKE THIS.** Every evening the 170 windows of the dull gray five-storey giant lit up, casting their light toward the asphalt courtyard with the stone girl in the fountain. Green-faced, mute, naked, with a jar on her shoulder, she gazed languidly into the round bottomless mirror all summer long. But in the winter a wreath of snow lay over her swirling stone hair. Each evening automobiles clattered and vibrated around the gigantic smooth semi-circle in front of the entrances; cute little lamps glowed on the ends of their shafts on smart horse-drawn cabs. Oh, what a famous building it was. The stylish Elpit Building.

For example, once at ten in the evening a 100 horsepower auto-mobile stopped at the main entrance with a merry, bouyant honk of its horn. Like shadows, two secret service men hopped up out of the earth and flitted into the shadows, while another darted through the back gates and from there along slippery steps into the yard-keeper's cellar. The door of a lacquered carriage opened and the dear guest exited, wrapped in a fur coat.

He visited Apartment No. 3, that of Cavalry General de Barrain, until three.

Until three, one spy kept vigil leaning against the base of a gray caryatid, exhausted by his lupine life. The other smoked on a semi-

---

1. First published in *Diaboliad*.

dark flight of stairs until three, listening to the carpet-muffled strains of a Hungarian rhapsody, *capriccioso,* or tempestuous bursts of Gypsy music:

> We drink today! We drink tomorrow!
> We drink all week—hey!
> Once, twice . . .

Until three, the third one sat in the senior yard-keeper's hole on a rubbish heap of cotton scraps. And cones of sharp white light burned on the semicircle until three. And from floor to floor, on an invisible telephone, the proud, whispered rumor ran: Rasputin is here. Rasputin. Boris Samoylovich Christy, the dusky-faced possessor of the safe, the trader in living goods, the most brilliant of all Moscow building superintendents, became somehow even haughtier and more mysterious after Rasputin's night at de Barrain's.

Glints of steel pride appeared in his black eyes, and he raised the rent of the apartments cruelly.

And in No. 2 . . . Christy, but who is Christy? . . . In storm or snow Elpit himself took off his Astrakhan hat to the woman in chinchilla if he ran into her getting out of her mirrorlike carriage. And he would smile. This woman's bills were liquidated by a man so elevated that he did not have a surname. He signed his first name with a sly flourish . . . What can one say. It was a real building . . . Important people—an important life.

On winter evenings when the devil, disguised as a snowstorm, was somersaulting and howling under the iron gutters on the roofs, adroit yard men pushed drifts along in front of them with plows and cleared the courtyard down to the asphalt. Four elevators moved up and down noiselessly. Mornings and evenings, as if by magic, the gray harmonies of the pipes in all seventy-five apartments poured forth warmth. Lamps burned in brackets on the landings . . . In the depths of the apartments there were white bathtubs, in the grand semidark anterooms a dull shine of telephones . . . Carpets . . . Noiselessly solemn in the studies. Massive leather armchairs. And prominent bigwigs lived even on the top floors. The bank director, a clever man, a government man with the face of Saint-Brie from *The Hugenots,*[2] flawed just a bit by his eyes, which were something like sick, or criminal; the factory owner (Athenian nights with magnesium flash cameras); golden-haired, well-fed women; the phenomenal, world-famous bass soloist; and the general; and . . . and minor ones—attorneys in morning coats, physicians specializing in abortions . . .

It was an important time.

And then there was nothing. *Sic transit gloria mundi!*

It is terrible to live when kingdoms are falling. And the very memory of it began to disappear. Could it really have been? Lord! . . . A Cavalry General! . . . What a title!

Yes . . . But the furniture remained. No one was allowed to take anything away.

Elpit himself left with only the clothes on his back.

It was then that the white list with the strange inscription "Rabkommun" on it was glued up beside the street light (the fiery "No. 13"). Unknown folk appeared in all seventy-five apartments. The pianos went silent, but record players were lively and often sang in ominous voices. Ropes were stretched across the living rooms, and there was wet underwear on them. Primuses hissed snake fashion; and acrid fumes floated along the staircases day and night. The lamps disappeared from all of the brackets, and every evening darkness set in. Through it stumbled shadows carrying bundles, crying out dolefully, "Manya, hey Manya! Where are you? Goddamn it!"

In two rooms of Apartment 50 the parquet floor was burned for heat. The elevators . . . However, what is there to tell in all this?

But a miracle did happen. Elpit-Rabkommun was heated.

The thing is that in two rooms of a semi-basement apartment one person remained—Christy.

2. An opera by Meyerbeer, frequently alluded to in Bulgakov's works.

The three men who got the lion's share of Elpit's carpets, and who hung the scrap of a sign "Directorate" on the floor of de Barrain's apartment on the first floor, understood that the Rabkommun's building would not remain standing for a month without Christy. It would fall apart. So they left this lusterlessly black wheeler-dealer in his service cap with the lacquered bill behind some green curtains in the semi-basement. A monstrous union: on one side the noisy, backward directorate, on the other—the "supervisor"! That was Christy! But it was the solidest union in the world. Christy was precisely that man who no less than the directorate wanted Rabkommun to stand as an unharmed, dull gray giant—and not fall into ruins.

And so, not only did they not insult Christy, they gave him a salary. Well, true, a trifle. About one tenth of what he had been paid by Elpit—who was now sitting in two crummy rooms on the other side of Moscow with absolutely no signs of life.

"To hell with them, to hell with the toilets, to hell with the wiring!" Elpit was saying passionately, clenching his fists. "Just keep the heat going. Save the main things. Boris Samoylovich, save my building until this is all over, and I will know how to thank you! What? Believe me!"

Christy did believe; he nodded his cropped, graying head and went away, gloomy and preoccupied after his report. As he rode up to the building he saw the directorate standing in the gateway, shut his eyes from hate, and turned pale. But this was just for a moment. And then he smiled. He knew how to have patience.

But the main thing was to keep the heat going. And, lo and behold, they got requisition orders and the oil was delivered. The pipes heated up. Fifty-three degrees! Fifty-three degrees! Whenever there was any hitch where they got the oil from, Elpit paid big chunks of money. His eyes would burn. "Well, all right . . . I'll pay. Give some to both of them—and the secretary. What? Stop? Oh no, no! Not for a minute . . ."

Christy was a genius. He laid a taboo on a fifth-floor apartment in the central section, one in which there had once been a studio.

"We'll put Nilushkin, Egor in there . . ."

"No, comrades, if you'll be so kind. I cannot get along without a storeroom. Why, it's for the building, for *you*."

Basically, it was rubbish. Some sort of stupid decorations, steel fittings. But . . . But there were also three cans of Elpit gasoline —plus something else in packages that Christy was saving for better days.

And gray Rabkommun No. 13 lived under an unslumbering eye. True, the lights in the left wing would go out once in a while . . . The electrician, who had begun to drink in January of 1918, the brutalized electrician who was as threadbare as felt, would shout at the peasant women:

"Why don't you drop dead! Slam the door on the panel again! What am I, your slave? It's overtime!"

Viciously and mournfully, the women howled in the dark, "Manya! Hey, Ma-anya! Where are you?"

Again they would go to the electrician, "You ba-a-astard! Sot! We'll complain to Christy."

Yes, sir, Christy was a real man.

He tormented the directorate until they got Nilushkin, Egor out of their way with the title "Sanitary Inspector." Nilushkin, Egor made the rounds of all seventy-five apartments every two weeks. His fists thundered on locked doors, and he barged through unlocked ones with no ceremony, even if there were naked women there. He would crawl under the wet underdrawers shouting hoarsely and horrifyingly, "Everyone who's been befouling this place is going to be booted out in twenty-four hours!"

And he fined those who were indicted.

And so they lived on and on until February, in the worst freeze, when again there was a hitch with the oil. And Elpit could not do a thing. They took the bribe and said, "We'll have it here in a week."

At his report to Elpit, Christy uttered painfully, "Oh . . . I'm so tired! If you knew how tired I am, Adolph Iosifovich. When will all this end?"

And indeed, at this point one could see that Christy's eyes looked mournful and exhausted. The steel Christy!

Elpit replied passionately, "Boris Samoylovich! Do you believe me? Well, I'm telling you: this is the last winter. And next summer, just as easily as I will smoke up this cigarette, I will toss them out and to hell. Well? Believe me. But I ask only one thing of you, very urgently I ask: this week you yourself check things— you yourself. God forbid them getting stoves in! The ventilation . . . isn't meant for them . . . I'm so afraid. But also see that they don't poke holes in the windows. Surely a week won't kill them! Or maybe six days. I'll make a trip to see Ivan Ivanych myself tomorrow."

That evening at Rabkommun, exhaling whitish steam, Christy said, "Well, how about it . . . We'll manage. Four or five days. But no stoves . . ."

And the directorate agreed.

"Of course. Is that thinkable? Those things aren't flues. Would it be long before disaster struck?"

And Christy himself made the rounds, he made the rounds himself, every day, especially on the fifth floor. He looked with an eagle-eye to make sure they hadn't pieced on black "Bourgeoises" [Franklin stoves] and led the pipes out through the openings that looked so treacherously and enticingly out of the corners of the rooms, just below the ceiling.

And Nilushkin, Egor made his rounds.

"If I see any of you guys . . . Those are not flues for you. Out in twenty-four hours."

On the sixth day the torture became unbearable. The building whip, Pylyaeva, Annushka, a light-haired woman, shrieked down the stairwell at the receding Nilushkin, Egor.

"Bastards! Getting fat behind our backs! All they know how to do is swill moonshine. And when it comes to worrying about the heating—they ain't nowhere to be seen! O-o-oh, you cursed scum! Well, I'll heat things up without moving from my spot. There ain't no rule says they can stop us! The one-eyed devil (this referred to Christy)! All he cares about is one thing: how to keep the building walls from getting smoked up. He's waiting for the owner—we all know that! It doesn't matter to him if a proletarian worker drops dead . . ."

And Nilushkin, Egor, retreating from step to step, muttered in confusion, "Oh, you're a pain, old woman . . . You are really a pain!"

But nevertheless he turned around and boomingly returned the fire, "I'll start the heating up! In twenty-four hours . . ."

From above: "Son of a *bitch!* I'll go to Karpov. What? Freezing workers!"

Don't condemn. The cold is torture. Anyone would be brutalized . . .

. . . At two o'clock in the morning, when Christy was asleep, when Nilushkin was asleep, when in all the rooms people were sleeping hunched up like little dogs under their rags and fur coats, in room 5 of Apartment 50, it became like paradise. Outside the black windows there was a devilish snowstorm, but in the small stove a small fiery prince danced, burning up the squares of parquet.

"Oh, it draws well!" Pylyaeva, Annushka said in rapture, glancing now at the tiny teapot with the bouncing lid, now at the black ring going out through the opening. "Remarkable draw. There, the dogs, Lord forgive! Do they begrudge it? Well, all right. It's all under cover."

And the prince danced, and sparks swept through the black tube and flew out into the mysterious maw . . . And there, in the black windings of the narrow ventilation passage lined with felt . . . And into the attic . . .

The flickering torches of the Arbat Square Station were the first to flash ... With one hand Christy had torn the telephone receiver from the hook, with the other ripped down a green curtain ...

... Give me the Prechistenka Fire Station! Queen of Heaven! Comrades! Nine hundred and thirty people woke up simultaneously. They saw that the windows were blood red with a serpentlike flicker. Holy Saints! Scre-eaming! The doors hammered like machine guns, in bursts. Lady! Oh, lady!! One—oh, twenty two ... eighteen. Eighteen ... Give me the Krasnopresnya Station!!

... Water poured down the stairs from the steps in cascades. A Niagara through the stairwells and elevators to the basement. He-e-elp! Give me the Khamovnichesk Station!!

Oh, brave firemen! Intrepid knights in red-gold helmets, in canvas coats. They extended their ladders, the gray hoses squirmed along like boa constrictors. Goddamn! Mother-fucker!! And thunder, thunder, thunder. At the twentieth minute came the City Station with sparks, fire, and helmets ...

But the gasoline, dear friends, the gasoline! The gasoline! We're done for, the gasoline! Next to Pylyaeva, Annushka, from room 5. An explosion ... one ... another!

... And many, many more times ...

And now not a small prince, but a fiery king started to play a rhapsody quite threateningly. And not *cappriccio,* but terrifyingly —*brioso.* Sretenka, give me water, from the alley!!! And there was such a boom in the left wing that in a twinkling of an eye not a window was left. A fiery abyss in the center section, and over the abyss iron sheets flew like flat, funereal butterflies.

Copper helmets stormed the left wing, and in the center one the devil blew up so that in 49 on the fourth floor Granny Pavlovna who sold toffee had no way out! And with a mortal howl, she flew out of the window with a flash of naked yellow legs. Ambulance! 1-22-31!! Take care of a bloody wafer! Saints of God! Vanyushka was burned up! Vanyushka!! ... Where's daddy? Oh! Oh! The machine, the machine! The sewing machine, fellows! Bundles out the windows onto the asphalt—plop! Stop! Don't throw them! Comrades! . . . And from the fifth floor in the left wing eleven plates in a bundle whapped down—former bourgeoise porcelain. And Nilushkin, Egor did exist, and now Nilushkin, Egor doesn't. Instead of Nilushkin's head—mash; instead of porcelain—fragments in a sheet. Comrades! Oh! You forgot Tanya! Cordon off from the corner! Hold them! Back! Mother-fucker! Goddamn!

Current electrocuted one of the intrepid knights in the basement. Another died a glorious death in a stream of gasoline sweeping downward through the furious flames. A beam tore loose, crashed down, and broke the spinal column of a third.

With a samovar in one hand, an ikon in the other—quiet, white old Serafim Sarovsky wearing a silver chasuble. Others wearing just their nightshirts. Screams, screams. The axes pound and pound through the screams. Hold them back!! The roof! When it collapses, when it crashes from the third floor to the second, from the second to the first.

And at this point it was hell. Pure hell. One's hair stands on end from the way it's whipping out of the central section. The last windows—the furthest away—bing, tinkle! Bing, tinkle!

The firemen are crushed in the smoke, they sway, the pressure tears the nozzles out of their hands. Bring up the reserves! What do you mean, reserves? Don't get any closer than ten yards to the central section any more! Your eyes will burst . . .

For the first time in his life Christy wept. Graying, steel Christy. By a damp column in a garden off a side street, where it was light enough that you could read small print. His fur coat was hanging down off his shoulders, and Christy's bare chest could be seen. But it was not cold. And Christy's face looked as if he himself had burned up in the fire, but he was mute and could not cry out at all. He was still looking without taking his eyes off it, to the place where the flaming motionless faces of the caryatids could be seen through the flickering black shadows. Tears oozed slowly down his bluish cheeks. He did not wipe them off, but kept looking and looking.

Only once did he shake his head, when Elpit touched his shoulder and said hoarsely, "Well, what more is there . . . Let's go, Boris Samoylovich. You'll catch cold. Let's go."

But Christy shook his head again.

"Go ahead . . . I'll just be a minute."

Elpit drowned among the shadows, among the torches, splashing through the melted snow, making his way toward a cabby. Christy stayed, but he shifted his gaze to the pale sky, across which a hot, sprawling, orange beast was swaying . . .

. . . Pylyaeva, Annushka was also looking at the beast. With stifled sighs and groans, she had been running through quiet snowy side streets, and her face looked like a witch's face from the soot and tears.

From time to time she would whisper some nonsense:

"They'll try me . . . Try me, I'm lost . . ."

From time to time she would sob.

Long, long ago the howling and the screaming and the naked people and the terrible flashes on helmets had been left behind. It was quiet in the side street, and there was a light dusty snow. But the beast's belly still hung in the sky. Everything was flickering and playing. And so exhausted and worn out with suffering was Pylyaeva, Annushka, from the black thought of "woe" from this fiery belly-reflection which was playing triumphantly across the sky . . . so worn out with suffering was she, that a dull calm came over her, and, more important, for the first time in her life there was an illumination in her mind.

Stopping to catch her breath, she bumped into a step and sat down. And the tears dried up.

She propped up her head and for the first time in her life she had this lucid thought.

"We are ignorant people. Ignorant people. We must be taught, fools that we are . . ."

Having caught her breath, she got up, set off walking slowly now, not looking back at the beast—she just kept smearing the soot across her face, sniffing her nose.

And when the sky grew pale, the beast itself began to grow pale, misty. It grew dimmer and dimmer, dwindled, curled up in black smoke, and vanished entirely.

And there was no sign left in the sky that the famous No. 13, the Elpit-Rabkommun Building had burned to the ground.

A Chinese Tale

Six Scenes in Place of a Story[1]

[I]

THE RIVER AND THE CLOCK

HE WAS A remarkable coolie, a real saffron representative of the Celestial Empire, about twenty-five years old, or maybe forty? The devil only knows! I think he was twenty-three.

No one knows why the mysterious coolie flew several thousand miles like a dry leaf and turned up on the river bank under a chewed-up, serrated wall. Now the coolie was wearing a cap with shaggy ears, a short fur jacket with ripped seams, quilted trousers torn in the seat, and fabulous yellow shoes. One could see that the coolie had somewhat crooked, but sinewy legs. As for money—the coolie had not a kopek.

An extremely unpleasant wind, as shaggy as his big-eared cap, was sweeping along under the serrated wall. One look at the river was enough to be convinced that it was a devilishly cold, alien river. In back of the coolie was an empty trolley line, in front of the coolie porous granite—beyond the granite on the slope a rowboat with a broken bottom, beyond the rowboat the same damned river, beyond the river granite again, and beyond the granite—buildings,

1. First published in *Diaboliad*.

146

stone buildings, the devil only knows how many buildings. For some reason the stupid river flowed through the very center of the city.

After admiring the long red chimneys and green roofs, the coolie shifted his gaze to the sky. And the sky was the worst thing of all. Gray, oh so gray—dirty, oh so dirty . . . and very low, clinging to the eagles and onion domes which jutted up behind the wall; thick clouds crawled across the gray sky puffing out their bellies. The sky was the final crunching blow on the coolie's shaggy cap. It was quite obvious that if not right now, then shortly after, a cold, wet snow would start pouring from the sky, and in general under a sky like this nothing good, satisfying, or pleasant could happen.

"O-o-oh!" the coolie murmured, even more dolefully adding a few words in a language incomprehensible to anyone.

The coolie blinked his eyes, and immediately a very hot, round sun floated up before him, a very yellow, dusty road, off to the side, like a golden wall, a kaoliang, then two spreading oak trees (which cast a keen-edged shadow of the earth, which was cracking from the heat), and the clay threshold to his *fanza*. And it was as if the coolie were a little boy squatting down, chewing some very tasty flat cake, and with his free left hand he was caressing the earth, which was burning like fire. He was extremely thirsty, but he was too lazy to get up, and he was waiting for his mother to come out from behind the oak trees. His mother had two buckets on a yoke, and in the buckets was ice-cold water.

The wind cut into the coolie like a razor, and he decided that he would again traverse the vast distances. Leave—but how? What does he have? Somehow. The Chinaman . . . Letee in laiload ca-a-al. The music of a bell tower began to play high above, beyond the corner of the serrated mass.[2] The bells babbled indistinctly, intermittently—but it was still obvious that they wanted to play some melody tunefully and victoriously. The coolie tramped around

2. It is clear from the description that the hero is standing beside the Kremlin in Moscow.

the corner, and looking up into the distance, he satisfied himself that the music was coming from the round black clock with the gold hands on the lofty gray tower. The clock played and played and stopped. The coolie sighed deeply, watched as a sputtering, beat-up motorcycle rode straight into the tower, pulled his cap down lower, and went off in an unknown direction.

[I I]

BLACK SMOKE. A CRYSTAL HALL

THAT EVENING the coolie found himself far, far away from the gray embrasures and the black clock with the musical trick. In the dirty outskirts of town, in a two-storey house off the second through courtyard, beyond which there was only a vacant lot covered with patches of foul gray snow and fragments of broken brick. Wood was burning with an ominous reddish flame in the tiny stove in the last room along a stinking corridor, behind a door covered with a tattered oilcloth. A very middle-aged Chinese was squatting in front of the shield with its fiery little round holes. He was about fifty-five, or maybe eighty. His face was like bark, and when the Chinese opened the shield his eyes seemed evil like a demon's; but when he closed it they seemed sad, deep, and cold. The coolie was sitting on a greasy piece of blanket on a warped slat bed inhabited by huge, bold bedbugs; and he was looking fearfully and vigilantly at the red and black shadows flickering and playing back and forth over the smoke-blackened ceiling, frequently shrugging his shoulders, sticking his hand inside his collar, scratching furiously, and listening to what the old Chinaman was saying.

The old man puffed out his cheeks, blew into the stove, and rubbed his eyes when the acrid smoke crept into them. At these times the story was interrupted. Then the Chinaman slammed the shield shut, disappeared into the shadows, and spoke a language incomprehensible to anyone but the coolie.

Something extremely mournful and humble came out of the Chinaman's words. In Russian it would be like this: "There's no bread. None. I'm hungry myself. There's nothing to sell at all. There is a little cocaine. No opium." The sly old Chinaman especially emphasized the latter. "There isn't any opium. No opium, none. Sad, but there's no opium." At this the old Chinaman's eyes completely disappeared in their slanted slits, and the fire from the stove could not penetrate their mysterious depth.

"What is there then?" the coolie asked desperately, and he convulsively jerked his shoulders.

"What is there?" There was something, of course, but all of it was stuff it was better to refuse.

"Cold there is. Trying to catch people, there is. I got stabbed with knife in vacant lot for packet of cocaine. The murderer was taking it away, the pig. Nastka's bastard."

The old man jabbed his finger toward the thin wall. Listening intently, the coolie made out hoarse female laughter, some sort of hissing and bubbling.

"Moonshine—there is."

Thus the old man clarified things—by throwing back the sleeve of his loose greasy shirt and pointing to a slanting, fresh, five-inch-long scar on his yellow forearm, crossed with knotty veins. It was obvious that this was the mark of a well-sharpened Finnish knife. When he looked at the crimson scar the old Chinaman's eyes hazed over, his dry neck turned dark. Looking at the wall, the old man hissed in Russian, "Bandits—there are!"

Then he bent forward, opened the shield, thrust two wood chips into the fiery maw, and puffing out his cheeks started to look like a Chinese demon.

In a quarter of an hour the wood was roaring evenly and mightily, and the black pipe was beginning to turn red. Heat flooded the room, and the coolie wiggled out of his jacket, climbed down from the bed, and squatted on the floor. Becoming kinder from the heat, the old Chinaman was sitting with his legs under him, weaving a hazy story. The coolie blinked his yellow lids, breathed heavily from the heat, and from time to time he muttered questions mournfully and uncomprehendingly. And the old man rumbled on. "Things made no difference to him—he was old. Lenin—there is. The main thing—there is. Bourgeoizees—there aren't, oh no! In place the Red Army there is. Much—there is. Music! Yes. Yes. Music, because of Lenin. In the tower with the clock—you sit, and sit. Beyond the tower. Beyond the tower—the Red Army."

"Go home? No, oh no! A permit—there isn't. Good Chinese sit quietly."

"I be good! Where to live?"

"Live? No, no, and no. The Red Army lives everywhere."

"L-l-led Almy?" whispered the coolie, finally, looking into the fiery holes.

An hour passed. The roaring had gone silent and the six holes in the shield looked like six red eyes. In the flickering shadows and reddish reflection the wrinkled-up coolie aged already, fell onto the floor, and stretching his arms to the old man, he implored him for something.

An hour passed, then another hour. The six holes in the shield went blind, and the sweet, black smoke was being drawn toward the partially opened *fortochka*.[3] The crack over the door was stuffed full of rags, and the keyhole pasted over with dirty wax. The spirit lamp flickered on the floor with its faint bluish flame, and the coolie was lying beside it on its side, on his jacket. In his hands he had a foot and a half-long yellow pipe with a dragon-lizard spreading across it. A small black ball was melting like a crimson point in its brass bowl, which looked like gold. The old Chinaman grumbler lay on the other side of the spirit lamp on a torn blanket with the

3. A *fortochka* is a small ventilation window within a larger window, usually at the top.

same kind of pipe. And around him, as around the coolie, the black smoke melted and floated, and was drawn toward the *fortochka*.

Toward morning, on the floor beside a dying tongue of flame, two rows of bared teeth could be seen—one yellow with black, one white. Where the old man was no one knows. But the coolie was living in a crystal hall under a huge clock which rang every minute as soon as the golden hands made a round. The tolling caused laughter in the crystal, and a very jovial Lenin walked out wearing a loose yellow Chinese shirt, a huge glittering and tightly wound hair lock, and a small cap with a button on the crown. He grasped the pointer pendulum by the tail and drove it to the right—then the clock rang to the left, but when he drove it to the left—the bells rang on the right. Having rung the bells loudly for a while, he took the coolie out onto the balcony—to show him the Red Army. "Live —in a crystal hall. Warmth—there is. Nastka—there is." Nastka, the undescribed beauty, was walking in front of a crystal mirror, and her feet in their shoes were so tiny you could hide them in a nostril. And Nastka's bastard, the murderer, the bandit with the Finnish knife, was going to sneak into the hall, but the coolie got up, terrible and brave, like a giant, and brandishing a broad sword, he cut off his head. And the head rolled off the balcony; the coolie grabbed the decapitated corpse by the scruff of the neck, and tossed it after the head. And the whole world felt relieved and joyful that a good-for-nothing like that would no longer be walking around with a knife. As a reward, Lenin played a thunderous melody on the bells for the coolie, and he pinned a jeweled star on his chest. The bells began to ring again, and finally they rang into being shoots of golden kaoliang growing on the crystal floor, a round hot sun overhead, and a keen-edged shadow by the oak tree . . . And his mother was walking along, and in the buckets on her yoke there was ice-cold water.

[I I I]

NO DREAMS. REALITY THERE IS.

IT IS NOT KNOWN what happened in the two-storey house during the next four days. It is known that on the fifth day, having aged five years, the coolie emerged into the dirty street, no longer wearing his jacket—but in a sack with a black stamp across the back "Storeroom No. 4712," no longer wearing fancy yellow shoes, but in beat-up, rust-colored footwear out of which his big red toes with their nacreous nails protruded. Under a crooked lamppost on the corner, the coolie looked fixedly at the gray sky, waved his hand decisively, and sang to himself, like a violin, "Le-e-d Al-my . . ."

And set off in an unknown direction.

[I V]

THE CHINESE COMRADE

AND TWO DAYS LATER the coolie found himself in a gigantic hall with hemispherical arches resting on wooden foundations. The coolie was sitting, his feet lowered into his worn shoes, as if he were in the *belle-étage;* and in the parterre clustered moustachioed and unmoustachioed heads wearing helmets with huge red stars on them. The coolie looked at the faces under the stars for a long time, and finally, feeling that it was essential to somehow call attention to himself, he first dressed his face in its best saffron smile, and then, melodiously and delicately, he said everything that he had learned during his terrible flight from the round sun to the capital of the bell tower clock.

"Bread . . . let in car . . . le-e-d . . . Chinesee . . ." and three other words, the joining of which produced an amazing combination which possessed a miraculous effect. The coolie knew from experience that this combination could open the doors of heated freight cars, but that it could also result in heavy blows with fists on his shaved Chinese head. Women fled from it, and men behaved in very different ways: sometimes they gave bread, sometimes, on the contrary, they rushed to beat him up. In this case the consequences were happy ones. A thundering wave of laughter struck the arched hall and washed up to the very ceiling. The coolie replied to this first roll with smile No. 2—it had a slight conspiratorial shade—and a repetition of the three words. After this he thought he would be deafened. A piercing voice cut through the racket.

"Vanya! Get over here! A Chinese volunteer does a great job of mother-swearing!"

Beside the coolie there was first a storm, then that quieted down, then they quickly gave the coolie some tobacco, bread, and turbid tea in a tin cup. In the wink of an eye the coolie ate the three chunks with animal fury, crunching it in his teeth, drank the tea, and greedily lit up the roll-your-own cigarette. Then the coolie was presented to *a certain man* wearing a green army field shirt. Sitting under a lamp beside a typewriter, wearing a creased service cap, the man looked at the coolie favorably, and said to a head which was stuck through the door, "Nothing unusual here, comrades. An ordinary Chinese . . ."

And immediately after the head vanished he took a sheet of paper out of a drawer, took a pen in his hand, and asked, "First name? Middle and last names?"

The coolie replied with a smile, but refrained from using any words whatsoever.

Perplexity appeared on the face of this certain man.

"Ahem . . . what is it, comrade, you don't understand? Russian? Eh? What's your name?" he jabbed his finger softly in the coolie's direction, "Name? From China?"

"Chi-na . . ." sang the coolie.

"Well, well! Chinese—that I understand. But what are you called, comrade? Eh?"

The coolie shrouded himself in a radiant and satisfied smile. Bread and tea were digesting in his stomach, imparting a feeling of pleasant languor.

"By a-a-ac-cident," the certain man murmured, scratching his left eyebrow resentfully.

"The Milcom (Military Commissar) will be here in a minute. Then you'll get it."

[V]

A VIRTUOSO! A VIRTUOSO!

Two months passed. And when the sky turned from gray into blue with puffy cream-colored clouds, everyone already knew that as Franz Liszt was born to play his monstrous rhapsodies on the piano, the coolie Sen-Zin-Po appeared in the world in order to shoot a machine gun. At first vague rumors got around, then they blew up into legends surrounding the head of Sen-Zin-Po. It began with the cow that was cut in half. It ended with the men in the companies saying the coolie cut off heads at 2000 paces. Heads or no heads, he really did make 100% direct hits, exclusively. The idea that 100% is unstable and arbitrary was born. Perhaps there is 105%? There had been a miraculous sighting field in his slanted agate eyes from birth—otherwise there was no way to explain such shooting.

To the shooting range came an important-looking, fluffy-moustachioed man in a gray overcoat; he looked curiously through his binoculars. Fixing his squinting eyes in the distance, the coolie squeezed the trigger of the thundering Maxim and cut down a grove of trees the way a peasant woman cuts down wheat.

"Really, the devil only knows what this is! It's the first time I've ever seen such a thing," said the fluffy-moustachio after the heated Maxim fell silent. And turning around to the coolie, he added with smiling eyes, "A virtuoso!"

"Viltuosi . . ." replied the coolie, and he looked like a Chinese angel.

Within a week the regimental commander told the commander of the machine gun squad in a bass, "Son of a bitch, he's good" and ecstatically shrugging his shoulders he added—turning to Sen-Zin-Po, "he should be paid a bonus!"

"Bo-noose . . . payee, payee," replied the coolie, emitting a yellowish glow.

The commander rumbled as if in a barrel, the machine gunners answered him with rolling shouts. That same evening at headquarters, under a broken tulip, the certain man in the service shirt reported that a paper had been received—the coolie was to be transferred to the international regiment. Blood rushed to the commander's face, and he struck lower "do."

"And Up-U-Ass," he said, and with that he made a hairy finger of colossal dimensions. Our certain man immediately sat down to compose a rough draft of a paper which began with the words: "Since machine gunner Sen-Zin-Po is the pride and virtuoso of the armored regiment . . ."

[V I]

A BRILLIANT DEBUT

A MONTH PASSED, and there was not a single small cloud in the sky, and the hot sun was sitting directly overhead. Blue copses a mile and a half away were thundering like a storm: behind and to the left the armored regiment rolled on making a dry, staccato sound, and disappearing into the ground. Covered with a heap of cartridge belts, the coolie hung out over his sharp-nosed machine gun on a slope. There was a certain pensiveness in the coolie's expression. From time to time he turned his gaze to the sky, then peered toward the copses, occasionally turning his head to the side and then seeing a fellow machine gunner. At forty paces you could see his head behind the bushes—and the tattered red decoration on his chest. After looking sideways at the machine gunner, the coolie again squinted and looked at the little sun which was baking his service cap; he wiped off the sweat and waited to see what turn all of these bubbling events would take.

They developed this way. Beneath the blue woods in the distance little black chains appeared, now sinking down to the very earth, now growing up, getting broader and denser—and they began to approach the coolie's sloping hill. The armored regiment behind and to the left of the coolie thundered faster and more furiously. A piercing voice rang over the hill behind the coolie:

"Fire!"

And immediately the machine gunner with the decoration began to fulminate from the bushes. It was echoed somewhere to the left, and a dusty haze began to rise in front of the chain which was growing up out of the earth. The coolie braced himself, laid his yellow virtuoso's hands on the handles of the machine gun, was silent for a few moments, barely moving the barrel from side to side, and then he fired briefly and challengingly, stopped . . . fired again, and suddenly, with a deafening rattle, he began to play his terrifying rhapsody. For a few seconds hot bullets spat at the chain from edge to edge. It fell, rose up, began to break and fall apart. An ecstatic, hoarse voice soared up from behind.

"Coolie! Start rattling! Fire! Fire!"

Through the haze and dust the coolie sent bullets at the second chain in an uninterrupted flood. And then, to the right, far away from the ground, dark stripes grew up, and pillars of dust stood over them. A current of distress ran invisibly across the face of the hill. The voice, going hoarse, breaking, yelled: "At the attacking ca-val-ry . . ."

A roaring noise made the earth shake all the way to the coolie, and the dark stripes began to approach with horrendous speed. At the moment that the coolie turned his machine gun to the right, the air over his head was split by a pale fire, and something threw the coolie's chest straight against the handles, and he went blind.

When he again perceived the sun and the machine gun, and the trampled grass again floated through the mist in front of him, everything around was breaking up and dashing off somewhere. The regiment behind sporadically burst into crackling and fell silent. Barely breathing because of the scalding pain in his chest, the coolie turned around and saw behind a mass of riders flying along in a cloud, attacking the spot where the armored division was firing. The machine gunner to the right had vanished. And running toward the hill in chains, surrounding it in a half-moon, were men wearing green, their shoulders flashing like gold spots. There were more and more of them with each moment, and the coolie could already make out their bronze faces. Moaning in pain, the coolie looked ahead in confusion, grabbed the handles, swung the barrel, and began to clatter. The faces and gold spots started to drop into the grass in front of the coolie. But on the right they grew up and headed toward him. The commander of the machine gun squad appeared alongside. The coolie saw, vaguely and momentarily, that there was blood flowing down his left sleeve. The commander shouted nothing to the coolie. Standing up to his full height, he stretched his right hand forward and impassively shot at the attackers. Then, before the eyes of the amazed coolie, he shoved the barrel of the Mauser into his mouth and fired. The coolie was silent for a moment. Then he began to thunder again.

Holding a rifle at the ready, catching his breath from running, outstripping the chain, a bronze-faced cadet tore toward Sen-Zin-Po from the right.

"Throw down the machine gun . . . you damned Chinaman!!"

he yelled hoarsely, bubbles of foam spitting from his lips, "Surrender! . ."

"Surrender!!" was howled from the right and the left, and the gold spots and sharp stingers were jumping around at the very foot of the slope. "Rat-a-tat-tat!" played the machine gun for the last time—and it fell silent all at once. The coolie stood up, by an act of will he suppressed the pain in his chest and the ominous distress which had suddenly made his heart twinge. During these last few moments, miraculously, a cracking earth and a keen-edged shadow and shoots of golden kaoliang managed to flash before him under the hot sun. Home, homeward bound. Stifling the pain, he called up a radiant halo on his slanting face, and now already feeling clearly that hope was fading, nevertheless he said, addressing it to the sky:

"Bo-noose . . . Led Almy viltuosi . . . payee! Payee!"

And heavily swinging his bayonet, the giant bronze-red cadet struck him in the throat in such a way that he broke his spinal column. The black clock with the golden hands managed to ring out a melody with rolling bronze bells, and the crystal hall flashed around the coolie. No pain can penetrate him. And the coolie, painlessly and calmly, with a frozen smile on his face, did not feel the cadets stabbing him with their bayonets.

The Adventures
of Chichikov

A Poem in Ten Items with a Prologue and an Epilogue[1]

"Hold it, hold it, you idiot!" Chichikov shouted to Selifan. "Why I'll give you a taste of my sword!" shouted a courier with yard-long moustachioes, galloping straight at them. "Can't you see this is a government carriage, the devil flog your soul!"

PROLOGUE

A BIZARRE DREAM . . . It was as if a joker-satan had opened the doors to the kingdom of shades—over the entrance to which an inextinguishable lamp inscribed "Dead Souls" flickers. The kingdom of the dead started to stir, and an endless line filed out of it.

1. First published in *Diaboliad*. This is the only story of the five which has ever been reprinted in the U.S.S.R., in *Rural Youth* (*Sel'skaja molodezh'*), XLII (January, 1966).

"The Adventures of Chichikov" is the title which censors made Gogol use along with *Dead Souls* for the first edition of his novel (1842). Gogol subtitled *Dead Souls* a "poem."

Manilov in a thick bear-fur coat, Nozdryov in someone else's carriage, Derzhimorda on a fire-wagon, Selifan, Petrushka, Fetinya . . .

And last of all *he* set off—Pavel Ivanovich Chichikov in his celebrated chaise.

And the whole band headed into Soviet Rus, and then astonishing events occurred there. And what sort they were—the following items show . . .

I

Switching from his chaise to a car in Moscow, and flying through Moscow gullies in it, Chichikov scolded Gogol violently.

"May blisters as big as haystacks bubble under his eyes, the son of a devil! He's befouled and polluted my reputation so badly there's no place I can show my nose. If anyone finds out that I'm Chichikov, they'll naturally toss me to the devil's mother in two shakes! And it's still all right if they just toss me and I don't end up sitting in Lubyanka, God forbid. And it's all Gogol's doing, may he and all his kith and kin . . ."

And meditating thus, he drove in through the gates of that same inn out of which he had driven one hundred years ago.

Absolutely everything in it was as before: the cockroaches peeped out of the cracks, and it was as if there were even more of them—but there were a few small changes too. Thus, for example, in place of the sign "Inn" hung a placard with the inscription "Dormitory No. Such-and-such," and, it goes without saying, the grime and filth was such as Gogol could not even have fantasized.

"A room!"

"Your order!"

But not for a second was the brilliant Pavel Ivanovich nonplussed.

"The manager!"

"Wham!" the manager is an old acquaintance: old Bald Pimen who one time ran "The Shark," and who had now opened a café on Tverskoy Boulevard—in the Russian style with German trimmings: orgeats, balsams, and of course, prostitutes. The guest and manager exchanged kisses, susurrated back and forth, and in a wink the matter was closed without any order. Pavel Ivanovich had a makeshift snack of leftovers and flew off to arrange for work.

II

He appeared everywhere and enchanted everyone with his bows slightly to the side and the colossal erudition which had always distinguished him.

"Fill out the questionnaire."

They gave Pavel Ivanovich a questionnaire a yard long, containing one hundred of the trickiest questions: where are you from, where have you been, and why? . .

Pavel Ivanovich had not been sitting there for more than five minutes before he had filled every bit of space on the questionnaire. But his hand was trembling as he handed it in.

"Well," he thought, "now they'll read what a treasure I am, and . . ."

And absolutely nothing happened.

In the first place, no one read the questionnaire; in the second place, it fell into the hands of the lady registrar who handled it as usual: she processed it as an outgoing instead of incoming document and then immediately stuck it somewhere, so that the questionnaire vanished as if into the waters of the sea.

Chichikov grinned and went to work.

III

And from then on everything got easier and easier. First of all, Chichikov looked around, and saw that wherever he spat, his old buddies were there, holding positions. He flew into an office where, he heard, rations were issued, and he hears:

"I know you, you skinflints, you'd take a live cat, skin it, and give it out as a ration! But you just give me a side of mutton and some oatmeal. Because even if you sugarcoat it I won't put that toad you call a ration in my mouth, and I won't take your putrid herring either!"

He looks—there's Sobakevich.

As soon as he arrived, Sobakevich made it his first duty to demand a ration. And by God he got it! Ate it and asked for seconds. Got them. Not enough! Then they dished out a second meal for him; they'd first given him a single one—now a shock-worker's ration. Not enough! They gave him some sort of reserve amount. He bolted that and demanded more. And he made a scandal about demanding it. He cursed them all as "Judases," said that scoundrel sits on scoundrel and persecutes scoundrel and that there is only one decent man, the clerk, and he's a pig, if you tell the truth!

They gave him an academician's ration.

No sooner did Chichikov see how Sobakevich handled the rations than he instantly finagled things for himself too. But, of course, he surpassed Sobakevich. He got rations for himself, for his nonexistent wife and baby, for Selifan, for Petrushka, for that same old guy about whom Betrishchev had told, for his old mother who was not in this world. And academician's portions for all. So that they started delivering the groceries to him by truck.

And having settled the food problem thus, he headed for other offices to find a position.

Once as he was flying along Kuznetsky in his car, he met Nozdryov. The latter made it his first duty to report that he had already sold the watch and chain. And indeed, he had neither watch nor chain on him. But Nozdryov did not despair. He told how he had made out at a lottery when he had won a half pound of vegetable oil, lamp glass, and soles for children's shoes, but how he had had no luck after that, and how he, dammit, had reported his six hundred million rubles to the government. He told how he had proposed that VNESHTORG [Foreign Trade Ministry] send a shipment of genuine Caucasian daggers abroad. And they did. And he would have made millions on it if it were not for the damned English, who had noticed the inscription "Made by Savely Sibiryakov" and rejected them all as defective. He dragged Chichikov to his hotel room and plied him with amazing cognac supposedly brought from France, in which, however, full-strength moonshine could be tasted. And, in the end, his cock-and-bull stories got to the point where he started maintaining he had been issued eight hundred yards of textiles, a baby-blue automobile with gold trim, and an order for living space in a building with columns.

When his brother-in-law Mizhuev expressed some doubt, he swore at him, calling him not a Sofron, but simply a bastard.

In a word, he bored Chichikov so much that he did not know how to get out fast enough.

But Nozdryov's stories gave him the idea of going into export trade himself.

IV

And so he did. Again he filled out a questionnaire and went to work and showed himself in all his glory. He shipped sheep across the border in double sheepskins with Brabant lace underneath; he smuggled in jewels inside wheels, shafts, ears, and the devil only knows what sort of places.

And in the shortest period he turned up with about five hundred oranges capital.

But he did not rest there—he submitted an application to the proper place expressing a desire to take a lease on a certain enterprise, and he used extraordinary colors to paint up a picture of the profits the government would have from it.

At the government office mouths simply gaped open—the profit was indeed colossal. They asked to be shown the enterprise. If you please. On Tverskoy Boulevard right opposite the Strastnoy Monastery, across the street—it is called "Pampas on Tverboul." They sent an inquiry to the proper place: "Is there any such thing there?" They were answered: "There is, and it's known to all Moscow." "Fine."

"Turn in a technical estimate."

Chichikov already has the estimate in his shirt.

They gave him the lease.

Then, without wasting any time, Chichikov flew off to the proper place.

"An advance, please."

"Present an authorization in triplicate with the required signatures and seals."

Two hours had not passed before he presented the authorization too. All in order. As many seals as stars in the sky. And the signatures all right there.

"Signing for the manager—Neuvazhai-Korito, for the secretary—Kuvshinnoe Rilo, for the chairman of the Tariff Estimate Commission—Elizavet Vorobey." [2]

"Right. Here's your order."

The cashier just gurgled when he saw the total.

Chichikov signed the receipt and carted away the banknotes in three carriages.

And then off to another office:

"A loan, my merchandise as collateral."

"Show the merchandise."

"By all means. Your agent, please."

"Get the agent!"

Tfu! The agent is an acquaintance too—Rotozei Emelyan.

Chichikov picks him up and takes him away. He takes him to the first cellar they come to—and points to it. Emelyan sees an enormous quantity of goods lying there.

"M-yes . . . And it's all yours?"

"All mine."

2. These are all names of dead souls (or serfs) from Gogol's novel, so the associations are not very flattering.

"Well," says Emelyan, "then I congratulate you. You're not a millionaire—you're even a trillionaire!"

And Nozdryov, who at this point had caught up with him, poured oil on the fire.

"See that," he says, "see that car with the boots in it, driving through that gate? Well, those are his boots too."

And then he got carried away, dragged Emelyan to the street and pointed.

"See those stores? Well, those are all his stores. Everything on that side of the street—it's all his. And the ones on this side—they're his too. See the trolley? His. The streetlights? . . . His. See? See?"

And he spins him in all directions.

So that Emelyan begged: "I believe it! I see . . . Just let my soul rest."

They went back to the office.

There they are asked, "Well?"

Emelyan just waved his arm.

"It's . . ." he says, "it's indescribable!"

"Well, if it's indescribable—give him $n + 1$ billion."

V

After that Chichikov's career developed in a dizzying fashion. What he was up to is beyond the mind's powers to comprehend. He founded a trust to pour iron from sawdust, and got a loan on that too. He became a shareholder in a huge cooperative, and he fed all Moscow on sausage made from already dead animals. Having heard that in Moscow "everything had been settled" now, the landowner Korobochka expressed a desire to acquire some real estate; Chichikov formed a company with Zamukhryshkin and Uteshitelny and sold her the Manège,[3] the exposition hall opposite

3. The Manège is a large government building, now an exhibition hall, in the center of Moscow. It is associated with con-men the way our Brooklyn Bridge is.

the university. He signed a contract for the electrification of the city—which is so big you can't get out of it even if you gallop for three years—and making contact with the former mayor, he set up some sort of wood fence, put in landmarkers so that it would appear some planning was going on, and as for the money dispensed for electrification, he wrote that it had been stolen by the gangs of Captain Kopeikin. In a word, he worked miracles.

And soon the rumor that Chichikov was a trillionaire was being trumpeted all over Moscow. Government organizations began to rush pell-mell to get him as a specialist. Chichikov had already rented a five-room apartment for five billion; Chichikov was already lunching and supping at the "Empire."

VI

But suddenly the crash came.

Chichikov was ruined by Nozdryov, as Gogol had correctly predicted, and he was finished off by Korobochka. Without any desire to do him dirty, but simply because he was drunk, Nozdryov babbled something in passing about sawdust and about Chichikov taking a lease on a nonexistent enterprise, and concluded all of this with words to the effect that Chichikov was a swindler and that he would have him shot.

The public fell to thinking, and the winged rumor took off like a spark.

And at this point, idiot Korobochka pushed into a government office to make inquiries about whether she could open a bakery in the Manège. Vainly they kept assuring her that the Manège was a government building, and that it was impossible to buy or open anything in it—but the stupid old crone understood none of it.

But the rumors about Chichikov kept getting worse and worse. People began to wonder what sort of bird this Chichikov was and where he was from. Slanderous tales got started, one more ominous and monstrous than the next. Uneasiness entered the hearts of all.

Telephones started to jangle, conferences began . . . The Commission on Construction with the Commission on Inspection, the Commission on Inspection with ZHILOTDEL, ZHILOTDEL with NARKOMZDRAV, NARKOMZDRAV with GLAVKUSTPROM, GLAVKUSTPROM with NARKOMPROS, NARKOMPROS with PROLETKULT, etc.[4]

They rushed to Nozdryov. That, of course, was stupid. They all knew that Nozdryov was a liar, that not a word Nozdryov said could be believed. But they summoned Nozdryov and he answered every item in order.

He announced that Chichikov had in fact leased a nonexistent enterprise, and that he, Nozdryov, saw no reason why he shouldn't have since everyone does it. To the question, was Chichikov a White Guard spy, he answered that he was a spy and that not long ago they had even wanted to shoot him, but that for some reason he had not been shot. To the question, is Chichikov a forger of counterfeit banknotes, he answered that he was a forger and even told an anecdote about Chichikov's extraordinary skill, how when he had learned that the government wanted to put out new notes Chichikov had rented an apartment in Marina Grove and issued from there 18 billion rubles worth of fake notes, and, to top it off, this was two days before the real ones came out, and when they had raided the apartment and sealed it shut, in one night Chichikov mixed the fake banknotes with real ones so that afterward the devil himself couldn't tell which were fake and which genuine. To the question, was it true that Chichikov was exchanging his billions for diamonds so that he could escape abroad, Nozdryov answered that it was true, and that he himself was helping him and taking part in the deal, and that if it weren't for him, nothing would come of it.

After Nozdryov's stories everyone was overwhelmed by the most complete depression. They see there's no possibility of finding out what Chichikov is. And it is unknown how all this would have

4. These are all transliterated acronyms for various People's Commissariats and Trade Departments.

ended if it had not been for one person in this company. True, like all the others he had never had a copy of Gogol in his hands, but he commanded a small dose of common sense.

So he exclaimed, "You know what Chichikov is?"

And when they all thundered, in chorus, "Who?"

He said in a sepulchral voice: "A swindler."

VII

Only at this point did the light dawn on everyone. They rushed to look for the questionnaire. Nowhere to be found. As an incoming document. No sign of it. In the filing cabinet—not a sign. To the registrar. "How should I know? Ask Ivan Grigorych."

To Ivan Grigorych. "Where is it?"

"It's none of my business. Ask the secretary, etc., etc."

And suddenly, unexpectedly, in a wastepaper basket—there it is.

They started reading and froze.

"First name? Pavel. Patronymic? Ivanovich. Surname? Chichikov. Social Status? Gogol character. Occupation before the Revolution? Purchase of dead souls. Draft Status? Neither fish, nor fowl—nor the devil knows what. Party Affiliation? Sympathizer [but with whom—unknown]. Have you ever been arrested? A wavy zigzag. Home Address? Turn into the courtyard, the third floor on the right, ask the field-officer's wife, Podtochina,[5] in the information office, she knows. Personal signature? A splotch!!"

They read and turned to stone.

They yelled to Instructor Bobchinsky,[6] "Get going over to Tverskoy Boulevard to the enterprise he leased, and the yard where his merchandise is, maybe something will turn up there!"

Bobchinsky returns. Round eyes.

"An extraordinary event!"

5. Podtochina is a character from Gogol's story "The Nose."
6. Bobchinsky and Dobchinsky are from Gogol's play *The Inspector General,* as is Lyapkin-Tyapkin below.

"Well?!"

"There ain't no enterprise at all there. He gave the address of
the Pushkin Monument. And the goods aren't his, they're the
ARA's."

Here they all howled, "Holy Saints! So that's the kind of goose
he is! And we gave him billions!! Now, it turns out we've got to
nab him!"

And they started trying.

VIII

A finger pressed a button.

"A courier."

The door opened and Petrushka presented himself. He had left
Chichikov a long time ago and become a courier for a government
office.

"Take this package immediately and be on your way immediately."

Petrushka said, "Yes, sir."

He immediately took the package, immediately got on his way,
and immediately lost it.

They called Selifan at the garage.

"A car. On the double."

" 'Medjutly."

Selifan shook himself, covered the motor with a pair of warm
pants, put on his jacket, hopped into the seat, whistled, honked,
and flew off.

What Russian does not love a swift ride?

Selifan loved it too, and therefore at the entrance to Lubyanka
he was forced to choose between a trolley car and a plate-glass
store window. In a brief instant of time Selifan chose the latter,
swerved away from the trolley, and like a whirlwind, screaming
"Help!" drove through the store window.

Here even Tentetnikov, who was in charge of all the Selifans and
Petrushkas, lost his patience.

Fire them both and send them pig farming!

They fired him. Sent him to the Employment Bureau. From there these orders were made: Plyushkin's Proshka was to replace Petrushka, Grigory Try-To-Get-There-But-You-Won't to replace Selifan. And meanwhile things were boiling along!

"The authorization for the advance!"

"Here, if you please."

"Ask Neuvazhai-Korito here."

This turned out to be impossible. Some two months before Neuvazhai had been purged from the Party, and then he purged himself from Moscow immediately after that, since there was absolutely nothing more for him to do there.

"Kuvshinnoe Rilo?"

He went off somewhere into the sticks to advise a GUBOTDEL.

Then they took up Elizavet Vorobey. No such fellow. True, there is a typist named Elizavet, but not Vorobey. There is Vorobey who is an assistant to the deputy of the junior clerk of the Deputy Manager of some subsection, but his first name is not Elizavet.

They got hold of the typist.

"It's you?!"

"Nothing of the sort! Why me? Here Elizavet ends with a hard sign, and I surely don't have a hard sign on my name. Quite the contrary . . ."

And she breaks into tears. They leave her in peace.

But meanwhile, as they were fussing around with Vorobey, the lawyer Samosvistov let Chichikov know on the side that a big fuss had begun over the matter, and naturally, all trace of Chichikov disappeared.

And in vain they raced by car to the address he had given: when they turned to the right, there was no information office there at all, of course; but there was a cheap public dining hall which had been abandoned and ruined long ago. And the cleaning woman Fetinya came out to them and said there weren't nobody there.

Next door, it's true, turning to the left, they did find an information office—but there was no field-officer's wife sitting there, only some Podstega, Sidorovna, and it goes without saying, she was ignorant not only of Chichikov's address but even of her own.

IX

Then despair fell over them all. The case had gotten so mixed-up that even the devil couldn't have found anything to his taste in it. The nonexistent lease got confused with the sawdust, Brabant lace with electrification, Korobochka's purchase with diamonds. Nozdryov was still stuck to the case, both the sympathizer Rotozei Emelyan and the non-Party member Antoshka the Thief turned out to be involved, and some sort of Panama hat with Sobakevich's ration cards in it was discovered. And the whole province was off on the light fantastic!

Samosvistov worked without rest, and stirred into the general stew some wanderings connected to trunks, and a case of falsified expense accounts for government trips (this alone turned out to implicate up to 50,000 people), etc., etc.

In a word, the devil only knows what had got started. And both those from under whose noses the billions had been requisitioned, and those who had to find it were rushing around in terror, and there was only one indisputable fact confronting them: "The billions were here and have vanished."

Finally, some Uncle Mityay got up and said, "Well, fellows . . . Obviously we can't get around appointing an investigative commission."

X

And right at that point (something you'll never see in a dream), I emerged like some *deus ex machina* and said,

"Let me handle it."

They were astonished.

"But . . . you . . . know how to?"

And I said, "Put your minds at ease."

They vacillated, then in red ink: "Assigned."

Here I got started (I've never had such a nice dream in my life!). Thirty-five thousand motorcyclists swept up to me from all sides.

"Do you need something?"

And I say to them, "I don't need anything. Don't interrupt your work. I'll manage by myself. Single-handedly."

I sucked in my breath and barked so loudly that the windows rattled.

"Get me Lyapkin-Tyapkin! On the double! On the telephone!"

"Then it's impossible to get him . . . The telephone's broken."

"Oh! Broken! The cord's torn loose? So that it doesn't dangle there for nothing, hang the one who's making the report to me with it!"

Lord! What had begun!

"Please, sir . . . What are you doing, sir . . . This . . . he, he . . . this instant . . . Hey! Repairmen! The cord! Fix it immediately!"

In two shakes they fixed it and gave it to me.

And I tore ahead.

"Tyapkin? The Bastard! Lyapkin? Arrest the scoundrel! Give me the lists! What? Not ready? Have them ready in five minutes or you'll find yourself on the lists of dead souls! Who's *that*? Manilov's wife is the registrar? Boot her out! Ulinka Betrishcheva is the typist? Boot her out! Sobakevich? Arrest him! That good-for-nothing Murzofeykin works for you? Shuller Uteshitelny? Arrest them! And the one who gave them the jobs too! Take him! And him! And this one! Out with Fetinya! Send the poet Tryapichkin, Selifan, and Petrushka to the accounting office! Nozdryov to the cellar! . . This minute! This second!! Who signed the authorization? Get him in here, the scoundrel!! Even if he's on the bottom of the sea!"

Thunder rumbled through hell . . .

"A devil's flown down on us! Where'd they get one like that?"

And I say, "Get me Chichikov!"

"I'm . . . I'm . . . impossible to find him. He's hiding . . ."

"Oh, hiding? Marvelous! Then you'll go to jail for him."

"Plea . . ."

"Shut up!!"

"This minute . . . This . . . Hold on just a second. They're looking, sir."

And in two instants they found him.

And in vain Chichikov crawled at my feet and tore his hair and coat and assured me that he had a disabled mother.

"Mother?!" I thundered, "Mother? . . Where are the billions? Where is the people's money?! Thief!! Cut the bastard open! He's got the diamonds in his stomach!"

They slit him open. There they were.

"All of it?"

"All, sir."

"A rock around his neck and down an ice hole with him!"

And it got quiet and all clear.

And I said on the telephone, "All clear."

So they answer me, "Thanks. Ask anything you want."

Thus I jumped around the telephone. And I almost poured into the telephone all of those estimated expenditures which had been tormenting me for a long time.

"Pants . . . A pound of sugar . . . A twenty-five watt bulb . . ."

But I suddenly remembered that a decent writer should be unselfish, I relented and muttered into the receiver, "Nothing but Gogol's works in a binding like the edition of his works I recently sold at the market."

And . . . pow! I have a gold-embossed Gogol on my desk!

I was so glad to have Nikolai Vasilievich—who had often comforted me on bleak, sleepless nights—that I bellowed, "Hurrah!"

And . . .

EPILOGUE

. . . OF COURSE, I woke up. And nothing—no Chichikov, no Nozdryov, and, most important, no Gogol.

"Oh, ho, ho," I thought to myself and started to get dressed, and again life went parading before me in its quotidian way.

Other Stories

A Treatise on Housing[1]

I

IT WAS NOT from the fine far-away that I studied the Moscow of 1921–24. Oh no, I lived in it, I tramped it back and forth. I went up almost every sixth floor that had some official bureau on it, and since there was definitely no sixth floor on which there wasn't an official bureau, I am familiar with absolutely all of those floors. For example,, you're riding along in a cab toward Zlatouspensky Alley to visit Yury Nikolaevich, and you recall, "Oy, what a building! Of course, I've been in there!" I was, on my word of honor! And I even remember just when it was. In January of 1922. And what the hell brought me here? If you please. It was when I had started work for a private trade and industrial newspaper and asked the editor for an advance. The editor did not give me the advance, but said, "Go to Zlatouspensky Alley, the sixth floor, room . . . , well, 343?" Or maybe 180? . . . I've forgotten. It's not important . . . In a word, "Go and get an ad from MAINCHEM," or was it CENTCHEM? I've forgotten. Well, it's not important . . . "Get the ad and I'll give you 25%." If someone had said to me, "Go get an ad," I would have answered, "I won't go." I have no desire to go for ads. I don't like to go for ads. It's not my specialty. But then . . . Oh, it

1. The stories "A Treatise on Housing," "Psalm," "Four Portraits," and "Moonshine Lake" all appeared in a small book entitled *A Treatise on Housing* (Moscow: Zemlya i Fabrika, 1926). "Moonshine Lake" was first published in *On the Eve,* No. 397 (Berlin, 1923). We have no information on the first publication of the other three stories.

was a different matter then. I put on my hat obediently, took that ridiculous ad book, and set off like a lunatic. It was absolutely un- believable how cold it was out—it's never so cold. I climbed up to the sixth floor, found room No. 300, and in it I found a balding red- haired man who listened to what I had to say and didn't give me the ad.

Apropos of sixth floors. It appears, if you please, that there are elevators in that building? There are. But then, in 1922, only people with heart trouble could ride in them. That's the first thing. The second is that the elevators didn't work. So that both people with certificates that said they had heart trouble and people who had no heart trouble (including me) walked up to the sixth floor the same way.

Now it's different. Oh, now it's a completely different matter. I was at my friend's place at Patriarch's Ponds just recently. As I was goodnaturedly going up to the sixth floor under my own power, about one hundred feet above sea level, in the encaged shaft be- tween the fourth and fifth floors I saw the completely motionless elevator hanging there all lit up. From it I could hear a female's crying and a booming masculine bass: "They should be shot, the bastards!"

On the stairway stood a man who looked something like a door- man; beside him was another man, wearing grease-covered pants, apparently a mechanic, and some curious peasant woman from apartment 16.

"What a mess," the mechanic was saying and smiling in astonish- ment. When I came home from my visit that night, the elevator was still hanging in the same place, but it was dark, and no voices could be heard from it. The two unlucky people had probably been hang- ing there for about two weeks and died of hunger.

God knows whether that CENT- or MAINCHEM still exists. Maybe there's some CHEMTRED there now, or something else. It's possible that neither that CHEM nor the red-haired bald man have been around for a long time, and the rooms have already been rented, and precisely in the spot where the desk with the ink on it stood there now stands a piano or a soft divan—and in place of a chemical man there is a seductive girl sitting there, her hair beautified by hydrogen peroxide, reading *Tarzan*. Anything is possible. The one good thing is that I will never climb up there again, either on foot or in the elevator.

Yes, many things have changed before my very eyes.

The places I've been! On Myasnitsky a hundred times, on Varvarka—in the Delovoy Dvor, on Staraya Square—in CENTRALUNION, dropping by Sokolniki, I was tossed out toward Devichie Field too. One desire drove me all across the strange and immense capital: the desire to find enough to live on. And I found it—true, it was skimpy, uncertain, and irregular. I found it in the most fantastic jobs—ones as transitory as galloping consumption, getting it in strange, precarious ways many of which seem ridiculous to me now that things are better. I wrote a trade-industrial chronicle for a newspaper, and nights I composed gay feuilletons which seemed no funnier than a toothache to me myself; I applied for a job in a fabric trust, and one night, in a mad frenzy caused by Lenten butter, potatoes, and holey shoes, I concocted a dazzling design for a neon industrial ad. That this design was a good one is shown just by the fact that when I took it to an engineer friend of mine to be checked, he embraced me, kissed me, and said that it was too bad I had not studied to be an engineer: it turned out that by pure force of intellect I had invented the very same construction which was already flashing over Theatrical Square. What does that prove? It proves only that a man who is fighting for his survival is capable of brilliant achievements.

But enough! The reader is, of course, uninterested in my ups and downs in Moscow, and I am relating all this with the single goal of making him believe me when I say that I know Moscow of the twenties perfectly well. I rummaged back and forth across every part of it. And I intend to describe it. But I wish to be believed when I am describing it. If I say something was so, it was really so.

I am keeping in reserve the job of guide—for a future time when famed foreigners start coming to Moscow.

II

> . . . Hey, an apartment!!
> —*The Barber of Seville*, Act III

Let us agree once and for all: living quarters are the foundation stone of human life. Let us accept this as an axiom: without living quarters man cannot exist. And in addition to this, I hereby inform everyone who lives in Berlin, Paris, London, and elsewhere—in Moscow there are no apartments.

"How do people live there then?"

"They live like this, sir."

"Without apartments."

But that's not the important thing. The last three years in Moscow convinced me quite definitely that Muscovites have forgotten the very concept of the word "apartment" and use the word for anything you can live in. Thus, for example, not long ago, before my very eyes one of the journalists whom I know got a paper: "Issue Comrade So-and-so an apartment in building No. 7 (the one where the typography is)." Signature and a round wax stamp.

Comrade So-and-so was presented with an apartment, and that evening I got hold of Comrade So-and-so. Cabbage soup had been slopped all over a handrail-less stairway, and across the stairway hung a frayed cable as thick as a garter snake. On the top floor, after passing over a layer of broken glass, past windows half of which had been stuffed with pieces of wood, I found myself in a dull and dark space, and in it I began to shout. A strip of light answered my shout, and going in somewhere I found my friend. What had I entered? The devil only knows! It was something dark like a mine shaft, divided by plywood partitions into five sections which resembled longish hatboxes. In the middle box sat my friend on a bed, beside the friend his wife, beside his wife, my friend's brother, and the aforesaid brother was drawing his wife's portrait on the opposite wall in charcoal without getting up from the bed, but just reaching out with his hand. His wife was reading *Tarzan*.

These three were living in a telephone booth. You people living in Berlin just imagine how you would feel if you were moved into a telephone booth. A whisper or the sound of a match falling on the floor was audible throughout the apartment, and their's was the center section.

"Manya!" (from the end box).

"What?" (from the opposite end).

"You got any sugar?" (from the end).

"In Lustgarten, in the center of Berlin, a demonstration of many thousands of workers carrying red banners took place . . ." (from the neighboring box on the right).

"I've got candy . . ." (from the opposite end).

"You're a pig!" (from the neighboring left).

"Let's go together at 8:30!"

"Wipe his nose, please . . ."

Within ten minutes a nightmare had begun: I could no longer distinguish between what I was saying and what other people were saying, and my ears kept picking up extraneous things. The Chinese, who are specialists in the area of tortures, are mere puppies. Things like this couldn't be invented.

"How did you get in here? He, he, he! . . . The Soviet delegation accompanied by the Soviet colony set out to see the tomb of Karl Marx . . . Ku?! I'll give you a Ku! Thank you, I didn't . . . With candy? . . To hell with your Ku! . . Pig, pig, pig! Throw him out! And where is he? . . In Kioto and Yokohama . . . Don't lie, don't lie, you animal. I've seen through you for a long time! What, isn't there any john?!"

My God! I left without wasting a second, but they stayed there. I spent a quarter of an hour in that box, but they've been living there for seven months.

Yes, dear citizens, when I got home I felt for the first time that everything on earth is relative and arbitrary. I imagined myself living in a palace, and there was a powdered lackey wearing a red livery at every door, and dead silence reigned. Silence is a great thing. Silence is the gift of the gods and paradise. But still I always have one door (just as I have one room), and this door opens directly into the hallway, and catercorner live the renowned Vasily Ivanovich and his renowned wife.

I swear by everything that is holy, every time I sit down to write about Moscow, the cursed image of Vasily Ivanovich stands before me in the corner. A nightmare wearing a jacket and striped undershorts blots out my sun. I press my head to the stone wall, and Vasily Ivanovich stands over me like the lid of a coffin.

All of you understand that this man can make life impossible in any apartment, and he did make it impossible. All of Vasily Ivanovich's acts are intended to harm his neighbors, and there is not a single section of the Law Code of the Republic which he has not broken. Is it bad to swear loudly using your mother's name? It is bad. But he does it. Is it bad to drink moonshine? It is bad. But he drinks it. Is rampaging allowed? No, no one is allowed to. But he goes on rampages. And so on. It is a great pity there is no section of the code forbidding playing accordions in apartments. Attention Soviet jurists: I implore you, take him away! Well, he used to play. I say he used to play because he doesn't any more. Perhaps, pangs of conscience stopped the man? Oh, no, strange people from Berlin —he sold it for drink.

In a word, he is not thinkable in human society, and even taking into consideration his descent I cannot forgive him. Quite the contrary: precisely taking that into consideration I cannot forgive him. I analyze it like this: he ought to set me (a man of dubious descent) an example of good behavior—and not me him. And just try to prove to me that I'm wrong.

And I have been living in the same apartment with Vasily Ivanovich for three years now, and how much longer it will be I don't know. Possibly until the end of my life, but now—after the visit to the box—I feel better. One need not get especially belligerent about things, citizens!

Yes, I feel better. I have become more patient and sympathetic toward people.

Doctor G., my friend, came to my place last week with this moan: "Why am I not married?"

From his lips—he is the biggest and best-known misogamist in Moscow—this deserved attention.

It turned out that his Building Directorate was making people double up. They put up a partition in his room and moved a married couple in behind the partition. The doctor floundered and howled in vain. Nothing came of it. The chairman kept repeating the same thing: "Now if you were married, it would be another matter . . ."

And the day before yesterday the doctor appeared and said, "Well, thank God, I never got married . . . Do you quarrel with your wife?"

"Hm . . . occasionally . . . how can I put it . . ." I answered evasively and courteously, glancing over at my wife. "Generally speaking . . . there are . . . occasionally . . . you see . . ."

"And who's to blame?" my wife asked quickly.

"Me. I'm to blame," I hastened to assure her.

"A nightmare! A nightmare! A nightmare!" the doctor started saying, swallowing some tea. "A nightmare! Every evening, you see, the same thing breaks out: 'Where've you been?' 'At Nikolaevsky Station.' 'Lies!' A half an hour later: 'Where were you?' 'At

Anya's 'Lies!' "

"The poor woman," said my wife.

"No, I'm the poor one," replied the doctor, "and I'm going away to Orekhovo-Zuevo, to hell with her!"

"With whom?" my wife asked suspiciously.

"That . . . that . . . the clinic."

This winter Natalya Egorovna threw a mop rag on the floor and couldn't unstick it because it was nine degrees above the table and on the floor there were no degrees at all—and it even lacked one (it was —1). And all winter she played Chopin's waltzes while wearing canvas boots, so Peter Sergeevich hired a servant, and within a week he fired her—but the servant wouldn't leave! Because the chairman of the Directorate came and said that she (the servant) was a member of the dwelling-place commune now and occupied her living space, and no one had a right to touch her. Now Peter Sergeevich dashes all over Moscow like crazy, asking everyone what he should do? And there is absolutely nothing he can do. In the servant's trunk she has a card from a bold Red army soldier who took Perekop, and a card from the dwelling-place commune. The end for Peter Sergeevich!

And a certain young man in whose "apartment" they settled a pious old woman, one Sunday when the old woman was returning from matins, met her with these words: "I'm sick of you, you pious old woman!"

And with that he whacked her over the head with a piece of steel. And I know all of four incidents like this lately. Am I condemning the young man? No. Categorically, no. For the feeling which made them settle an old woman into my apartment—or even a second Vasily Ivanovich—is a virtuous feeling. But I would pick up a piece of steel myself, in spite of the fact that since childhood I had inculcated in me the idea that one ought never to arm oneself with pieces of steel.

And Sasha offered 300 rubles if they would just get Anfisa Markovna out of his room . . .

But enough!

What is the source of such a strange and unpleasant life? There is only one source—the overcrowding. It's a fact—Moscow is overcrowded.

What can be done?

One can do only one thing: use my project. And this plan consists of the following: Moscow must be built up.

Psalm

A T FIRST it seems to be a rat scratching at the door. But a very
courteous human voice is heard.

"May I come in?"

"Yes, please."

The door hinges sing.

"Come and sit on the couch!"

(From the door.) "But how do I get acwoss the floow?"

"You just walk softly and don't slide. Well, now, what's new?"

"Nuffing."

"What? And who was that bawling in the hall this morning?"

(A painful pause.) "I was bawling."

"Why?"

"Mama spanked me."

"For what?"

(A tense pause.) "I bit Suwka's eaw."

"Really."

"Mama says Suwka's a no-good. He teases me, and he took some
kopeks away."

"Still there's no law saying people's ears should be bitten over
kopeks. You end up looking like a foolish kid."

(Offense.) "I'm not going to cawe what you say."

"And you don't have to."

(A pause.) "Papa will come, I'll tell him." (A pause.) "He'll soot you."

"Oh, I see. Well, I won't make any tea then. Why should I? If I'm going to be shot . . ."

"No, you make tea."

"You'll have some with me?"

"With some candy? O.K.?"

"Definitely."

"I'll have some."

Two human bodies squatting down—a big one and a small one. The teapot boils with a musical ring, and a cone of hot light lies across a page of Jerome Jerome.[1]

"You've forgotten Tikhi, probably?"

"No I haven't."

"Well, read."

"Well . . . I'll buy myself some shoes . . ."

"To match the frock coat."

"To match the frock coat, and at night I'm going to sing a . . ."

"Psalm."

"Psalm . . . And I'll get myself . . . a dog . . ."

"And . . ."

"And we will have a beau . . ."

"A beautiful life."

"Beau-ti-ful life."

"Exactly so. The tea's boiling, let's have some. A beautiful life." (A deep sigh.) "Beau-ti-ful."

Ring. Jerome. Steam. Cone. Parquet shines.

1. The allusion is apparently to a story by Jerome K. Jerome (1859–1927), the English humorist. Jerome's writings frequently resemble the feuilletonistic manner and humor of Bulgakov (both had fathers with theological backgrounds, both wrote novels which have been called mystical). Jerome visited Russia in 1899 and was very popular there. A twelve-volume edition of his works was published in Russia in 1912. Which story Bulgakov has in mind we have been unable to determine.

"You ah' lonely."

Jerome is falling on the floor. The page falls out of the light, is extinguished.

(A pause.) "Who told you that?"

(Undisturbed innocence.) "Mama."

"When?"

"When she was sewing youw button on. She was sewing and sewing. Sewing and saying to Nataska . . ."

"So. Wait, wait, don't squirm, or I'll spill it on you . . . Oh!"

"Hot?"

"Take whatever piece of candy you want."

"I want this big one hewe."

"Blow on it, blow and don't kick your feet."

(A woman's voice off-stage.) "Slavka!"

Knock at the door. The hinges sing pleasantly.

"Slavka is here. Slavka, go home!"

"No, no, we're still drinking tea."

(Quiet frankness.) "I . . . I haven't had any."

"Vera Ivanovna, come in and have some."

"No thanks, I was just . . ."

"Come in, come in, I won't let you go . . ."

"My hands are wet . . . I'm hanging up clothes . . ."

(The uninvited defender.) "Don't you dawe gwab my mama."

"Well, all right. I won't grab her . . . Vera Ivanovna, please sit down."

"Wait a minute, I'll go hang the clothes and then come back."

"Fine. I won't turn the stove off."

"And Slavka, you drink up and get home to bed. He's bothering you."

"I'm not bothewing. I'm not messy."

The hinges sing unpleasantly. Cones in various directions. The teapot is silent.

"Are you ready for bed already?"

"No, I'm not. You tell me a stowy."

"But your eyelids are already drooping."

"No, not little ones. Tell me."

"Well, come here to me. Put your head here. There. A fairy tale? What fairy tale should I tell you? Eh?"

"About the little boy, the one . . ."

"About the little boy? That's a hard fairy tale to tell, brother. Well, for you, so be it."

"Well, sir, so there lived this little boy in the world. Yes, sir. He was small, approximately four years old. In Moscow. With his mama. And the little boy was named Slavka."

"Oh . . . Like me?"

"He was pretty good-looking, but unfortunately he was always starting fights. And he used everything he could—fists and feet and even his galoshes. And one day there was a little girl on the stairs from number three, a fine little girl she was, quiet, a beauty—and he smacked her in the face with a book."

"She stahts fights huhself . . ."

"Wait, this is not about you."

"A different Slavka?"

"Completely different. Now, where was I? Oh yes. . . . Well, naturally this Slavka got whippings every day, because really, one can't allow fighting, you know. But Slavka didn't relent anyhow. And things got to the point where one fine day Slavka quarreled with Shurka (he was another such little boy), and without thinking much about it, wham, he grabs his ear between his teeth and half of his ear gets bitten off. There's a furious uproar, Shurka howls, Slavka is whipped, he howls too . . . Somehow they stick on Shurka's ear with a glue. Slavka was put in the corner, of course . . . and then suddenly the doorbell rings. And a complete stranger appears, he has a huge red beard and blue glasses and he asks in a bass, 'And may I ask which of you is Slavka?' Slavka answers, 'That's me, I'm Slavka.' 'Well, listen to this,' he says, 'I am the supervisor of all bullies, and I'm going to have to move you, esteemed Slavka, out of Moscow, to Turkestan.' Slavka sees things are bad, and he sincerely repents, 'I confess,' he says, 'that I have been fighting, and I did play pitch penny on the stairs—and I lied shamelessly to mama, I said I hadn't been . . . But it's not going to happen again, because I'm starting a new life.' 'Well,' says the supervisor, 'that's a different matter. Now you should get a reward for your sincere repentance.' And he immediately took Slavka to the reward distribution room. And Slavka sees that there are various visible and invisible things there. Balloons and cars and airplanes and striped balls and bicycles and drums. And the supervisor says, 'Pick out what you really want.' And Slavka picks out . . . oh I forget . . ."

(A sweet, sleepy bass.) "A bicycle!"

"Yes, yes, I remember—a bicycle. And Slavka got right on his bicycle and rode straight to Kuznetsky Street. He rides along and blows the horn, and the public stands on the sidewalk amazed. 'Well, what a remarkable person that Slavka is! And how does he keep from falling under a car?' But Slavka gives signals and shouts to the drivers, 'Keep to the right!' Horse-drawn cabs fly by, cars fly by, and Slavka is all enthusiastic, and soldiers are going by, marching along so that one's ears ring . . ."

"Already? . . ."

The hinges sing. Corridor. Door. White arms, bare to the elbow.

"My Lord, let me undress him."

"Come on. I'll wait."

"It's late."

"No, no . . . I don't want to hear that."

"Well, all right."

Cones of light. It begins to hiss above the wick. Jerome Jerome isn't necessary, it's lying on the floor. A small sweet hell in the mica window of the kerosene lamp. At night I'm going to sing a psalm. Somehow we'll have a beautiful life. Yes, I'm lonely. The psalm is sad. I don't know how to sing. The most tormenting thing in life is—buttons. They drop off as if they were rotting off. One of them flew off my vest yesterday. Today one on my jacket and one on my pants—behind. I don't know how to live with buttons, but I see everything and understand everything. He won't come. He won't shoot me. That time she said to Natashka in the hall: "My husband will soon return, and we'll move to Petersburg." He won't ever return, believe me. He's been gone seven months, and accidentally I've seen her cry three times. You can't hide tears, you know. But he's really lost a lot by abandoning those white, warm arms. That's his business, but I don't understand how he could forget Slavka . . .

How joyfully the roosters crowed . . .

No cones. Black darkness in the mica window. The teapot fell silent long ago. The light of the lamp peeks through the worn sateen cover like a thousand small eyes.

"You have remarkable fingers. You should be a pianist."

"When I go to Petersburg, I'm going to play again . . ."

"You're not going to Petersburg. Slavka doesn't have the same kind of curls on his neck that you have. But you know, I'm sad. It's boring down there, extremely so, somehow."

It is impossible to live. Buttons, buttons, buttons all around . . .

"Don't kiss me . . . Don't kiss me . . . I have to go. It's late."

"Don't go. You'll start crying there. You have the habit of doing that."

"That's untrue. I don't cry. Who told you?"

"I know myself. I live myself. You are going to cry, and I am sad . . . so sad . . ."

"What am I doing? . . . What are you doing? . . ."

No cones. The lamp is not shining through the worn sateen. Darkness. Darkness.

No buttons. I'll buy Slavka a bicycle. I won't buy myself any slippers or frock coat, I am not going to sing psalms at night. It's all right, somehow we'll have a beautiful life.

Four Portraits

———————

"WELL, GENTLEMEN, please sit down," said our host amiably, and with a regal gesture he indicated the table.

Without making ourselves be asked a second time, we sat down and unfolded the napkins which were standing on end.

Four of us sat down: the host—a former attorney; his cousin—also a former attorney; a female cousin—the former widow of an Actual State Councillor, subsequently a clerk in SOVNARXOZ,[1] and now simply Zinaida Ivanovna; and a guest—me, a former . . . but that makes no difference . . . now a man with occupations called indefinite.

The early May sun struck the window and began to play on the frames.

"Spring is here, thank God; the winter has exhausted me," said our host, delicately taking a small carafe by its neck.

"Don't remind us!" I exclaimed, and dragging a sprat from a box, I stripped the skin from it in an instant, then spread some butter on a piece of bread, covered it with the knife-torn body, and amiably baring my teeth in Zinaida Ivanovna's direction, I added, "Your health!"

And swallowed.

1. Bureau of Soviet Agriculture.

"It isn't too weak . . . ahem . . . too diluted?" inquired the host solicitously.

"Just right," I replied, taking a breath.

"A trifle weak, perhaps," responded Zinaida Ivanovna.

The men protested in a chorus, and we drank a second glass each. The maid brought in a tureen of soup.

After the second glass a divine warmth suffused my insides, and geniality took me in its embrace. In a moment I fell in love with my host, his cousin, and decided that in spite of her thirty-eight years Zinaida Ivanovna was still not bad at all, and that Karl Marx's beard—which was located directly across from me beside a railroad map on the wall—was not as huge as is commonly assumed. The story of the appearance of Karl Marx in the apartment of an attorney who hated him with all his soul goes like this:

My host was one of the most cautiously thoughtful men in Moscow, if not *the* most cautiously thoughtful. He was virtually the first to sense that what was happening was a serious and long-lived thing, and therefore he entrenched himself in his apartment not in any haphazard, amateurish way, but formidably. As his first duty he called Terenty, and Terenty befouled the entire apartment for him, fixing up something like a clay coffin in the dining room. The same Terenty poked huge holes in all the walls, through which he shoved thick pipes. After this my host said, admiring Terenty's work, "They can cut off the steam heat, the bandits," and he set off for Plyushchik. From Plyushchik he brought Zinaida Ivanovna and settled her in the former bedroom, a room on the sunny side. Three days later his cousin arrived from Minsk. He willingly and rapidly took in his cousin, putting him in the former reception room (to the right from the entrance hall) and set up a small black stove for him. Next he put five hundred pounds of flour in the library (straight down the hall) and locked it with a key, put a bookstand on the rug in front of it along with empty bottles and some old newspapers, and the library vanished—the devil himself couldn't have found the entrance. Thus, of six rooms only three were left. He installed himself in one with a certificate that he had a heart disorder, and he took down the doors between the remaining two rooms (the living room and the study), turning them into a strange double chamber.

It was not one room because there were two of them, but living in them as two was impossible, all the more so that in the first (the living room) he put a bed immediately under the statue of a woman's head and beside the piano, and calling Sasha out of the kitchen, he told her, "Those guys will come here. So you say they sleep right here."

Sasha smiled conspiratorily and replied, "Very well, sir."

The door of the study he papered over with mandates one of which proclaimed that this was the law office of such and such an organization and was given "extra space." In the additional space he constructed such barricades—from two bookcases, an old bicycle with no tires, chairs with nails sticking out of them, and three cornice boards—that even I, who knew his apartment quite well, smashed both of my knees, my face and hands, and tore my jacket from back to front in a very sensitive spot on my first visit after the apartment had been put on battle status.

On the piano he pasted a certificate that Zinaida Ivanovna was a music teacher; on the door to her room a certificate that she worked in SOVNARXOZ, on the cousin's door that he was a secretary. He began to open the doors himself after the third ring, and while he did that Sasha would lie down in the bed beside the piano.

For three years men in gray greatcoats and moth-eaten black overcoats, and women carrying briefcases and wearing canvas ponchos, tore into the apartment like infantry through barbed-wire barriers, and not a damned thing could they find. Having returned to Moscow after three years—I had left frivolously—I found everything in its former place. The host had just gotten a bit thinner and complained that he was absolutely persecuted.

It was then that he bought the four portraits. Lunacharsky he placed in the living room in the most visible place, so that the Narkom[2] was visible from absolutely every spot in the room. He hung the portrait of Marx in the dining room, and in his cousin's room over a marvelous yellow mirrored bureau he pinned Trotsky —who was depicted wearing a pince-nez, as is customary, and with a rather genial smile on his lips. But as soon as the host rammed the four tacks into the photograph, it seemed to me that Trotsky frowned. And he remained frowning. Next the host pulled Lieb-knecht out of the folder and headed for his female cousin's room. She met him on the threshold, and striking herself on the thighs, which were enveloped by a striped skirt, she screamed, "That's all I need! While I'm alive, Alexander Ralych, there aren't going to be any Marats or Dantons in my room!"

"Zin . . . what has Marat got to do with . . ." he started to say, but the energetic woman turned him around by the shoulders and shoved him out. He turned over the colored photograph in his hands pensively—and then put it away.

Exactly a quarter of an hour later the regular attack ensued. After the third ring and a pounding of fists in the colored magic of the main door's glass, the host—having pulled on a greasy field jacket in place of his suit coat—admitted three people. Two were wearing gray, one in black with a reddish briefcase.

"You have extra rooms here . . ." the first gray one began, look-ing around the anteroom in astonishment. As a precautionary meas-ure the host had not turned on the lights, so that the mirror, hang-ings, expensive leather chairs, and the deer antlers remained dis-solved in the darkness.

"What are you saying, comrade! ! !" yelped the host, waving his arms, "Where are there any extra rooms here? Do you know that there have been six commissions here before you this week. Not only aren't there any extra rooms, there aren't even enough for me. Just look," and he pulled a piece of paper out of his pocket, "I've

2. Also *Narkompros*—People's Commissar of Education, who was Luna-charsky.

been assigned sixteen additional square yards, and all I have is thirteen and one half. Yes, sir. Where am I to get the other two and a half square yards I'd like to know?"

"Well, we'll see," said the second gray one gloomily.

"Come in, please, comrade!"

Immediately Lunacharsky appeared before them. The three of them, mouths open, stared at the Narkompros.

"Who's in here?" asked the first gray one, pointing to the bed.

"Comrade Elishina, Alexandra Ivanovna."

"Who's she?"

"A technician," the host replied, smiling sweetly, "she washes clothes."

"She isn't your servant, is she?" asked the black one suspiciously.

In reply the host burst out in convulsive laughter.

"What are you saying, comrade? What am I—a bourgeois or something, to keep a servant?! I don't have enough for food, and you say servant! He, he, he!"

"Here?" asked the black one laconically, pointing to the hole into the study.

"The additional thirteen and one half for the office of my organization," replied the host very rapidly.

The black one stepped slowly into the nearly dark study. A second later a basin crashed thunderously in the study and I heard the black one hit his head against the bicycle chain as he fell.

"There, you see, comrades," said the host ominously, "I warned you, hellishly overcrowded."

The black one made his way out of the wolves' den with a distorted face. Both of his knees were torn.

"Did you bruise yourself?" asked the host in fright.

"Oh . . . fu . . . fu . . . yr . . . yr . . . mothe . . ." the black one mumbled something indistinctly.

"Nastrushchina is here," the host led on, pointing, "I am in here," and he gestured broadly to Karl Marx. Amazement kept growing on the faces of the three. "And in here, Comrade Shcherbovsky," and he waved triumphantly to Trotsky.

The three looked at the portrait in terror.

"What is he, a Party member?" asked the second gray one.

"He is not a Party member," the host simpered sweetly, "but he is a sympathizer. A Communist in his soul. Just like me. We are all responsible working people living here, comrades."

"Responsible, sympathizers," the black one growled gloomily, rubbing his knee, "but with mirrored bureaus. Objects of luxury."

"Lux-ur-y?!" the host yelped reproachfully. "What's wrong with you, comrade? The last of the linen is lying right here, torn. Linen, comrade, is an object of necessity." At this point he reached in his pocket for his keys, and stopped instantly, turning pale because he remembered that just yesterday evening he had shoved six silver teacup holders between the torn pillow cases.

"Linen, comrades, is an object of cleanliness. And our dear leaders," the host pointed to the portraits with both hands, "constantly point out to the proletariat the necessity of keeping oneself clean. Epidemics . . . typhus, plague, and cholera, are all from someone. What is this, comrades, do we still not sufficiently realize that our sole salvation, comrades, is in maintaining oneself in a state of cleanliness. Our leader . . ."

At this point it seemed quite apparent to me that a shudder passed across the face of the photographic Trotsky, and that his lips fell apart as if he wanted to say something. Apparently the host saw the same thing, because he fell silent abruptly and quickly changed the subject.

"Comrades, here's the toilet, here's the bath, but, of course, it's ruined, as you see, there's a box full of rags lying in it—there's no time for baths now. There's the kitchen—it's cold. No time for kitchens now. We fix things on the primus. Alexandra Ivanovna, what are you doing here in the kitchen? There's a letter for you in your room. And that, comrades, is all! I intend to petition for another additional room for myself—otherwise, you know, I smash my knees every day—that, you know, is really awful. Where should I go to have them give me another room in this building? For the office."

"Let's go, Stepan," said the first gray one, waving his hand hopelessly, and all three started out, stomping their boots through the anteroom.

When the steps died on the stairs, the host fell into a chair.

"There, how do you like that," he exclaimed, "and the same thing every blessed day. I give you my word of honor, they are doing me in."

"Well, you know," I said, "it's still not known who is doing whom in!"

"He, he," the host giggled, and then bellowed merrily, "Sasha! Bring the samovar!"

Such is the story of the portraits, and in particular that of Marx. But I return to my story:

. . . After soup we ate beef stroganov, drank a glass each of white "A-Daniel" put out by VINDELPRAVLENIYA,[3] and Sasha brought in the coffee, and at that point there was a brittle telephone ring in the study.

"Probably Margarita Mikhailna," smiled the host amiably, and he flew into the study.

"Yes . . . yes . . ." we heard from the study, but in a few moments a howl burst out.

"*What!*"

The receiver quacked hollowly, and again the howl:

"Vladimir Ivanovich! But I asked! We're all civil service workers! How can this be?"

"Oh," moaned the cousin, "have they taxed him?"

The receiver was slammed down thunderously, and the host appeared in the doorway.

3. Bureau of Wine Production.

"Taxed you?"

"Congratulations," the host replied furiously, "you've been taxed, my dear!"

"What?" his female cousin stood up, her face blotchy. "They have no right! Why I told them at the time that I was a civil service worker!"

"I told them, I told them!" mocked the host. "Telling them wasn't what you had to do—you should have looked yourself to see that that bastard of a building supervisor was writing it on the rolls! And you," he turned to his other cousin, "you kept asking and inviting, come on up, come on up! And now how do you like it: he's put a mark beside all three of our names for taxes!"

"*You* are the fool," his cousin replied, blood rushing to his face, "what have I to do with it? I told that pig twice to mark us down as civil service workers! It's your fault! He's your acquaintance. You should have asked him yourself!"

"He's a bastard, not an acquaintance," the host thundered, "calls himself a friend! The miserable coward! All he cares about is avoiding responsibility."

"For how much?" yelled the lady cousin.

"Five!"

"But why only me?" she asked.

"Don't worry," the host replied sarcastically, "it'll get to me and to him. Obviously, the word didn't get through. But if they're taking you for five, what'll they slap on me! But here's what we'll do—there's no reason to loll around here. Get dressed and go to the regional inspector, explain that it's a mistake. I'll go too. Quickly, quickly!"

His cousin flew out of the room.

"What is this?" the host's voice rang dolefully. "They don't give a person a moment's rest, or even set deadlines. If it isn't the door, it's the telephone! They gave up the requisition, and now a tax. How long will this go on? What else have they thought up?"

He raised his eyes to Karl Marx, but he sat there motionlessly and silently. The expression on his face suggested that he wanted to say, "This does not concern me!"

The tip of his beard was gilded by the early April sun.

Moonshine Lake

A Narration

At ten o'clock on the evening before Easter Sunday our damned hallway fell silent. In this blissful silence an electrifying idea was born in my mind—that my dreams had come true and Pavlovna, the old crone who sells cigarettes, had died. I decided this because there were no screams from her tortured son Shurka coming out of her room. I smiled voluptuously, sat down in a beat-up chair, and opened a volume of Mark Twain. Oh, blissful moment, radiant hour! . . .

. . . And at quarter after ten a rooster crowed three times in the hall.

A rooster is nothing special. After all, a pig lived in Pavlovna's room for six months. In general Moscow is not Berlin—that's the first thing—and the second is that no man who has lived off hall No. 50 for six months can be surprised by anything. It was not the fact of the unexpected appearance of a rooster which confused me —it was the circumstance that the rooster was crowing at 10:00 P.M. A rooster is not a nightingale—in prerevolutionary times they crowed at dawn.

"Do you suppose those bastards have been getting that rooster drunk?" I asked my unhappy wife, tearing myself away from Twain.

But she did not have time to answer. After the rooster's prefatory

fanfare an unbroken crowing began. Then a male voice began to
bellow. And how! It was the uninterrupted bass howl on C-major,
the howl of spiritual pain and desperation, an anguished mortal
howl.

All of the doors began slamming, footsteps began to rumble.
I threw down Twain and rushed into the hall.

In the hall under a light, in a tight circle of the astonished inhabitants off this renowned hall, stood a citizen whom I did not
know. His legs were set wide apart like the letter "V" upside down,
he was staggering, and without closing his mouth he was emitting
the insane howl which had frightened me. In the hall I heard an
inarticulate long note (*fermato*) change into a recitative.

"So-o-o," the unknown citizen howled and choked gutterally,
drenching himself in huge tears. "Christ is risen! A fine way you
act! Nobody gets it like that! A-a-a-a!"

And with these words, he started pulling clumps of feathers out
of the tail of the rooster which was flopping in his hands.

One glance was enough to convince one that the rooster was quite
sober. But inhuman pain was written all over the rooster's face. His
eyes were jumping out of their orbits, he was flapping his wings
and trying to pull out of the chainlike hands of the unknown man.

Pavlovna, Shurka, the chauffeur, Annushka, Annushka's Misha,
Duska's husband, and both Duskas were standing in a circle in
absolute silence, and as motionless as if they had been driven into
the floor. But this time I don't blame them. They had even lost
the power of speech. They, like I, were seeing this scene, the pluck-
ing of a live rooster, for the first time in their lives.

The apartment head of No. 50, Vasily Ivanovich, was smiling
crookedly and desperately, grabbing the rooster now by an elusive
wing, now by the legs, trying to grab it away from the unknown
citizen.

"Ivan Gavrilovich! Have some fear of God!" he was yelling,
growing sober before my very eyes. "No one is taking your rooster

away, may it be damned three times. Don't torture the bird on Easter eve! Ivan Gavrilovich, come to yourself!"

I was the first to come to my senses, and with an inspired blow I knocked the rooster out of the citizen's hands. The rooster dashed around madly, plunged heavily into the light, then went down lower and disappeared around the corner by Pavlovna's storeroom. And the citizen went silent instantly.

It was an extraordinary event, if you wish, and just because of that it ended well for me. The apartment head did not tell me that if I didn't like the apartment, I could go look for a private mansion. Pavlovna didn't tell me I keep the light on until five o'clock in the morning, occupied with "business of an unknown nature," and that in general there was absolutely no reason why I should intrude where she lived. She has a right to beat Shurka, because he's her Shurka. And I can raise "your own Shurkas" and eat them with oatmeal. "Pavlovna, if you hit Shurka in the head again, I will take you to court and you will get a year for torturing a child," helped but little. Pavlovna threatened to file a "petition" with the directorate to have me moved out. "If someone doesn't like it here, let him go where there are educated people."

In a word, this time none of this happened. In deathly silence all of the inhabitants of the most renowned apartment in Moscow dispersed. The apartment head and Katerina Ivanovna led away the unknown citizen down the stairs. He went along, crimson, shaking and staggering, silently throwing back his murderous, dimming eyes. He looked like *atropa belladonna*.

Pavlovna and Shurka caught the exhausted rooster under a tub and took it away.

Returning, Katerina Ivanovna said, "My son of a bitch (read: the apartment head, Katerina Ivanovna's husband) went to the store like a good man. He bought a fifth at Sidorovna's. He invited Gavrilych—'let's go, he says, let's go and try it.' All people are human, so they got plastered, God forgive my trespass, the priest had still not rung the bell in church. I simply can't make out what happened to Gavrilych. They drank up and mine says to him: 'Why you going in the toilet with a rooster, Gavrilych, let me hold him.' And he ups and explodes. 'So,' he says, 'so you want to snitch my rooster for yourself?' And he started to yell. What was wrong with him, God knows! . . ."

At two o'clock in the morning, breaking his fast, the apartment head smashed all of the windows, beat up his wife, and explained his deed by saying she had eaten away his life. I was at matins with my wife at the time, so the scandal passed without my participation. The populace of the apartment shuddered and called up the chairman of the Building Directorate. The chairman of the Directorate appeared immediately. Red as a flag, with flashing eyes, he took a look at Katerina Ivanovna—who was black and blue—and he said, "I'm surprised at you, Vasily Ivanych. The head of a household and you can't manage a woman."

This was the first time in the life of our chairman that he was not made happy by his own words. He personally, along with the chauffeur and Duska's husband, was forced to disarm Vasily Ivanych, during which he cut his arm. (After the chairman's words, Vasily Ivanovich had armed himself with a kitchen knife in order to cut up Katerina Ivanovna. "I'll show her.")

Having locked Katerina Ivanovna in Pavlovna's storeroom, the chairman impressed upon Ivanych the idea that Katerina Ivanovna had run away and Vasily Ivanovich fell asleep with the words, "O. K. I'll cut her up tomorrow. She ain't going to get out of my clutches."

The chairman left with the words, "That's some moonshine Sidorovna has. A devilish moonshine brew."

At three o'clock in the morning Ivan Sidorych appeared. I declare publicly: if I were a man and not a rag, I would of course throw Ivan Sidorych out of my room. But I'm afraid of him. He is the most powerful figure in the Directorate next to the chairman. Maybe I won't succeed in getting him moved out (but maybe I will too, the devil only knows), but he can poison my existence quite easily. For me that's the most terrible thing. If my existence is poisoned, I can't write feuilletons, and if I can't write feuilletons, there'll be a financial crash.

"H'lo . . . Mister Journ . . . list," said Ivan Sidorych, swaying like a weed in the wind.

"I've come to see you."

"Very nice."

"About the Esperanto . . ."

"?"

"I'd like you to wri . . . an article . . . I want to start a society . . . Write that, Ivan Sidorovich the Esperantist wants, he says . . ."

And suddenly Sidorych started speaking Esperanto (incidentally, it's an amazingly repugnant tongue).

I don't know what the Esperantist said before my eyes, but then he suddenly closed up, the strange duck-tailed words—like a mixture of Latin and Russian—began to break off, and Ivan Sidorych switched to a generally understandable language.

"However . . . excuse . . . Tomorrow I'll . . ."

"You're welcome," I replied warmly, seeing Ivan Sidorych to the door (for some reason he wanted to exit through the wall).

"Is it impossible to drive him out?" asked my wife as he left.

"No, dear, it's impossible."

At nine in the morning a holiday began—with a song played by Vasily Ivanovich on an accordion (Katerina Ivanovna dancing) and a speech addressed to me by Annushka's Misha, who was totally smashed. Misha expressed the esteem held for me by himself and by other citizens whose names I did not know.

At ten the junior yard man came (he was slightly drunk), at ten-twenty the senior one (dead drunk), at ten-twenty-five the furnace man (in a horrible state—he was totally silent and silent he went away—and he immediately lost the five million rubles I gave him in the hall).

At noon Sidorovna brazenly failed to fill Vasily Ivanych's fifth by three fingers. Then, taking his empty fifth, he went to the proper authority and declared, "They're selling moonshine. I want them arrested."

"Aren't you mixed-up?" the proper authority asked him morosely. "According to our information there's no moonshine in your section."

"None?" Vasily Ivanovich sneered bitterly. "I find your words quite remarkable."

"Well, there isn't any. And how would you turn up sober if you had moonshine? Better go home and sleep a while. Tomorrow you turn in a declaration about who's got moonshine."

"So-o . . . I see . . ." Vasily Ivanych said, smiling dazedly. "So there's no rules for them? Let 'em pour even more out. And as for how sober I am, take a whiff of this fifth."

The fifth turned out to have "clear signs of the odor of intoxicating beverages."

"Lead on," they said to Vasily Ivanovich then. And he led on.

When Vasily Ivanovich woke up, he said to Katerina Ivanovna, "Run over to Sidorovna's and get a fifth."

"Come to your senses, you cursed soul," Katerina Ivanovna replied, "Sidorovna's been shut down."

"What? How did they sniff her out?" Vasily Ivanovich said in surprise.

I felt triumphant. But not for long. Within half an hour Katerina Ivanovna appeared carrying a full fifth. It turned out a fresh well had been drilled two doors down from Sidorovna's—at Makeich's. At seven that evening I tore Natasha out of the arms of her husband, Volodya the baker. ("Don't you dare hit her!" "She's my wife!" etc.)

At eight that evening when the jaunty song boomed out and Annushka started dancing, my wife rose from the couch and said, "I can't take it any more. Do whatever you must, we have to get out of here."

"My dear," I replied in desperation, "what can I do? I can't get another room. It'll cost twenty billion. I get only four. Until I finish my novel we have nothing to hope for. Be patient."

"It's not for me," my wife answered. "But you will never finish the novel. Never. Life is hopeless. I'm going to take morphine."

At these words I felt that I had become like iron.

I answered, and my voice was full of metal, "You will not take morphine, because I will not allow you to. As for the novel, I will finish it, and I dare say confidently that it will be a novel that will set the heavens on fire."

Then I helped my wife dress, locked the door with key and latch, asked Duska I (she drinks nothing but port) to see that no one broke the lock, and took my wife away for a three day holiday at my sister's on Nikitinskaya.

CONCLUSION

I have a project. I undertake to dry out Moscow in two months, if not completely, then by 90%.

My conditions: I am in charge. I will personally choose a staff made up of students. They must be set a very high salary (400 gold rubles—it's worth it). One hundred of them. I get an apartment with three rooms and a kitchen—and one thousand gold rubles all at once. A pension to my wife in case I am murdered.

Unlimited powers. My order to be carried out at once. Court examination within twenty-four hours, and no fines can be substituted.

I'll smash all of the Sidorovs and the Makeichs—also smashing along with them all of the "Corners," "Flowers of Georgia," and "Tamara's Castles" and similar places.

Moscow will be like the Sahara, and in the oases under neon signs "Open Until Midnight" there will be only light red and white wines.

Moscow, 1923.

The Raid

In a Magic Lantern[1]

<hr />

T HE BLACK JUMBLE of the storm exploded in a slanting white flame, and immediately after this long, dark horses' muzzles tumbled out of the cloud.

Snorting. Then a second fiery explosion. Abram fell into the deep snow, and from the impact of a formless muzzle and terrifying chest, he went flying, without dropping his rifle from his hands . . . Trampled and crushed, he stood up in pearly columns of swirling snowflakes.

He did not feel the cold. On the contrary, a rather dry heat coursed through his entire body, and this heat gave way to sweat all over his body. It was then that Abram realized what mortal fear means.

The snowstorm blew and pasted his eyes over so that for several moments he could see nothing whatsoever. The cold blackness blew at a slant, and fiery rings floated up before his eyes.

"Just try to shoot . . . go ahead, you son of a bitch," said a voice from above, and Abram understood that the voice was coming from atop a horse.

Then for some reason he remembered the fire in a little black stove and an unfinished watercolor on a wall—a winter day, home, tea, and warmth. He understood that precisely that absurd and

1. Published in the Moscow newspaper *Gudok* [The Whistle], No. 1984 (December 25, 1923).

terrible thing had happened which he imagined as he stood at his post, timidly and vigilantly peering into the swirling storm. Shoot? Oh, no, he had no intention of shooting. Abram dropped his rifle into the snow and shudderingly sighed. It was useless to shoot, the horses' muzzles jutted out in the diminishing column of the storm; nearby stood the black sentry box, and the snow screens, thrown into a heap, looked like a gray heap of rags. Wearing a peaked hood, the second sentry, Streltsov, appeared quite close-by, dark and formless; but the third, Shchukin, was done for.

"What regiment?" asked the voice hoarsely.

Abram sighed, cast his eyes upward apparently striving to look at the sky for a moment, but black and cold poured down from above, a screw was twisting upwards—there was no sky at all there.

"Well, start talking!" was said, also from above, but on the other side, and immediately Abram had a keen sense of great but restrained malice coming through the howling of the storm. Abram did not have time to protect himself. Something hard and black flashed before his face like a bird, and then a furious, scalding pain cracked his jaws, brain, and teeth, and it seemed to him that his entire head had burst into flame.

"A-a-a-a!" Abram cried, shuddering, crunching down on the mash of bones in his mouth and choking on salty blood.

At this moment Streltsov flared up for an instant, pale blue and in agony, at the edge of the electric flashlight's field; and the third sentry, Shchukin, could still be distinguished quite clearly, bent up in a snowdrift.

"Which one?!" screamed the storm.

Abram knew that the second blow would be even more terrible than the first; he sighed and answered, "The Guard Regiment."

Streltsov faded, then again flared up. The storm's snowflakes swept along in benign swarms, jumping and somersaulting in the bright cone of light.

"Tfu! We got a Kike!" cut a voice in the darkness beyond the flashlight, and the flashlight was turned away, extinguishing

Streltsov, and it fixed its big protruding eye right in Abram's eyes. Its pupil was flashing. Abram saw the blood on his hands, a foot in a stirrup, and the sharp black muzzle sticking out through a wooden holster.

"A Kike! A Kike!" a hurricane behind his back rumbled joyfully.

"What about the other one?" a bass replied greedily.

Only Abram's left ear was hearing, the right had turned numb, just as his cheek and brain were numb. Abram wiped the thick, sticky blood off with his hand, causing a fiery pain to pass from his cheek down into his chest and heart. The flashlight extinguished half of Abram, but showed all of Streltsov in its circle of light. An arm from the saddle knocked Streltsov's big hat from his head, and a shock of his hair stood on end.

Streltsov shook his head, opened his mouth, and suddenly he said faintly in the rustle of the snowstorm, "O-oh, rotten bandits. May you rot in hell."

The light jumped upward, and then to Abram's feet. They had struck Streltsov with a hollow thump. Then the horse's muzzle pressed forward again.

Both Abram and Streltsov were standing beside a dried heap of snow screens, still in the same bluish glare from the light; and directly in front of him men in gray overcoats were dismounting and darting about. Into the cone would fall now a rifle with a hand, now a red tail with galoons and tassels on a big hat, now a clinking, chewed-up bit made of white meerschaum.

Two lights were burning—a white one at the station, cold and high up—and on the other side a low, funereal one in the snow beyond the roadbed of the tracks. The gusts of wind came less and less often, more and more lightly, and it was not roaring, and not squalling. As it poured cold, dry clouds into one's face and down one's neck, the diminishing storm swept evenly and smoothly through the cone.

Streltsov was standing there, his face smeared over with a red mask—they had beat him long and heavily for his effrontery, pounding his head to a pulp. He grew wild from the blows, became totally insensate, and staring ahead with one eye, a seeing and hateful eye—the other was seeing and crimson—and leaning his stretched-out arms on the stack, he said, croaking and coughing blood, "O-oh, rotten bandits. O-oh, you mother-fuckers . . . You'll all be caught, they'll shoot you all."

Occasionally a figure with a black bone-handled pistol in his hand dashed into the cone of light and pounded Streltsov with the butt. Then he completely lost strength, moaned, and his legs slipped away from the stack; and he was left with only his arms to support himself.

"Make it faster!"

"Faster!"

A volley could be heard fanning out from the direction of the white station light, and then it ceased.

"Go ahead, beat me, beat me, faster!" Streltsov cried hoarsely, "Why torture people for no reason."

Streltsov was standing there in just his shirt and yellow, quilted pants; he had on no overcoat or boots, and his unwinding, bespattered leg wrappings trailed behind him when his legs slipped away from the snow screens. But Abram was wearing his miserable overcoat and canvas leg covers. They did not tempt anyone, and the golden straw peered peacefully out of the torn right toe just as always.

Abram's face was something the world has never seen before.

"The Kike is laughing!" said the surprised darkness outside the cone.

"He's laughing at me," answered the bass.

Tears oozed from Abram's eyes of themselves, not ticklishly and not painfully; and his mouth was torn—as if he were smiling at something, and it remained that way. His unbuttoned overcoat was thrown open, and for some reason he was holding onto the piping of his black trousers with his hands; he was silent and looking into the protruding eye with the blinding pupil.

"So it's all over now," he thought, "just as I supposed. I won't see the watercolor or the light again in any case. And nothing will happen. There's nothing to wait for—this is the end."

"Well," the darkness lay in waiting. The cone moved, the eye shifted to the left and straight ahead in the darkness, opposite the sentries, in the barrels of rifles, the end he expected lay concealed. At this point Abram went weak all at once and started to slip—his legs were going. Because of this he did not even feel the flashing end.

The snowstorm swept off like a whirlwind across track bed, and an hour later everything had changed. It stopped pouring from overhead and the sides. Far away over the snowy fields clouds exploded, and were swept away, and from time to time the edge of the golden moon's corona peered through in the clear spaces. Then a thin, milkish, treacherous reflection lay across the field, and the tracks stretched into the distance; and the heap of snow screens started to look black and ugly. The high light at the station grew dim, but the low, yellowish one was unchanged. Abram was the first to see it, as he raised his eyelids and stared at it for a very long time as if welded to it. The light was unchanged, but Abram's eyelids kept opening and closing so that it seemed to him that the light was blinking and flickering.

Abram's thoughts were strange, painful, inexplicable, and languid —why had he not gone out of his mind, this amazing miracle, the yellow light.

He dragged his legs as if they were broken, worked along the snow on his elbows, stretched out his wounded chest, and spent a very long time crawling over to Streltsov: five minutes for five paces. When he reached him, he felt him with his hand, convinced himself that Streltsov was cold, covered with snow, and started to crawl away. He got up on his knees, then staggered, bent over, and got to his feet and pressed his chest with both hands. He walked a little ways, fell down, and again started crawling toward the roadbed, never losing sight of the yellow light.

"Who's there? Lordy! Who is it?" the woman asked in fright, holding onto the door latch. "I'm here alone with a sick child. Go on to the station, go on."

"Let me in, let me. I'm wounded," Abram repeated persistently, but his voice was dry, thin, and singsong. He grabbed the door with his hands; but his hand would not obey, and it slipped off, and Abram feared more than anything else that the woman would close the door. "I'm wounded, do you hear," he repeated.

"Oh, it's too much," the woman answered, closing the door part way.

Abram crawled into the black porch on his knees. The woman's eyes disappeared in circles, and she watched the crawling man, but Abram was looking ahead at the yellow light and he saw it quite closely. It was hissing in a triangular lamp.

Only toward morning did the night effloresce completely. Ice cold and scattered with stars all over. In crosses, bushes, and squares the stars lay over the plowed-up earth and up at the zenith, and far beyond, over the mute forests on the horizon. On the slope of the sky, near the moon, there was a rainbowlike corona, frost, and cold.

In the watchman's hut beside the tracks it was suffocatingly hot, and the light which had been tireless and yellow before was now barely burning, with a hissing sound. The watchman's wife was sitting sleeplessly on a bench by the table, staring past the light at the stove where, under a pile of rags and a sheepskin coat, Abram's body was still alive.

The heat swept in waves from his brain to his legs, then returned to his chest and strove to blow out the icy candle sitting in his heart. The candle expanded and contracted rhythmically, counting off the seconds, marking them quietly and evenly. Abram did not feel the candle, he felt the even hiss of the light in the triangular glass, but as he did so it seemed to him that the light existed in his head; and Abram told this light the story of the screw of the storm, the throbbing pain in his cheekbones and brain, Streltsov buried in the snow. Abram wanted to pull Streltsov out of the drift and drag him to the stove, but he was too heavy and burdensome, like a stake anchored in the earth. Abram wanted to pull the tormenting yellow light out of his head and throw it away, but the light sat there stubbornly scorching everything that was in his deafened head. The icy arrow in his heart skipped a beat, and the clock of life began to do a strange thing—reversing, and cold instead of heat passing from his head to his legs, the candle was shifted into his head, and the yellow light into his heart; and Abram's body was racked by quick shudders in musical thirds, out of time and syncopation with the pounding of life; and now there was too little sheepskin fur over him, and he wanted to pile the whole watchman's shack full to the ceiling with them, to curl up, and lie down on heated bricks.

The years passed. And an event occurred which was just as joyous as it was unnatural: firewood was brought to the club.

Of course, it was wet, but wet wood will burn—and it did burn. The mouth of the stove vomited ugly fiery devils; the heat swam out and danced on the dried fir branches, on the bunting on the portrait, catching at the edge of a beard, on the floor, and on Bronya's face. Bronya was squatting down right at the mouth of the stove, staring into the flames, her arms wrapped around her knees, and the toes of her shaggy fur boots sticking out being warmed by the fiery devil. Bronya's head was poppy red from the ever-present scarf twisted into a neat knot.

The others were sitting on broken chairs in a semicircle, listening to what Gruzny was telling. In his base, Yak told about attacks, about ice-cold nights, about the searing war. It came out in such a way that Yak was a brave and untiring man. And he really was brave. When he finished, he spat into a gray bucket with metal hoops around it, and let out a cloud of awful smoke from cheap, rotten tobacco.

"Now Abram," said Bronya, "he's a regular professor. He can tell a few interesting little things too. It's your turn, Abram," she said smoothly, because Abram was the only recent arrival whom she addressed with the formal "you."

Small, hair mussed up like a sparrow, he climbed out of the back row and came into the flame's light in all his beauty. He had on a padded jacket of the sort that wheat sellers once wore, and trousers remarkable for the whole Workers' Faculty, and no doubt the only ones in the entire world: brown with a strange greenish tint, wide up above and narrow down below. For some reason, they never covered up the right flap of his right boot, and they rested higher, allowing everyone to see a strip of Abram's gray sock.

The possessor of these trousers was deaf, and therefore he always kept a polite confused smile on his face, and in cases which required it, he cupped his hand over his left ear.

"Your turn, Abram," ordered Bronya loudly, as everybody spoke to him, "you probably were not in the war, so you just tell us anything at all."

The ruffled sparrow stared into the stove and, restraining his voice so as not to speak more loudly than he had to, he started to tell his story. Finally, he got carried away, and addressing the flames and Bronya's poppy-red scarf, he told his story with passion. He wanted to put everything into the story: the screw of the storm, and the sudden muzzles of the horses, and what formless terrible fear there is when you are dying and there is no hope. He spoke in the third person of two sentries in a guard regiment; pityingly raising his brows, he told how one of them was not shot dead, and how he crawled in a straight line, always heading for the yellow light, about the woman, the watchman's wife, the hospital in which the doctor swore that the sentry would never survive, and how the sentry did survive . . . Abram was keeping his left hand in his jacket pocket, and pointing to the fire with his right, as if that other fire and light were here and were drawing this picture for him. When he finished, he looked into the stove with horror and said, "That's the way it was."

Everyone was silent.

Yak looked at the brown trousers condescendingly and said, "That was . . . But why . . . That was in the Ukraine . . . And who did it happen to?"

The sparrow was silent for a moment, and then answered bashfully, "It happened to me."

Then he was silent for a moment and added, "Well, I'm going to the library."

And he went away, slightly limping in his usual way.

All heads turned to follow him, and everyone kept looking at the brown trousers for a long time, until Abram's feet had crossed the whole large hall and disappeared through the door.

The Crimson Island

A Novel by Comrade Jules Verne
Translated from the French into Aesopian
by Mikhail A. Bulgakov[1]

PART I

THE ERUPTION OF THE
FIRE-BREATHING MOUNTAIN

I HISTORY AND GEOGRAPHY

IN THE OCEAN which from ancient times has been called Pacific
because of its tempests and gales, below the forty-fifth parallel,
there was a huge uninhabited island populated by fine native tribes
—red Ethiopians, white Arabs, and Arabs of an indefinite color who
had for some reason got the nickname "double-dyed" from seafarers.
When the *Hope*, the celebrated Lord Glenarvan's ship, first came
to the island, it discovered odd customs there: in spite of the fact
that the red Ethiopians were ten times more numerous than the
white and double-dyed Arabs, the Arabs has exclusive control of the
island's government. On his throne in the shade of a palm tree sat
the sovereign Sizi-Buzi, decorated with fish bones and sardine cans,

1. Published in *On the Eve* in Berlin (April 20, 1924).

and beside him his high priest and also the commander of the army, Riki-Tiki-Tavi.

The red Ethiopians, on the other hand, occupied themselves with the cultivation of the cornfields, fishing, and the gathering of turtle eggs.

Lord Glenarvan began the same way he was accustomed to beginning everywhere he went—he raised a flag on a hill and said in English, "This island . . . will be mine somewhat."

A misunderstanding occurred. The Ethiopians, who understood no language other than their own, made pants out of the flag. Then the lord began to flog the Ethiopians under the palms, and having flogged them all, he entered into negotiations with Sizi-Buzi, and from the latter he learned that the island was his, Sizi-Buzi's, and that "the flag isn't necessary."

It turns out that the island had already been discovered twice. First the Germans, and then some guys who ate frogs. As proof Sizi cited the sardine cans and sweetly hinted that "firewater is very tasty, yes."

"They smelled the place out, the sons of bitches!" the lord grumbled in English, and slapping Sizi on the shoulder he generously allowed him to consider the island his in the future too.

An exchange of goods followed. The sailors unloaded onto the shore from the *Hope* glass beads, rotten sardines, saccharin, and firewater. Celebrating wildly, the Ethiopians brought beaver pelts, elephant ivory, fish, eggs, and pearls to the shore.

Sizi-Buzi took the firewater for himself, the sardines too, the beads too, but gave the saccharin to the Ethiopians.

Orderly relations were established. Ships came into the bay, threw off English treasures, and gathered up the native trash. A correspondent from *The New York Times,* wearing white pants and smoking a pipe, settled on the island—and he immediately contracted tropical gonorrhea.

In geography textbooks the island was named Ethiopian Island (l'Isle d'Éthiope).

II   SIZI DRINKS FIREWATER

After this the island flourished in an incredible way. The high priest, the commander of the army, and Sizi-Buzi himself were literally swimming in firewater: finally Sizi-Buzi's face got to look lacquered and somehow round, without wrinkles. The army of the white Arabs, decorated with beads, left their forest of spears flashing near the tent.

Passing ships frequently heard victorious cries coming from the island.

"Long live our sovereign, Sizi-Buzi, and the high priest too! Hurrah, hurrah!"

The Arabs shouted—and the double-dyed ones loudest of all.

On the part of the Ethiopians there was a loud silence. Not getting a ration of firewater, and working until they were dropping on their feet, the Ethiopians were in a languid state which even bordered on dull dissatisfaction. And since there are troublemakers among the Ethiopians, as there are among all people, it happened that incendiary ideas were born among them.

"What is this, brothers? Why it doesn't work out in any godly way. They (the Arabs) get the vodka, they get the beads, and we get a fig with saccharin. And who works—we do that too."

This ended with a great unpleasantness, again for the Ethiopians. As soon as this ferment of minds began, Sizi-Buzi sent a punitive expedition of Arabs to the Ethiopians' wigwams, and in two shakes it reduced them to a common denominator.

Flogged viciously, they bowed down and said, "And our children will obey too."

And then peaceful times began again.

III A CATASTROPHE

The wigwams of Sizi-Buzi and the priest were located on the best part of the island, at the foot of a fire-breathing mountain which had been extinguished for 300 years.

One night it awoke quite unexpectedly and the seismographs in Pulkovo and Greenwich showed an ominous piece of nonsense.

Smoke flew out of the fire-breathing mountain, next flames, then some sort of rocks, and next, like boiling water from a samovar, hot lava.

And by morning it was all clear. The Ethiopians learned that they had been left without their sovereign, Sizi-Buzi, and without the priest, and with just the commander of the army. On the site of the royal wigwams lay mountains of lava.

IV KIRI-KUKI THE GENIUS

At first the Ethiopians were thunderstruck and there were even tears in the crowd, but soon a quite natural question flashed through the heads of the Ethiopians and the surviving Arabs, including the commander of the army: "What happens next?"

This question was followed by a rumbling, at first vague, and then loud; and it is unknown what this would have turned into had it not been for an amazing event.

Over the crowd, looking like a poppyfield with a few white spots and curlicues, flapped someone's drunken face and darting eyes; and then, getting up on a barrel, Kiri-Kuki, a drunkard and loafer known to the whole island, presented his whole self to the crowd.

The Ethiopians were thunderstruck a second time, and the reason for this was Kiri-Kuki's striking appearance. From youngest to eldest they were used to seeing him staggering around by the bay where the fiery goodies were being unloaded, or beside Sizi's wigwam, and they knew that Kiri was an absolutely pure double-dyed

Arab. And now Kiri appears before the crazed islanders painted from head to toe in red Arab war paints. The most experienced eye could not have distinguished the flighty sneak from an ordinary Ethiopian.

Kiri swayed to the right of the barrel, then to the left, and opening his big mouth he boomed astonishing words which were immediately entered in the notebook of the ecstatic *Times* correspondent.

"Now that we've become free Ethiopians, I announce my thanks to you."

Not a single one of the Ethiopians of the sea understood just why Kiri was announcing his thanks—or what the thanks were for?! And the whole huge crowd answered him with an astonished, thunderous, "Hurrah!!!"

For a few minutes it rolled across the island, and then it was pierced by another cry from Kiri-Kuki.

"And now, brothers, get down and swear allegiance!"

And when the ecstatic Ethiopians howled, "To whom?!!"

Kiri answered piercingly, "Me!!!"

This time the Arabs were stunned. But the paralysis did not last long. A shout came:

"He figured it, the rascal, to a 'T,'" and the commander of the army was the first to rush and throw Kiri-Kuki up in the air in celebration.

All night long on the island gay bonfires burned, their reflections flashing in the sky; and Ethiopians danced around them, drunk from joy and firewater which had been opened by efficient Kiri.

Passing ships anxiously barraged the sky with radio telegrams and got ready to fire on the island to restore order, but soon the entire civilized world was pacified by a telegram from the *Times* correspondent.

"The idiots on the island are having a national holiday stop the swindler is a genius."

V BOUNT[2]

After that, events rolled along with preternatural speed. The very first day, to please the Ethiopians, Kiri named the island "Crimson Island" in honor of the basic Ethiopian color; and this did not flatter the Ethiopians, who were indifferent to fame and glory, but it did embitter the Arabs. The second day, to please the Arabs, he reaffirmed the Arab, Riki-Tiki, as commander of the army; and this did not please the Arabs, because each of them wanted to be boss, but it did embitter the Ethiopians. The third day, to please himself, he fixed up a floppy headdress made from sprat cans, which looked very much like the late Sizi's crown. This did not please anyone, but embittered them all, for the Arabs considered that each of them was worthy of a bottle and the Ethiopians, who were debauched by the firewater, were in general against a can which reminded them extremely painfully of being reduced to a common denominator.

Kiri-Kuki's last measure was directed at the firewater, and Kiri was completley ruined by this. Kiri announced that everyone would get an equal amount of firewater and did not carry out the promise. Very simple. If all got it, then they would need a great deal. But where could they get it? Kiri sent off the regular corn harvest in exchange for the water—he did not get much water, and not only the Ethiopians, but even the Arabs' stomachs were beginning to growl—and that caused unrest.

One fine hot day when Kiri was lying in his wigwam, as usual, unfit for any use, a certain Ethiopian came to Riki-Tiki, his physiognomy clearly written over with rebellious tendencies. At the moment of his arrival Riki was drinking firewater to the accompaniment of a crunching on roast suckling pig.

"What do you want, Ethiopian snout?" the gloomy commander asked drily.

2. This is the Russian for "revolt."

The Ethiopian paid no attention to the compliment and went straight to the point.

"Now just what is this," he complained, "what's going on? You get vodka *and* suckling pig? So it looks like the old ways again."

"Oh. So you want a suckling pig?" asked the warrior, restraining himself.

"What do you mean? I think an Ethiopian is a person too," the visitor replied impudently, and he brazenly put a leg forward.

Riki took the pig by the crunched leg, and winding up like a screw, he clobbered the Ethiopian so hard in the teeth that juice squirted out of the pig—and blood out of the Ethiopian's mouth—and tears from his eyes, interspersed with large green sparks.

"Out!!!" Riki ended the discussion.

It is unknown what the Ethiopian did when he got home, but it is very well known that by the end of the day the whole island was already humming like a beehive. And that night when the frigate *Chancellor* was passing by the island, it saw two glowing reflections in the southern bay of Blue Calm, and upset the entire world with a telegram.

"Fires on the island all signs of holiday again for the Ethiopian asses Hatteras."

But the respected captain erred. True, there were fires, but there was absolutely nothing festive about them. It was simply that the Ethiopians' wigwams by the bay had been set fire to by Riki-Tiki's punitive expedition.

In the morning the fiery columns turned to smoky ones, and there were no longer just two, but nine. Toward nightfall the smoke turned into serrated glowing reflections again (sixteen in number).

The world was disturbed by headlines in Paris, London, New York, Berlin, and other cities: "WHAT'S GOING ON?"

And then came a telegram from the *Times* correspondent, astounding the world.

"The Arabs' wigwams have been burning for six days. Hordes

of Ethiopians . . . (indecipherable). Kiri the scalawag is runni . . . (indecipherable)."

And a day later an astonishing telegram boomed to the whole world—and not from the island, from a European port:

"Ephiop sakatil grandiosni bount. Ostrov gorit, polnaja tschouma. Gori troupov. Avanson piatsot. Korrespondent.[3]

3. A garbled macaronic message: "Ethiopia has been struck by a great revolt, island burning, Total plague. Heaps of corpses, Advance 500. Correspondent."

PART II

THE ISLAND IN FLAMES

VI   MYSTERIOUS CANOES

At dawn sentries on the European shore shouted, "Ships on the horizon!"

Lord Glenarvan came out with his telescope and studied the black dots for a long time.

"I don't understand," said the gentleman, "they look like native canoes!"

"Thunder and lightning!" exclaimed Michel Ardan, throwing his Zeiss aside. "I'll bet a Washington dollar against a holey Russian rublé of 1923 that those are Arabs!"

"Naturally," affirmed Paganel.

Ardan and Paganel had guessed it.

"What does this mean?" asked the Lord, surprised for the first time in his life.

Instead of answering, the Arabs just giggled. They really were a horrible sight to see. When they had caught their breath a bit, terrifying things became clear: hordes of Ethiopians. The damned rebels had burned out these idiots. Their demand: to hell with the Arabs. Riki sent an expedition and it was smashed. That bastard Kiri-Kuki was the first to sneak off in a canoe. The remains of the expeditionary force, headed by Riki, were now here—in the canoes. They had barely made it to the lord.

"A hundred and forty devils and a witch!!" boomed Ardan, "They're planning to live in Europe. *Comprenez-vous?*

"But who's going to feed you?" Glenarvan said in fright. "No, you go back to the island."

"Your Excellency, it's impossible for us to show our noses on the

225

island now," the Arabs wept. "The Ethiopians will kill us all off. And in the second place, our wigwams have been shot all to hell. Now if you have some military forces to send, to pacify those bastards . . ."

"Thank you, no," the lord replied ironically, pointing to the correspondent's telegram. "You have the plague there. I have not yet lost my mind. One of my sailors is dearer to me than your whole crummy island. Yes."

"Precisely so, Your Excellency," agreed the Arabs. "It's well known we aren't worth a damn. And the correspondent is telling the truth about the plague. It's cutting people down left and right. And there's famine again."

"So," said the lord pensively, "all right. We'll see," and he commanded, "quarantine them!"

VII   THE TORMENTS OF THE ARABS

It is impossible to express what the Arabs suffered as the lord's guests. It began with them being washed with carbolic acid and kept behind a fence like some kind of asses. They were fed regularly, just enough so that they wouldn't die. And since it is impossible to set up an exact norm for a method like that, a quarter of the Arabs gave up their souls to God.

Finally, after having kept the Arabs waiting in quarantine, the lord sent them to work in the stone quarries. There were overseers there, and the overseers had whips made out of ox sinews . . .

VIII   THE DEAD ISLAND

Ships got orders to circle the island at cannon-shot range. So they did. Nights, a weak, dying glow could be seen, and days, the island burned with black smoke. Next, a suffocating putrid smell was added. The stench of corpses stretched across the blue waves.

"The end of the island," said the sailors, looking at the treacherous strip of green along the shore through binoculars.

The Arabs, who had turned into pale shadows on the lord's rations, expressed schadenfreude as they trudged through the stone quarries.

"That's what they deserve, the rascals. Let them die and feed the pigs. When they all drop dead, we'll return and occupy the island. And wherever we find that Kiri-Kuki dead we'll tear out his entrails with our hands."

The lord maintained a calm silence.

IX   THE TARRED BOTTLE

A wave cast it up on the European shore one day. It was unsealed after carbolic acid precautions, in the lord's presence, and it turned out to contain illegible scrawls in an Ethiopian hand. A translator deciphered it and presented the lord this document:

"We're dying of hunger. Children are dropping dead. The plague's the same. We are human, aren't we? Send food. The loving Ethiopians."

Riki-Tiki turned blue and snarled, "Your Excellency! . . . Absolutely not! Let them die! Why, if after their rebellion you feed them too . . ."

"I have no intention," the lord replied coldly, and he sent a lash across Riki's ear so that he would not annoy people with his advice.

"In essence, that's swinishness," Michel Ardan muttered through his teeth, "we could send them a little corn."

"I thank you for your advice, monsieur," Glenarvan replied drily, "I wonder who's going to pay for the corn. As it is, this mob of Arabs has gobbled up the devil only knows how much. I have no need of stupid advice."

"So that's how it is?" asked Ardan, screwing up his eyes. "Be so good as to tell me, sir, when we are going to shoot. And I swear, dear sir, that at twenty paces I will hit you as easily as the Notre Dame Cathedral!"

"I will not congratulate you, monsieur, if you find yourself twenty paces from me," replied the lord, "The weight of your body will be increased by the weight of the bullet which I will put in you through one of your eyes, take your pick."

Phileas Fogg was the lord's second, Paganel Ardan's. Ardan's weight remained unchanged, and Ardan missed the lord. He hit one of the Arabs, who had been sitting behind a bush out of curiosity. The bullet entered between his eyes and came out through the back of his head. The Arab died when it was half way through—in the center of his brain.

Ardan and Glenarvan shook hands and departed.

But the story of the bottle did not end with this. That night fifty Arabs fled the European shore in canoes, leaving the lord an impudent note.

"Thanks for the carbolic acid and overseers' ox sinews. We hope to break their legs with them some day. We're going back to the island. We'll make peace with the Ethiopians. Better die of the plague at home than from your rotten sardines. Respectfully yours, the Arabs."

The escapees had filched a telescope, a broken machine gun, one hundred cans of dried milk, six shiny doorknobs, ten revolvers, and two European women.

The lord flogged the rest of the Arabs and entered the value of the stolen items in his account book.

PART III

THE CRIMSON ISLAND

X AN AMAZING DISPATCH

Six years passed. The dead, isolated island was forgotten. Occasionally, from their ships seamen looked through binoculars at the luxuriant greenery on its shores, the cliffs, and the foaming surf. Nothing else.

Seven years was the period set for the plague to run its course and the island to become safe. At the end of the seventh year it was proposed that an expedition should be sent to the island, toward the goal of resettling the Arabs there. Thin as skeletons, the Arabs were languishing in the stone quarries.

And then at the *start* of the seventh year the civilized world was shaken by amazing news. The radio stations of America, England, and France received a radiotelegram.

"The plague is over. Glory to God, we are alive and well—and wish you the same. Your esteemed Ethiopians."

The next morning papers all over the world came out with extralarge headlines:

THE ISLAND SPEAKS!

MYSTERIOUS RADIOS!

THE ETHIOPIANS ARE ALIVE!

"I swear by my grandmother's flannel pajamas!" roared M. Ardan, "it's preternatural. It's not so surprising that they survived, but they're sending *telegrams!* Where the devil did they get a radio station?"

Lord Glenarvan received the news pensively. The Arabs were utterly stunned. Riki-Tiki-Tavi giggled and asked the lord, "Your

Excellency, now there's only one course: smash them—send an expedition. Why, what's going on here? It's your island by heritage. How long are we going to languish here?"

"I'll see," replied the lord.

XI CAPTAIN HATTERAS AND THE MYSTERIOUS LAUNCH

One marvelous May day a twist of smoke appeared over the sea near the island, and soon after, a ship under the command of Captain Hatteras, commanded by Lord Glenarvan, came to shore. Sailors manned the jacks and sides and looked at the island with curiosity. Their eyes were met by the following picture: the water dozed calmly in the bay, and right by shore an unknown launch stood out amid a whole fleet of new canoes, apparently just cut out. The riddle of the radiotelegram was explained here too: the tower of an extremely unattractively built radio station looked out in the distance from the emerald tropical forest.

"A hundred devils!" cried the captain. "Those blockheads have built that crooked monstrosity!"

The sailors laughed merrily, looking at this lopsided fruit of Ethiopian creativity.

A longboat from the ship moved to shore and let off the captain and a few sailors.

The first thing that struck the bold seafarers was the extreme abundance of Ethiopians. Hatteras was surrounded not only by grown-ups, but by a whole gang of children. The shore itself was garlanded with fat little Ethiopians sitting with their feet in the blue water, catching fish.

"I'll be damned if the plague hasn't worked to their benefit!" Hatteras was surprised. "They have mugs that seem to have been fed on 'Hercules' oatmeal. Well, sir, we'll look further . . ."

Further he was struck specifically by the old launch sheltered in the bay. One experienced glance was sufficient to be convinced that the launch was from a European shipyard.

"I don't like this," he said through set teeth, "if they didn't steal that holey galosh, then the question arises, what rascal came loafing onto this island during the quarantine? It very much seems to me that it's a German launch!" And turning to the Ethiopians, he asked, "Hey, you! Red-mugged devils! Where'd you filch that boat?"

The Ethiopians smiled slyly, showing their pearly teeth, and they did not answer.

"You don't want to answer? All right," the captain frowned, "I'll make you more talkative."

With these words he headed for the launch. But the Ethiopians barred the path of him and his sailors.

"Out of the way!" bellowed the captain, and he reached for his hip pocket with his usual gesture.

But the Ethiopians did not get out of the way. In an instant Hatteras and his sailors found themselves in a tight and strong ring. The captain's neck turned crimson. In the crowd he suddenly recognized one of the white Arabs who had escaped from the stone quarries.

"Aha! An old acquaintance!" exclaimed Hatteras. "Now I understand where the revolt comes from! Come here, you good-for-nothing!"

But the good-for-nothing did not desire to come there. Thus he answered, "I will not."

Captain Hatteras looked around in a mad fury, and his neck turned violet, making a lovely contrast with the white field of his hat. The thing is that he noticed in the hands of many of the Ethiopians weapons which looked extremely like German rifles, and in the hands of an Arab an automatic pistol stolen from Glenarvan. The sailors' faces, which were usually jaunty, turned gray and serious. The captain glanced at the scorching blue sky, then at the gulf where his ship rocked. The sailors who had remained on board were clustered like white spots on the yards, calmly watching the shore.

Captain Hatteras knew how to control himself. Gradually, his neck acquired its normal color, indicating that this time the paralysis had been ended.

"Let me go back to the ship," he said in a courteously hoarse voice.

The Ethiopians stepped aside, and escorted by the seamen, Hatteras left for the ship. Within an hour its anchor chains began to grate, and within two it was visible only as a small puff of smoke on the horizon of the sunny sea.

XII   THE INVINCIBLE ARMADA

Something indescribable took place in the huts occupied by the Arabs. The Arabs emitted victorious cries and stood on their heads. That day they were served thick golden bouillon by the bucketsful. There were no longer rags on the Arabs. They were issued fine calico pants and all the paint they wanted for war tattoos. New rapid-firing rifles and machine guns stood by the huts in stacks.

Most interesting of all was Riki-Tiki-Tavi. Rings glittered in his nose, multicolored feathers waved in the wind. His face shone like a very pious priest at Easter. He was walking around like a man possessed, saying just one thing, "All right, all right, all right. Now, you guys will hop to for me. Take it easy, we'll get there. And as soon as we get there . . ."

And with this he made gestures as if tearing out some invisible person's eyes.

"Into ranks! Attention! Hurrah!" he shouted and flew along in front of the bouillon-burdened Arabs.

Three armored hulks at the port started to take on the Arab battalions. And then an event occurred. A ragged and tattered figure shaved like a hedgehog crawled out from the middle of the line of troops. The astonished Arabs looked at him closely and recognized in this figure none other than Kiri-Kuki himself, who had been wandering around God knows where all this time.

He had the brazenness to come out in front of the Arabs and address himself to Riki-Tiki with a spasmodic smile.

"Did you forget me, brothers. Why, I am one of you. An Arab too. Take me to the island too. I'll come in handy for . . ."

He did not manage to finish his speech. Riki turned green and pulled a broad, sharp knife from his belt.

"Your Lordship," he said to Lord Glenarvan with quivering lips, "he's the one . . . he is Kiri-Kuki, the one who started all this strife. Will you allow me, Your Excellency, to cut his little throat with my own hands?"

"Why not? With pleasure," replied the lord amiably, "only be quick about it, don't hold up the boarding process."

Kiri-Kuki managed to squeal only once before Riki, with a masterful stroke, slit his throat open from ear to ear.

Then Lord Glenarvan and Michel Ardan came out before the troops and the lord made a parting speech.

"Go, conquer the Ethiopians. I will help, shoot from the ship. You will be paid for this after."

And with music playing the battalions of Arabs boarded the ships.

XIII AN UNEXPECTED FINALE

It was a blinding day, and the island appeared, shining like a pearl. The ships drew near the shore and the armed ranks of Arabs began to disembark. Full of battle fire, Riki hopped out first, and brandishing his saber he commanded, "After me, brave Arabs!"

And the Arabs streamed after him.

Then the following happened: an indescribable Ethiopian force rose up out of the fruitful earth of the island to meet the uninvited guests. The Ethiopians moved along in very thick columns. There were so many of them that the green island turned red in the wink of an eye. They swept along like clouds from all sides, and over the red ocean of them, a thick bristling layer of lances and bayonets crept along like the bristles of a toothbrush. Sprinkled here and there those same Arabs who had escaped from the stone quarries rushed along, acting as separate commanders. These marked Arabs were covered all over with Ethiopian markings, and they were brandishing revolvers. It was clearly written on their faces that they had nothing to lose. Only one thing soared from their gullets—the imperious, martial cry, "Attack!!"

To which the Ethiopians replied with a howl which made one's blood run cold, "Smash the sons of bitches!!!"

When the enemies met it became clear that Riki's army was nothing but a white island in the middle of a tempestuous crimson ocean. It splashed all over and submerged the Arabs from the flanks.

"I swear by the horns of the devil!" M. Ardan moaned on board a Flemish ship, "I've never seen anything like it!"

"Give them supporting fire!" Lord Glenarvan ordered, tearing away from his telescope.

Captain Hatteras supported them. A fourteen-inch cannon boomed and the shell, finishing its flight, burst right between the Arabs and Ethiopians. It tore 25 Ethiopians and 40 Arabs to shreds. The second shell had even greater success: 50 Ethiopians and 130 Arabs. No third shell followed, for Lord Glenarvan, having observed the results of the barrage through his telescope, grabbed Captain Hatteras by the throat and dragged him away from the cannon with a howl, "Cease fire, damn you! You're smashing the Arabs!"

After Hatteras's first noisy gifts a most incredible screeching and screaming arose from the ranks of the Arabs, and their rows faltered.

Even Riki-Tiki screamed, and a mad whirlpool began to swirl around him. Suddenly the distorted face of one of the rank-and-file Arabs bobbed up out of the whirlpool. He ran up to the crazed leader and yelled hoarsely—foam coming out along with the words, "What is this?! Wasn't it enough to drag us into the stone quarries and marinate us for seven years!! Now this too!! You made us pack animals! Now the Ethiopians in front and shells on the noodle from behind?!! A-a-a-a-!!!"

In a flash the Arab snatched out a knife and plunged it inspiredly into Riki-Tiki, extremely skillfully guessing the place between the fifth and sixth ribs on the left side.

"Hel . . ." the leader moaned, finishing the "p" in the next world before the throne of the Almighty.

"Hurrah!" thundered the Ethiopians.

"We surrender!! Hurrah! Peace, brothers!!" roared the shaken Arabs, spinning around in the tempestuous waters of the boundless Ethiopian army.

"Hurrah!!" answered the Ethiopians.

And everything on the island got mixed-up into an incredible stew.

"Seven hundred fevers and the Siberian plague!!" cried M. Ardan, his eyes fixed through Zeiss's lenses. "May I be hanged if those numbskulls have not made peace!! Look, sir! They're acting like brothers!"

"I see," replied Lord Glenarvan in a sepulchral voice, "it would be very interesting to know what reward I'm going to get for having fed that filthy gang of traitors."

"Forget it, dear sir," M. Ardan suddenly said sincerely, "you won't get anything here except tropical malaria. And in general I advise you to weigh anchor immediately. Save yourself!" he suddenly exclaimed and ducked. And the lord ducked mechanically beside him. Just in time too. Like a light gust of wind, a flashing cloud of Ethiopian arrows and Arabian bullets passed over their heads.

"Give it to them!!" roared the lord to Hatteras.

Hatteras gave it to them—unsuccessfully. It exploded high in the air. The united Arab-Ethiopian regiment replied with a repetition of the cloud of arrows—which flew in lower and with his own eyes the lord saw seven sailors turn crimson and fall, writhing in pain.

"To hell with this expedition!!" bellowed the far-sighted Ardan. "Get going, get going, sir!! They have poisoned arrows! Get going if you don't want to take the plague to Europe!!"

"Give them a parting shot!!" the lord yelled hoarsely.

The well-known cursing artillery officer Hatteras gave them a parting shot which went off somewhere, crooked, at an angle, and the ships weighed anchor. The third cloud of arrows landed harmlessly in the water.

Within half an hour the hulks were moving away, shrouding the horizon in smoke, cutting apart the smooth surface of the ocean. In the foaming wake bobbed the seven poisoned bodies of the sailors who had been thrown overboard.

The island was touched by light smoke, and in it the sun-drenched emerald strip of shore disappeared.

XIV   THE FINAL SIGNAL

That night the tropical sky was covered with a fiery glow over Crimson Island, and the ships lashed out to all radio stations with the words:

"The Island has a hangover of exceptional dimensions stop the devils are drinking coconut vodka!!"

And then the Eiffel Tower received green lightnings which formed into an incredibly impudent telegram: "To Glenarvan and Ardan. At a united holiday we suggest you go . . . (indecipherable) your . . . (indecipherable) MOTHER. Respectfully, the Ethiopians and Arabs."

"Shut down the receivers," bellowed Ardan.

The tower went dead in an instant. The lightnings were extinguished, and what happened after that is not known to anyone.

Translated by Mikhail Bulgakov

Date Due

JUL 06 1987			
OCT 21 1999			
NOV 16 1999			